THE ECHO

Also by James Smythe

The Testimony
The Machine

THE ANOMALY QUARTET
The Explorer

JAMES SMYTHE

THE ECHO

Book Two of The Anomaly Quartet

HARPER
Voyager

HarperCollins*Publishers*
77–85 Fulham Palace Road,
Hammersmith, London W6 8JB

www.harpercollins.co.uk

First Published by Harper*Voyager* 2014
1

A catalogue record for this book
is available from the British Library

ISBN 978 0 00 745679 6

This novel is entirely a work of fiction.
The names, characters and incidents portrayed in it are
the work of the author's imagination. Any resemblance to
actual persons, living or dead, events or localities is
entirely coincidental.

Set in Sabon LT Std by Palimpsest Book Production Limited,
Falkirk, Stirlingshire

Printed and bound in Great Britain by
Clays Ltd, St Ives plc

MIX
Paper from
responsible sources
FSC **FSC™ C007454**
www.fsc.org

FSC™ is a non-profit international organisation established to promote
the responsible management of the world's forests. Products carrying the
FSC label are independently certified to assure consumers that they come
from forests that are managed to meet the social, economic and
ecological needs of present and future generations,
and other controlled sources.

Find out more about HarperCollins and the environment at
www.harpercollins.co.uk/green

PART ONE

The scientist is not the person who gives the right answers;
he's the one who asks the right questions.

— Claude Lévi-Strauss

1

The sense of pressure on us is immense. There is a feeling that if this fails – and if it were to fail it would be because of me and Tomas, and we are both far too acutely aware of that – but that if this fails, we might not try something like this again. I have seen the receipts for this project of ours. Tomas has signed off on them on my behalf, and we have decided that this is an endeavour that we should undertake. The weight of this endeavour falls onto our shoulders: his and mine. We are separated by only thirty minutes, and soon to be hundreds of thousands of miles. It feels like more already: because he is down there, in the comparative safety of his little bunker, dressed in his shirt and drinking his drink and smoking his cigarettes; and I am here, waiting to leave. I still find it hard to believe that I am the one going. We decided it, as with so many things in our life, on a game. The top bunk of our beds? The front seat of our mother's car? Always on a game, because somehow that made it fair. If he won, he went to space; if I did, I was the lucky one. Maybe part of the reason that we both wanted it so much is only because the other one did.

But here I am. I am the one up here, and I will be the one going out there into the dark. Tomas has safety: of the lab, the bunker, the hotel that sits adjoining; and of a ground underneath his feet that will not rumble and shudder and shake, and that has no danger of tearing itself apart or falling out of the sky. And he has the girlfriend, the nice house, the nice car. In reality, it's better that I am the brother who came up here. The only goodbye that I had to say was to him. We shook hands, which we have never ever done before.

I came up here with the crew yesterday. One of the things that Tomas and I decided, when we began this process, was that we would launch from the International Space Station. We decreed changes that would need to happen – the changes that transformed it into the New International Space Station, the same as the old but with what amounts to a loft conversion, a conservatory bolted onto the side, the prefix at the start of the name – and they all happened. Every single one. This is, for now, important. We are important. From here, I can see the planet we left. I have put marks on my window with black marker pen, just to check that we and it are moving as we should. But of course we are: how could we not be? And, on the other side, I can see the moon. I can see all of it. Now, here, I see Mare Fecunditatis and Langrenus. I know these features – a lake and a crater, essentially, named by gravitas and a Latin education rather than utility – almost by heart. I have studied them all my life.

I am worried. I cannot remember when I was last not worried, but that makes perfect sense. My mother once said, Man wasn't meant to go into space. If he was meant to go into space, God would have made us all angels.

I feel better knowing that Tomas is on the ground, though. That he is watching over us. He is rooted, and that's a nice feeling. If something goes wrong on the trip (which it will not, because we have covered every single eventuality, because we are those sort of people) he will be there to steer us home. He can override the controls, and there might be lag, there might be a delay, but he would get us home. I am comfortable in that knowledge. It makes me feel good; we have always steered each other.

I call him from the computer. It amazes me: how we can speak from here, with this distance between us. I understand the science completely, and yet. Sometimes I forget how rational this all is, and how explainable, and I revel in the magic. It gets me carried away.

'You're up early,' he says. No platitudes or hellos. We have never had them. It has always been, Pick up where you left off. There is no need to pretend that you don't know each other. 'I'd have thought you would be sleeping still.'

'No,' I say. 'I didn't sleep much at all, really.' I do not sleep well. I never have.

'It's not like you won't get the chance,' he says. I switch the call to video, to see his face. He isn't paying attention: I see the side of his head, cigarette in his mouth. He is looking at something off-screen. When he turns to the screen he notices me, and he grins. 'How are you feeling about it?'

'I am not exactly happy,' I say. I am terrified of being put to sleep. The plan with the ship was that we would accelerate at a rate so much faster than we could from Earth, burning less fuel than if we had to break the atmosphere on this trip, less drag; and then we could coast. Constant acceleration, controlled by the ship itself. The ship has levels she can reach, speeds she cannot surpass, and we would control all that. Tomas and I, we are in control. But when we first move, the acceleration will be such that we will need to be asleep. We have constructed and designed beds that the crew can lie in to protect them, and we will be surrendering to chemicals to make it easier. I despise the idea: I have spent hours (by which I mean days, weeks, months of thought) looking into ways to make this part of the process easier for me. I have argued until I am blue in the face that I will stay there still and silent, and that it will be fine. Tomas has argued in turn that my body might not want to do what I tell it. He's right, of course: there's no way I could stand the pressure being put onto us. I would probably end up doing something – moving slightly, fidgeting – and getting myself killed. The concoction that we are using to induce sleep will also introduce a mild skeletal paralytic into our bodies, to ensure stillness and calm. It's all part of the drive towards efficiency.

This is what Tomas and I offered to the committee with our plan: our sense of efficiency. Everything was to be different to the way that they did it last time. The last trip into space was twenty-three years ago, and they were a ruinous lot. They set us back decades, I believe. When they disappeared, never to be heard from again – as if space is a fairy story, something less than tangible – all funding went. Private investors, the life-line to the modern scientist, disappeared. Everything they did was wrong. I can pick holes. They launched from Earth, even though it made no sense, even back then. They spent money on automated systems because they believed they would add efficiency. They were wrong, as proven by their disappearance. They spent billions developing ridiculous gravity systems, something that the Russians prototyped back in the previous decade concerning gravitomagnetism. And why? So that they could rest! So that they could feel the sensation of a ground beneath their feet! They took a journalist with them, because they spun

6

their mission into something commercial, something outside science. They took a man who didn't serve a purpose with them on a mission that could have meant something. What did that cost them, that folly? They played everything badly, a product of moneymen rather than scientific design. It drove Tomas and myself insane. And when they went missing, the balloon deflated overnight. No more space travel. There is nothing new out there to find, and no glory to be garnered from dying in the cold expanse of space as they surely did. All the corporations involved distanced themselves, because that isn't a visual that marketeers like: drink our cola as we spin out into the nothing. Most of us – scientists – felt as if they let us down. That's a hard truth, but a truth nonetheless. When Tomas and I decided that we would do this, we decided that we would do everything better. This – space, discovery – it deserved better.

So I lie to Tomas now, and tell him that I am fine with the process. 'It won't matter to me,' I say. 'I will sleep and then I'll wake up.' He will know that I am lying, but this is what we do: it's the way of twins, I suspect. 'This is nothing worth worrying over. It's only sleep.'

'It's not natural though, is it?' I can hear him smirking as he prods. His voice and mine are exactly the same. The same tone and timbre, and when we speak English – which we do all the time, because somehow, over the last twenty years, it's actually become easier to do it than revert back to a language that is now so close to dead it almost hurts to say the words – when we speak it, our accents are the same. We both got this from watching English-language television when we were children. We learned how to say words exactly the same way. American/English/Swedish. A curious hybrid. So we sound the same, and our mouths move the same way. Of course, we never used to hear it; it's like when you listen to yourself on the radio, and you never sound as you expect. But now, after years of it, I can tell the sound of his smirk because it is the sound of mine. It has the same intonation, the same rise and fall. 'So, listen to me,' he says, 'you'll be fine. Nobody ever dies from sleeping in those things.' He knows that somebody did, in the last trip. They woke up and the captain was dead, gone while he slept.

'What do you want?' I ask him.

'You called me,' he says. I don't remember it being that way, but instead of arguing we discuss the breakdowns of the fuel delivery, which is still ongoing: reserve tanks being fitted, able to be connected via a channel that we can manually open if needed. The fuel is kept frozen – I mean, it's far more complicated than that, but essentially – until it is needed, so that we can control its release perfectly, down to the last, ensuring that nothing is wasted. And frozen it's compressed, meaning we can take more than we need, in theory. I sit at my computer while he talks and I cycle the cameras, so that I can see the ship: plugged in, docked to the NISS by rigid arms that we designed ourselves, that we had built, that we had installed. She doesn't drift. She moves with us, like an appendage. There have been, over the past few days, people out there working on her. Checking her final systems, making sure that everything is as it should be. There is a crane arm attached to the NISS that was helping them, delivering the fuel and the provisions. Now, the crane is silent and still. There is only one man out there, on his own. I don't know what he's doing exactly. It will be logged somewhere, and I am intrigued, so I call up the spreadsheets and systems while Tomas talks, and I look for activity. The answer: he is cleaning the cameras. There are no exterior windows on the ship, only cameras, and he is cleaning them for us. Tomas can see what I am looking at, the computer screens and videos mirrored down there. Everything is parity.

'I have thought it might be nice, you know,' Tomas says, breaking his own chain of thought, changing the subject.

'What?'

'Doing that. Cleaning. Just something menial, you know? You're still in space, but that's like, I don't know. It's free, I think. Without this responsibility.' He sounds almost wistful.

'We're privileged, Brother,' I say. 'We get to travel to the stars instead of waiting and watching them.'

'You get to, you mean.' We haven't argued about our roles, not ever. He has always maintained that he is happy with the result: that he has his life down there, and he would have hated to leave it. I am alone, and still it remains so up here. 'For me, it's in the future. Another time.' That was the deal we made. After this, if we run another, he goes up and I stay down. 'This is good, though. Running things here, Mira: you wouldn't believe the minutiae.'

'I'm sure,' I say.

'But now you have what you wanted. I am happy for you, Brother. Relish it.' So we both look out of the window, me here and him watching on a computer screen two hundred and fifty miles below in a part of Florida that seems as if it has only ever really existed for the purpose of launching humanity into space. Neither of us says goodbye. That's how our conversations end, as they begin: one running into the other in a constant flow, as if no time has passed between us at all.

All of this was done before we came up here, the crew and myself. The ship was primarily constructed on Earth, then brought up for tweaks and reworking. The final layer of spit and polish. But we have only been up here a few days. We wanted to give our crew as much time on Earth as possible, as much time with their families. It's a litany of ways that the last trip really messed these things up: they sent their people to space camp for months before. As if that would help! We relocated the families of the people that we wanted, the people that were best for the job, and we gave them houses and put their children in schools. We wanted them to have as much of their life as possible. A happy crew, Tomas has always maintained, is a positive and productive crew. Some of them have families: Hikaru Morgan, one of our pilots, has a newborn baby, only a few months old. By the time we return, she will be crawling. We have even paid the money to fast-track her, so maybe it'll be more than crawling. Maybe talking. We wanted to make sure that they never resented us for taking them away, no matter how great the cause. Everything we have done has been to ensure that, yes, they are as efficient as possible.

I do not have a wife and children, or anything worth me missing. I am not well liked; I have no friends, no lovers. Tomas and I were nearly alone at our mother's funeral, and it was only after she died that he began to look for women. I said to him, This is you seeking a way to replace her. He said, And so what? It's better that I know that when I begin this. He found some women online, the sort of women he was looking for; the sort who were looking for the same thing as him. I told him that I couldn't stand the thought of forcing myself to connect with people like that; that conventional wisdom, everything I have seen in my life, tells me that there needs to be something organic. He told me that saying that was an admission of how alone I was anyway, and how willing I was to stay that way. He said, A relationship forged on mutual desperation can absolutely work, because you both know that you are starting from rock bottom. You are both already as alone as each other. In this way he met his girlfriend, and they began dating. She moved in with him after I don't know how many weeks. Far too few. She is a flake, and I don't find her physically attractive, which makes me wonder if he really does. We have the same tastes in most other things, I know that. She doesn't understand our work, also, which would be a barrier for me. She is a baker. She works in a bakery, and she understands cakes and breads. I sometimes think that she must find everything he says about our work so impressive because she cannot understand a word of it.

We have gathered the crew together for a meal, one last hurrah before we leave. I am uncomfortable with the lack of gravity: I am pitiably ungraceful, and I am forced to cling to the guide rails that have been installed. We have a system of magnetic carabiner clips that we developed to help us lock onto them, to keep us stable. They are all throughout the NISS, and they are all throughout the ship. Safety, efficiency: these are easy watchwords. The crew have all been told that today is free: no work. The safety checks are run by others. Today, they can talk to their loved ones, send messages, relax. The meal we have laid on is special: prepared by a chef from Earth, not freeze-dried and preserved, but something actually cooked for this occasion. He made it down there and we had it brought it up here on the last transport. We have champagne as well, and I pass out the boxes with the food in and the flasks with the alcohol.

'Go easy,' I say. 'Remember that it will hit you like a wall, here. You don't want a hangover for launch, do you?' They laugh, and Wallace – actually Andy Wallace, but he likes to be called by his surname, as if he is constantly being ordered around – he mimes drinking it down in one. He even mimes the gulps, and he smirks. He is a funny guy. Not a practical joker, though, and usually dry with his humour, but he's funny. 'And remember,' I say, 'this is the last proper meal you'll have for a while. After this, everything is vacuum packed or dried, okay?' They groan, but really, it's not an issue. The food that we have selected is fine for the purpose. We – Tomas and myself – have had control over every single aspect of this trip. The food, the way that the ship looks, the technology we have used inside it, the people that we hired. We made demands that the United Nations Space Agency initially balked at, but that's the beauty of demands: they can cause a standstill until you get what you want. We insisted on extra fuel, because you cannot be too cautious where that is concerned. We insisted on the development of the proxy system, where Tomas can control the ship from the ground if needs be. Tomas developed the entire system, in fact, working hard on it from day one. We insisted on decent meals, privacy in the bed pods, the development of a far better communication bandwidth than had been previously afforded. We didn't have to make many concessions either, because what were they going to do? We showed that we could bring the project in on time and on budget. And we were so up against the clock. That's the crucial thing, I suppose: as soon as the anomaly became visible and on their radar, there was no way for them to back out. Something had to be done, and we would do it. So a huge amount of technology on the ship is ours, either developed by us, or in conjunction. We bought licences and patents and hired the people who would make what we needed. We made the ship exactly what it needs to be to do this mission. Anything less and we would be running so many risks, more than were acceptable, just as the *Ishiguro* did twenty-three years ago.

So I fluster and try to control myself, and I drift next to Wallace and I hold my flask up to clink it against his. He was chosen because he had a background on jets, which made sense. He used to work on the commercial atmosphere planes, and he was the one responsible for their fuel systems, their landing systems. He was the one who was developing the guidance proxy, meant to be able to be used to guide in planes in hazardous conditions, and to prevent terror attacks. We bought it, and him, because they will be invaluable. We may never use that particular aspect, but the fact that we have it and that it works is cause for such a sigh of relief.

On the other side of me, Tobi White. I am flanked by the Americans. She's a pilot, absolutely the best that we could find. She flew as a teenager, taught by her father, who was a United States Air Force pilot, so she went that route herself when she could. Honours, all the rest. Top of her class. One tour of duty, injured – crashed, but survived – in Palestine, and we stepped in when she was healthy again. We had carte blanche to take whomever we wanted from the various armies and air forces, but we wanted the pilots to want it as well. We wanted everybody to see this as the opportunity that it is. What Tomas and I liked about Tobi is that she is driven by instinct. It's innate and inside her: acting before she even knows what she's doing. We liked that, and so we sought a balance with our other pilot, Hikaru. Asian by way of Wales, in the United Kingdom, and the single calmest man I have ever met. He is – and Tomas laughs at this cliché, always has done – but he is very zen. Something like that. He isn't a Buddhist; instead, he follows one of the religions that sprang up in the last decade, one of those new ones designed to help organize your life, straighten out your way of thinking, promote productivity. It is not my business what you believe in or how you worship, only that you are good at your job. He eats nothing but white food, wears only white clothes. No pressure for us: we made sure that as many of the meal bars were bleached as possible, and he has his own supply. We are very accepting.

Next to him, my research assistant, Lennox Deng. He's young and eager and irritating. Top of his year, I am told, although that means nothing to me. Tomas was top of our class, which leads to him believing that it's a lofty achievement. I was third, but that was because I was attempting other things. I was pushing the envelope, trying to see further than just the research we were tasked with. Lennox, to me, is a follower, therefore. I see him as the sort of person who will do as I say because he wants to get the best report. Perhaps this is what you want from an assistant in a place like this. He is insistent and obsessed with the wonder of this endeavour, as a child might be. I am perhaps more practical now. Not that the stars are not magnificent, because they are: but I have seen them. I have spent my life looking at them. With this mission, perhaps there is a chance for something else? Answers, rather than wonder. What we will find out there might not be visually stunning, it might not be something that decorates a postcard, but it might be an answer to something. What is the question? Well, we don't know that yet either. But Lennox: he is two birds with the one stone, a degree in engineering and a doctorate in astrophysics. Maybe he wasn't my first choice, but he's a sensible one. Besides which, it was an easy win I could give to Tomas.

Then there is our doctor, but she isn't here yet. She is arriving tonight. She has been in last-minute training sessions, because she was a replacement. Our original doctor, some prick from Los Angeles, as they so often are, he bailed at the last minute. I said to Tomas that I could see it coming. He was that sort of person. We went through uniforms, training: millions of dollars spent on him, essentially. He kept asking questions about what happened on the *Ishiguro*, why it didn't come back, and we kept saying, We don't know, it just didn't, but we have taken every precaution, blah blah blah. We told him, categorically, that it wouldn't happen to us, but that didn't make any difference in the end. He disappeared. So we went to the backup: Inna Gulansky. She's amazing, really. She's older than Tomas and myself by some years, and she's been a field surgeon for most of her life. Tomas found her file, and I went with his choice, so that we could sign her off as quickly as possible. I didn't question the choice once I saw her history. She was the doctor who came up to operate on the ISS last decade, so she's already done zero-g triage, things that the guy she's replacing could have only dreamed of. But her final stages of training have been happening without us, tucked away in some warehouse in Moscow, and that training prevented her coming up here with the rest of us. They wanted to ensure that she was absolutely ready. I have only met her a handful of times, but I can already tell that she will be an invaluable asset. I have told her, This will be an injury-free trip, that's my decree, and she said, Well, why am I coming then? That is a good question! I said. She is full of good questions.

Now, here, when we're nervous, everybody wants to talk

with Tobi and Hikaru. She's bright and bubbly, and she's got so many stories about her life that it's almost distracting; whereas he's a picture of perfect calm, so much that it's almost infectious. He tells us first about meditative techniques we can use when we are nervous about situations such as this, and then she tells a story about her father taking her up in a plane, about her first crash – her first landing where the plane didn't survive but she walked away – when she was sixteen.

'It's all about knowing how to meet the ground,' she says.

'Not a lot of that where we're going,' Wallace says. His quip disarms her, throws her story off. She tilts her head at him and squints. She does that, I've noticed, when people make a joke at her expense. It rolls off. I seize the opportunity, the gap in the conversation. Tomas told me that I should make a speech to rouse them, to make sure that we're all on the same page. I cough for attention, and I push slightly away from the wall, into the middle of the room. They all look at me. I do not know that I am much of a leader, but I am something. I am what they've got.

'Hello,' I begin, 'I just wanted to say a few words. There will be more tomorrow, and the press will be involved, but this is just all of us, now. We have important work to be doing out there. Very important work.' They are all smiling. Maybe they are just humouring me, because I know that I am bad at speeches, bad at all of this stuff. I know that I am not making eye contact with them; I am looking at my hands, at the paper that I wish I had to read from. I know all of this. 'We all remember when they did this last. We remember how it all went wrong. But they were different, because they didn't have you people as a crew.' I have lost their smiles. I haven't thought this through. I ask myself how Tomas would save this, and I remember the

16

champagne substitute. I raise my flask. 'So, you know,' I say, and I start clapping my hand against the flask, 'applaud yourselves! To us!' I raise it high, and then I say it again. 'To us!' They all repeat it, and we all drink, and I see them looking at each other, little glances out of the sides of their eyes. I have fucked this up, I know.

I quietly mumble at them that I have to go and do some final checks, so I fluster to the rail, leaving my food but taking my flask, and I pull myself along and back to my room. It takes too long, and when I am there I fasten myself to the chair with the magnets and I call Tomas, and I swallow the remains of my drink back in one, sucking it through the little semi-permeable straw and feeling it spark and fizz on my tongue and the back of my throat.

'Did you inspire them?' he asks. He was listening, I am sure. Why would he not have been listening? So this is a lie, his asking me. It's him giving me a chance.

'I did my best,' I say. 'What are you doing?'

'We're watching projections of what could happen if it all goes wrong.' I don't ask him any more about them. I've seen the projections myself. We are sure that we will be fine; but in case we're not, we have to run these things. They are terrifying, because there isn't a single one in which any of the crew manage to survive.

The reason for this mission is to examine something that we do not understand. We know it as an anomaly. We first knew about the anomaly – and, by we, I mean the world – six years after the *Ishiguro* went missing. The world was not told about the anomaly at the time, and so when they disappeared and didn't come back, it was a complete disaster. Tomas and I watched it on the news: the desperate wait for any sort of news from the lost shuttle. There were so many cameras in the launch centre, with the men and their computers and the branding everywhere. Showing endless, constant VT of the various astronauts as if they were participants in a reality show. Eventually the cameras packed up, and the news cycle was reduced to a small notice at the end that simply stated how many days they had been missing for. Everybody moved on. There was a funeral when it was decided that their fuel would have run out, that their life support would have disappeared. And then, after a while, they worked out where the ship must have dropped off the radar, and then later, they announced more details. A drip-feed of updates, holding things back when they were not ready for public consumption. Records from the ship's journey; information from the journalist, useless and garbled.

Then one day the newly named UNSA announced that they knew of something, out there in space, out where the *Ishiguro* had been. The UNSA was little more than a conglomerate of companies and investors and governmental bodies plucked from the remnants of NASA and other space agencies, given a ridiculous name to seem important. They disclosed that the thing first appeared a decade before. There was patch of space that nobody could see properly: as if it was nothingness. It had been designated the catalogue number 250480 – they could only give it a number because nobody knew what it was. There were hundreds of thousands of these things up there somewhere: things that we didn't understand, but that were catalogued with their little numbers and a file on a hard drive somewhere. It had been discovered before by Dr Gerhardt Singer, and he had been on the *Ishiguro* to try and learn more about it. It wasn't important, that was the party line – that Inspire the world! bullshit was the primary reason for the launch of the *Ishiguro* – but it was clear that it was the important thing about their trip to him. He knew that there was a differential in the readings from it, simply because you could ping it and get nothing in return. The stars that used to be forthcoming, eventually, with their locations, he got nothing back from them. The anomaly was, as best every telescope could tell, nothing. There was nothing inside it. Nothing past it. And yet, it had to be *something*. Even a definite nothing is always a something. Dr Singer's readings were correct, but they were brushed to one side as something to worry about another time.

When they announced the anomaly – and I say announced, but what I'm talking about is an update on a website, not a press release – they pointed out that they had singularly failed to get readings from the thing, because the probes that they sent to it malfunctioned. That didn't mean anything: there's a margin of error with anything technological. Two probes they sent, over a six-year period, both ostensibly to find the wreckage of the *Ishiguro*, but checking out the anomaly as they went, and they returned nothing, as if the thing wasn't there. No readings: machines could not do what humans were needed for. And that's where Tomas and I came in. We had worked with Dr Singer before he left, when we were students, in deep admiration of his work – of his role as an explorer – and we attempted to carry on his work, when we had the time. We were fuming after they spoke publicly about the anomaly, because they were denying that it was important. Tomas and I, we knew that it had something to do with the disappearance of the *Ishiguro*. Nothing is coincidence. Everything that happens anywhere happens with purpose and meaning. We went to the UNSA and we showed them our results, based on Dr Singer's research. Extrapolations and summations, but with some immutable, incontestable facts: the anomaly was either moving or growing, because the space that it occupied was different. At that distance, it was hard to gauge almost infinitesimally small movements on that scale. But it was, one way or another, closer to us – to the Earth – than it had been when Dr Singer found it, and when the *Ishiguro* went out to examine it. It was moving. (Or, as Tomas surmised, unfolding. He has his own theories, and I have mine. We are not that similar; or, we try and cover all bases.) We plotted exactly where it was, using readings from every telescope and satellite available to us. When you concentrate and focus, you see the things that others miss. Stars that were registering as present from one satellite at any given point might not return a ping from Jodrell Bank. We focused on the anomaly, put our careers into it, our reputations. Tomas said, It's better to be an expert in one thing that might be important than in many things that matter only a little bit.

The UNSA panicked then. They worried. More probes were sent, and they were lost as well. Everything there was lost. One of them, one of the people who approved the funding – he was the most desperate, his hands ready to sign funds to us before we even finished our first presentation – asked us what would happen if it reached the Earth. We said, We don't even know what it is, yet. Let us find out. We showed them a map we'd made, and expressed in real terms the actual scale of what we were dealing with. They didn't take long to reach the decision of a green light, on one condition: one of us would need to be up there, knowing what we were looking at. The other would stay at home and guide the operation from there.

One job sounded like what we had always wanted to do,

the excitingly childish dream; the other somehow more prosaic role. Drier, certainly. We played for it. We have always played for it. Whoever won was going onto the ship, up into space, to the anomaly, the prize of this thing. It was decisive, my victory: I had fought for it, and I deserved it. I never gloated, because that wasn't our way. We just got on with it. We planned the entirety of the trip meticulously. No room for error, and no error likely. Tomas framed the plan, seventeen printed A4 sheets of times and dates, and mounted it on the wall of our lab. I asked him why he framed it, and he said, It's not going to change, so I might as well.

Our launch time has been set for over a year now. I look at my watch and I've got four hours. In two hours I have to report for duty, then I have to be sedated and strapped into my bed, and I will be made to sleep.

When it is time, we will all go into that darkness out there.

Tomas was first born, by three hours and forty-one minutes. I was if not a surprise, then a miracle, because they had no idea I was stuffed in there as well. The people who delivered me, who were not real doctors, started to tell my mother to rest rather than to keep pushing, because her job was done. Her baby, Tomas, had been born, and with that they assumed she was finished. My mother was a hippie, back when such a name meant something. She was into free love or whatever, and she was eighteen and had run away from home and lived on a reservation near these marshlands in Sweden and she didn't believe in doctors. (We would argue, as she lay dying in the hospital bed that we forced her to lie in, that at least they fucking existed in the first place, so it wasn't something she could contest. I don't believe in them, or anything that they do, she told us, and we said, Well they're real! And they could have saved your life! Instead of doctors, she believed in angels and psychic energies and trees that breathed at night.) Because of this lack of faith – a denial of scans and tests performed before she slid into her birthing pool and spread her thighs – she didn't know that I was coming. I was a miracle. Tomas was abandoned, pushed to one side as they held me aloft. We are not equal, not completely. He has a birthmark stretched across half of his face, a wine stain that truly was there from birth. As she cradled him before I appeared, she apparently reasoned his mark away. It would clear itself up, was her logic. (A doctor might have told her differently, of course, but no.) When she finally held me, three hours after I began my climb out, she proclaimed me to be a *mirakel*: my looks, my health, my name. Mirakel – Mira, because I would never use that horrifying name, so gauche, a name that is such a product of who my mother was rather than anything resembling sense or logic, a name that would have lost me any respect within the scientific community – Hyvönen, brother of Tomas, son of Lära and some man who never existed, for all that I know of him. One of many people in a photograph of hundreds, drunk at some festival or other. I am the product of my mother's loose virtues, and I am a scientist.

The names were competition for us, as she didn't change my brother's name to something more impressive; so he had to prove himself. He was older, wiser, in theory, and he shrugged it off in what he said and how he acted. Not underneath. Underneath, as we raced each other through school – excelling in the logical subjects, with proper results reliant on knowledge and skill and being able to use your brain, and thus attain results that could be gauged, pitted against each other – then university, and doctorates, neck and neck the whole time, I was still the *mirakel*. I would still be there second but more perfect, and his face bore that scar the whole time. Not a scar, no, that's unfair: in my darkest moments, as we fought, that's what I would call it. It's a mark. It singles him out. It allows people to tell us apart, as otherwise we would be identical, monozygotic. We are in our forties now, and tired. Both of us are tired. And this trip, this excursion, it's our dream. When we stopped fighting, we joined forces. When we stop competing, we're unstoppable.

I'm the second to arrive at the gateway to the *Lära*. It was in our contract that we could name the ship, that Tomas and I would be able to choose what we would call it by ourselves. Her name is a word that means a theory, like a scientific supposition; and it was also our mother's name. It seemed appropriate: taken from the centuries-old tradition of naming ships after women. Gods or women, that's how you named a ship – never mind that the *Ishiguro* broke those traditions, celebrating the engineer who designed the engines.

Wallace is already here. He's leaning against the wall, and he looks weary. I can't blame him. He looks at me and nods. He will have just said his goodbyes to his family, and I assume that he would like it to stay quiet for a while longer; I don't have an issue with that. From the windows here, I can see the hull. I can see the panels, the bolts and fixtures holding them to each other. I know how they're held in place, and what's under each one. The design of this ship is entirely our own. We built this for practicality. There is a reason that spaceships look like they do. With the *Ishiguro*, that was just another in their colossal series of egomaniacal fuck-ups. They built a ship that looked like something from a film, that had no place being in space. It was built for its toyetic qualities, the design licensed out before they even took off; ours has been constructed to work perfectly, efficiently. To actually serve its purpose.

From here, down the tunnel, is an airlock. The other side of it leads you to a changing room, outfitted with benches and suits for exterior walks. One room off that is the bathroom, of our own design. Nobody likes shitting into a suction tube, I told Tomas, but that's what has to happen. Might as well make it as comfortable as possible. So it's a pod, and there's a seat, and there's a vacuum seal around your ass made by the seat, which is of a jelly, almost, malleable. It fits to you. There is no hose or inverted gas mask. No good for urination, though, so that's still into a funnel, but that's easier to deal with. The shower uses a vacuum as well, pulling through a grate at the bottom, and the water is pressure-pushed from the top. In theory, on a good day, it's like a waterfall or a car wash, fast and hard and maybe not very pleasant, but it'll get you clean.

Through from there is the bedroom, which has the beds set at a 40-degree angle off the floor, arranged around each other in a circle. We paid for a special darkening finish on the glass, which goes black on both sides, blocking light if you want, because it means that people can sleep while others work. No need to have lights out, or bedtime. This doubles as our sick bay as well, in case. Through from there is our living quarters, and at the neck of that room the cockpit, all built into one area. Less space than our predecessor, but theirs was extravagant. We've reserved more room for the essentials – fuel, food, the communications system that we had built – and taken away space for play. Tomas and I both agreed that it was unnecessary. The cockpit is state of the art. In the old Apollo spacecraft, they had open panels, hundreds of buttons. Every part of the process had to be performed under a strict regimen, an order in which things had to be done. They were suffering a basic lack of understanding of automated processes, but that is a hobby of mine. Ergo, we have tried to make this easier but still retain the functionality. We have cut down on what can go wrong, that's all. A lot is controlled by computer – life support, air supply, fuel intake – but we can take control back if we need to. We can do it from here, and Tomas can do it from Earth. That's thanks to the communications system, and how we've managed to get the signal to carry enough data, relaying it with satellites. Back in the *Ishiguro*'s day, such an undertaking would probably have been impossible. We haven't had a chance to test it, not outside of satellite commands, but that's always the way with new technologies. So much of it is theoretical until it suddenly works and you're proven correct.

Hikaru is next to arrive, and he is grinning.

'This is exciting,' he says. We have a special cupboard of food especially for him, of white bars of soya and tofu and processed chicken. He's not fussy about drink colour, apparently: just the food. Tobi and Lennox arrive together, and with them is Inna. Tobi pulls herself to the side and waves her hand out, allowing Inna past, as if this is some sort of formal greeting. Everybody smiles and greets her. They've all met her before, but only briefly, when she wasn't originally a part of this team. Bonding was low on the list of our desired achievables before launch; far lower than making sure that she was ready for this challenge.

'Hello,' she says. She shakes our hands, reintroducing herself. None of us have forgotten her name, because she's vital to this, and because we've all been talking about when she would join us.

'Great to have you,' Hikaru says. 'You as excited as we are?'

'Just about,' she says. Her accent is curious. She's from Georgia – Soviet, not American – but lived in England for most of her life. Her voice is very soft, only giving a hint of its origins on her Rs. She's ten years older than Andy and myself, and in better physical shape than almost anybody else here, which is really saying something. Not sure how much of it is tinkered. 'Can't pretend that I'm not nervous,' she says. She stretches the letters out, then the whole word. It sounds different, almost alien in its delivery. My own accent has been softened and lost if it was ever there in the first place; the rise and fall of my own language washed out. Hers is still there, and still prominent. Nerrrvous, she says, or it sounds.

'You'd be crazy if you weren't, I reckon,' says Tobi.

I feel sick, and this feels loose. Wrong. I need to speak with Tomas one last time. I can feel the lack of gravity inside me. My guts, swollen up and churning, and like the slightest movement could upset me, could end this for me. I back away from them all, down the corridor, around the corner, and I open a connection and whisper at him that I need to hear his voice.

'What's wrong now?' Tomas asks.

'Are you sure we've done everything we can?'

'Have a safe flight, Brother,' he replies – he calls it a flight, which sounds so demeaning for what this actually is – and I hear the click of him cancelling the connection. Over the speaker system, the launch crew announce that they are opening up the airlock entrance. We're boarding.

Every part of this process has been designed to ensure that nothing can go wrong. I cannot stress that enough: the level of control that we have enacted on this entire operation. Entry to the *Lära* is as controlled as everything else. There is no room for error. Everything must be checked, processed, run through before we are allowed on. There are exacting checklists full of bullet points that take days to tick off. It's these things that can mean the difference between life and death. This is how the systems can be guaranteed to work when we need them to, how we can streamline them and make them user friendly while still retaining the safety: they are prepared and perfected, and instigated with absolute care and diligence.

'Are we getting on anytime soon?' Tobi asks. She looks at the clock on the wall. Less than half an hour until we leave. Sedation takes only a few minutes to completely set in; the paralysis less. We don't control the boarding process from the ship: we are nothing but passengers for now.

'Not long,' I say. I am running through their final checks

in my head, and as I reach the final one, the door opens. It slides satisfyingly and the launch crew inside the ship move backwards, grinning. They've got balloons and a banner, both hanging in the middle of the air. My crew laughs, almost hysterically. *Bon Voyage*, the banner says. *From the moon to the stars*, under it in smaller type. They applaud, and we applaud them. We walk through to the corridor in single file as the ground crew start pulling aside the decorations, and we all find the bed labelled with our names. (I pretend to not know which one is mine, even though I dictated where the beds lie. I arranged them, like chess pieces.)

'I want to go last,' I say to Inna. She nods.

'You're nervous?' Nerrrvous.

'No,' I say. 'I've been sedated before. Nothing to be scared of.'

'Good,' she says. 'I always think it takes better the less wary you are.' She preps her injections. She clicks the first one in, a bullet into the hypo's chamber. I catch a glimpse of a mark – a tattoo, I think – on her collarbone as she moves, as the fabric of her shirt pulls away, but not enough to see what it is. I wonder what it is of. I wonder how big it is. 'Who's first?' she asks the group. Hikaru raises his arm, and, in one motion, starts to roll up his sleeve. 'Neck,' Inna says. 'It's better there. It takes faster.' He shrugs and lies back on the bed. The magnets click in, holding him in place, and she folds herself down a little to reach him. The hypo seems to fizz as it empties the contents of the pod into him. He winces, and then shudders, shaking the injection off.

'Nothing to it,' he says. The others line up one by one, and they all act as if it's nothing, but I see in their hands the mild tremble of fear at the injection itself; or, maybe, at the thought of being asleep and not being in control. I never used to drink, for that loss; I never used to take painkillers, for the same. Tobi goes first, then Lennox, then Wallace, and then Inna turns to me. 'You next,' she says.

'One second,' I say, as she readies the hypo. I pull myself to the cockpit and open a connection to Tomas. 'Can you hear me?' I ask him.

'What is it?' Tomas sounds annoyed at the sound of my voice. I know how busy he must be. I speak quietly, and turn away from the rest of the crew. I don't want anybody to see that I'm worried.

'Is everything okay?'

'It's fine. Why would it be anything other than okay?'

'I just wanted to check.'

'You think that I would let the launch happen if everything wasn't okay?'

'No,' I say.

'I have work to do, Mira.' And then he's gone. I turn back to Inna, who's waiting. 'Let me get into the bed,' I say. 'Do it there.' I am next to the central controls on one side, with Inna on the other.

'You can't,' she says. 'You have to do me after I've done you.' I nod and sit on the edge of the bed, unbuttoning the top of my shirt, and I pull it down to show the part she needs. She leans in: I feel the press of the needle. Like a bore, followed by the break of the skin, and the liquid. That's the worst part: feeling it rushing inside of you, something where it should not be, mingling. It hurts for a second, nothing more. 'It'll only be a couple of minutes before you feel it,' she says, and she pulls her top to one side and exposes the tattoo again. I can see more of it: the head of a bird, blue and yellow, eyes wide, mouth open. An eagle's beak. It seems to run lower, towards her chest itself. She puts the capsule in and then hands me the hypo, and points with her finger to where I should place the nib.

'Ready?' I ask.

'Of course,' she says. The hypo rests against the peak of the bird's head. I press the button and she barely reacts; I pull it away. She folds her top back up. 'Now,' she says, 'time for sleep.' She swings her body round into the bed and I hear the hiss of the magnets. 'They lower the doors for us?' she asks.

'They will, but you can do it yourself if you want.' I glance over at the others, their frontages still up. 'Sleep well, everybody,' I say. They murmur; they're already under. It hits you like you don't know it's coming, and you're suddenly elsewhere, in total darkness. It's brutal, how fast it is. Inna lies back.

'See you when we wake up,' she says. She reaches for the lid; her touch alone makes it descend, bringing it down around her. The glass darkens as it lowers. I flatten myself against the bed as well, and I fasten the magnets, and I try to stay still, because I am still not used to this; the feeling of never being flat, of never being orientated one way over the other. I rest my head on the bed, snug inside the plastic form that's been moulded around our individual physical shapes. I wait until a click comes over the intercom, and I hear Tomas' voice.

'This is the first milestone on the road to the stars,' Tomas says. 'Beds closing in five. Four.' He finishes the countdown and the glass slides down and seals me in. Enough air to breathe, to sustain, that's the deal. When you sleep you naturally need less. Your body rights itself, puts itself into a state of optimum intake. It aids the depth of your sleep as well, having less air. I shut my eyes and wait for sleep to take me. I know that it cannot be long now.

I hear the engines kick in, and the rumble that they send throughout the entire ship. For that second, it feels like an explosion. I hear the joining door being retracted, and the order that it be so, and I hear Tomas' voice over the intercom telling the ground crew to prepare for launch. I keep my eyes shut and think about the path we're going to take, and how the launch will look. We've run so many simulations – and a simulation was how we knew to launch from the NISS in the first place, how the money saved on building an extension here to do it was proven to be the right choice by another simulation – and I can see them all running at the same time.

When I used to fly in airplanes I would shut my eyes for a second as we took off and picture the plane exploding, bursting into flame. They say that if a plane is going to crash, it's statistically most likely to happen as it takes off. I figured that if I got past that I was pretty safe. I imagine this ship exploding. I imagine the pieces floating all around me in space. I imagine me floating amongst them.

Tomas does the other checks, his voice talking through every stage, and I start to wonder why I'm not asleep yet. I should be, by now. This is crucial. Sometimes people need a few minutes to really let the sedative sink in, I remind myself. Sometimes the body's natural adrenalin, the endorphins, they need longer to be counteracted and swallowed by the sleep. But then: now I am worrying that I am not asleep. In my life I have insomnia, I suppose, of a sort: when pressure mounts and the following day carries any sort of importance, I will worry all night, worry that I am not going to achieve the required amount of sleep to function at an optimum the following day. This is a self-fulfilling prophecy, as the worry is then the thing that conspires to keep me awake, rolling around in my head in circular patterns that never stop looping in on themselves. Only when I have given up all hope do I stand a chance of actually falling asleep: when I have managed to pass that point, to realize that there is nothing I can do now, and that the day I was so worried about is likely ruined. It is a hindrance; a horror. I sleep so badly, because almost every day carries that pressure. Tablets do not help, not really: all they do is render me more tired than I would ordinarily be when I awake. Eventually nature takes over and I sleep: but it is fitful, and it is not what I want. This injection: this is to be my salvation for this leg of the journey. After this, I will worry about it as and when.

I cannot see a clock from here. There's nothing. That's an oversight, and I should have thought about that. There are no microphones in the beds either, another oversight. It's to protect the seal: the fewer holes there are, the less chance of there being a crack. The pilot on the *Ishiguro* died before they even woke up, probably because of a gap in the seal, something like that. So we were cautious. It'll settle in. I'll sleep soon, because this is medically controlled. This is something I cannot avoid. On occasions, when I have been at my most desperate for sleep, I have taken painkillers: something strong enough to dull everything else, to remove my faculties from worrying about the sleep itself. This is like a better version of them: unavoidable, inevitable.

'Launch crew prepare,' I hear through the ship. You can't open the beds from the inside once they've been sealed. If you could, you could accidentally do it, and there's nothing worse than that thought. The speeds that the ship will reach as it pushes off from the NISS – free of the trappings of any real gravitational pull, free of the resistance offered by an atmosphere – are so ridiculously powerful that they could – or would – damage the human body. Our bones, our bodies, they are not strong enough. The beds are pressure sealed to provide an environment that the body can cope with. They create their own pressure level inside them; protect the crew from the g forces. It's another of mine and Tomas' innovations. Another way that we are making this expedition work. If any of the crew were to be out of their beds – and the controlled environment created therein – they would likely die. Their body would be found pulverized, as if it had been beaten to death. But I am not loose. I am in here, awake. I don't know if this is dangerous. I cannot think about how dangerous this is. I shout.

'Help,' I shout, 'I am not asleep yet!' I call Inna's name, hoping that I'll see her descend and open my bed, and inject me again, triple-strength, able to level me to slumber while this flight happens. I was always scared of flying as well: of seeing the Earth get smaller underneath me. Not like I will see it from space, that doesn't faze me, because you can see everything in one go: more the sensation of suddenly glimpsing people as specks, and cars as ants, and then everything smaller and smaller, houses like dust, and then whole towns. But Inna doesn't come, and everything is dark, soundtracked by the rumble of the engines proper: through everything, right through the hull. Everything underneath me feels like vibration, nothing else. I feel my bones rattle, and my teeth in my jaw. 'I should be asleep!' I shout, but my voice dulls itself against the inside of my bed, and against the growling of the ship, and against the paralytic. My words slurred.

The engines fire for launch in three phases. First phase is a warm-up, bringing the temperature of the engines up to the necessary point. The second phase – the phase that I feel kick in through the rumble, like a foot on a gas pedal while the handbrake remains pulled on – adds the injectant and coolant into the burner, readying to add it to the engines themselves. 'Please,' I hear myself say – an echo through the rumble – and then the third phase.

'Countdown time,' Tomas says. He goes through the numbers, twenty to one. I brace myself. I don't know what will happen. Why did we have to be asleep for this part of the launch? Because it made sense. Because we were liable to panic. Because the vibrations of the ship would be so violent that we weren't to struggle against them. I have always hated sleep. Not been afraid of it, that's wrong, but felt it a waste. Tomas slept less than I did, and he would play pranks on me as I overslept, as I lazed about; but it's more than that. He would have achieved so much by the time that I woke up. He would have done things. Found things. Now, he's meant to be awake and guiding me, and I'm meant to be asleep, and letting him, but I'm not. I want to be. I don't want to die, here. I don't want to be shaken apart. I tell myself not to struggle. I have the self-control to do this, I tell myself. I say it aloud; or I think that I do.

The engines accelerate to a point where we break a faster speed than any man-made machine before. In the glory days of space travel, when we were still trying, the shuttles hit speeds of nearly twenty thousand miles per hour, when they were in orbit. We're doubling that; more, even, when we reach maximum acceleration. Tripling it. And then we will coast, using that momentum, slowing to maintain that speed only, holding it as long and as far as we can. That's the rumble. Every part of this ship is made from materials built to withstand that pressure, joists and fixtures made with composite materials that didn't even exist a decade ago. The metal of the hull is our own: we bought the man who designed it, all of his patents, all of his designs. I think of this, of the blueprints now: flashing through my mind. His metal shakes like everything else, though. No amount of stress testing can prevent it feeling as if it is falling apart. We didn't tell the crew that. We told them that every possibility had been accounted for. We lied, because how else do you get people to agree to something like this?

'One,' Tomas says, or I think it's Tomas. Maybe I've been counting down with him, speaking at the same time, my voice along with his. The launch happens, and the craft shakes and lurches, and I hit my head, over and over, on the hard plastic part of the bed that is moulded to me instead of being a pillow, practicality not comfort, and I think that that's yet another oversight. We should have had a pillow; then, maybe my head wouldn't hit this so hard.

Everything gives way to darkness. This isn't sleep: this is my body giving up.

Man wasn't meant to see this. Man was meant to stay on the ground. My mother said that she believed in angels, and maybe she was right. What are the implications of travelling as fast as we're suggesting? That's what I asked Tomas. I said, Really, the actual implications. Do we know? We put carcasses in the centrifuge, reaching g forces equivalent to this, and we watched them quiver and be pulverized. So I said, Are we sure that this is the right thing? What are the implications? He said, The implications are that you'll have travelled faster than anybody before you. You know what I mean. He sighed. It could break you. You'll feel it, whatever happens. It'll pull every part of you. So we make them sleep, I suggested, because then they'll not know. They'll wake up feeling like they've been in a fight, and not knowing who hit them. Oh, they'll know, he said.

I open my eyes, like instinct, but it hurts. Everything's glowing white, I would swear: even though the lights are off and my glass is dimmed, it glows.

White, white, white. Almost painful, it's so bright.

I try and open them again, to see, and it feels like they're being pressed on, forced and pushed down, and everything's white when it should be black. My body can't move, I discover. I wish I was like the others, safe and asleep. They don't know what their bodies are going through. I can feel the bones in my face – the very essence of my skull, everything, underneath the skin, underneath all of me, every little part – and it feels as if it is being pulled apart.

I am in hell.

3

When I next open my eyes, it's quiet. The rumble is gone, and it's dark. My eyes hurt: all I can really see, apart from the darkness, are after-images of flashing white, as if I've been staring too closely at the sun. The beds hiss open, including mine. I hear Tomas' voice.

'Time to wake up, rise and shine,' he says. The pressure of the sealed beds is meant to keep us asleep until the time the beds open, and the lights are turned on. The blackness around the sunspots in my eyes goes white as well, brighter than the rest, and I can't see. I shut my eyes but the glow comes through the eyelids, so I try to turn my head. The beds are fully open. I hear voices.

'Wow,' says Lennox. 'Holy shit, that hurts.' He's floating upwards, arching his back. 'Oh my word.' I hear something click.

'What was that?' asks Tobi, and Lennox laughs.

'My bloody back,' he says. 'That noise was my bloody back.'

'Move slowly, all of you,' Inna says. 'Stretch, sure, but be gentle with it.'

37

'You never warned us about this,' Wallace says. 'Jesus Christ, I feel like I've been in a bar fight.' The others laugh. 'Tomas, where are we?' There's a slight pause as the transmission is sent back to Tomas, on Earth still. I wonder if he's slept yet.

'You're in space,' Tomas eventually says, his voice coming through a slight crackle. (Only a few seconds' wait. That will get longer, I know.) The crew laugh again, and then coo. This is realized: we're out here, wherever here is. 'Call up the maps, that'll show your position.'

'How fast are we going?'

Another wait, then Tomas answers. 'Forty-six,' he says. 'And that's locked in. Engines resting.' The delay here is really nothing. It'll get worse the further we go. And it's crystal clear. Used to be that, this far out, you'd be speaking through the hiss, hoping the message would get through, biting your nails. Another piece of technology that made all of this possible. 'Is everybody awake, everybody okay?' None of them say anything, but their silence is enough. I still haven't opened my eyes, but I can feel theirs on me: wondering why I'm lying as I am, stretched out and strapped in still. They stay silent. I can hear them wondering. Tomas guesses. 'Mira, are you up? Are you awake?'

'No,' I say. 'Not yet.' I try my eyes again, and they work – I can see the blurred shapes of the crew past the spots – so I swing my legs out, haul my body up. It feels worse than I ever imagined. I've never been a fighter. I never knew what this might feel like, when the analogy was presented. I could only guess.

'Up and at 'em,' Tomas says. 'I need you to start running tests. Begin with the batteries. We need to make sure they're recharging properly for when we need to decelerate.'

Everything that isn't the engine here is run off a battery. We took very few things from the previous space-flight attempts – the previous and failed attempts, by the South Asian Space Agency in the twenties, the *Ishiguro* not long after them – but we took their battery systems. Piezoelectric energy. It converts the vibrations of the ship into power. The rumble that we went through during launch, the slight shudder of the engines through the hull, even the repercussions of us being inside here and interacting with the ship herself, it all ends up as energy. It's what keeps the lights on, the ship warm, and us alive. In a worst-case scenario, we've even posited that it could get us home, powering the tiny boosters that we would otherwise use as stabilizers. Worst-case. But the power is therefore precious. If they had to – we're adrift, the fuel fails, something – the batteries are what would keep us alive. Though, they burn power a lot faster than they generate it. When we decelerate, when we're reaching the anomaly, we need to sleep again: the pressure change, all over again. I cannot even think about that now. 'I'll give you a minute,' Tomas says.

I feel a hand on my arm, and a face close to mine. 'Are you okay?' Inna asks. Her breath smells of mint, already, as if this is something she has taken care of before anything else. I dread to think about mine. That is such a small thing.

'I'm okay,' I say. 'Something went wrong, with the injection.'

'What do you mean?'

'I didn't sleep. I was awake through the launch.'

She squeezes my arm. Her nails: I can feel them on my skin, pressing down. 'That's a common dream, I think. When people are sedated, they manifest dreams of what they feel that they're missing. It's really a very common thing.'

'I was awake,' I protest, 'and then I passed out. I hit my head.'

'Well, you seem okay now,' she says. She runs her hand behind my skull, to feel for a lump, maybe. She doesn't believe me. It doesn't matter. 'Open your eyes for me,' she says.

'It's too bright,' I tell her.

'Let me look.' I feel her hand on my forehead, shielding me from the light. She stands in front of me, casting me in shadow. I open my eyes, and I can see her, past the after-image. She's close, peering at me. 'They're fine,' she says. I can feel her breath on my face, somehow both cool and warm. 'Pupils dilated, but that's okay. They'll settle. You're fine,' she says. She steps back, and I blink. Only the spots remain, but everything else starts to slip into focus. The crew are all staring at me.

'I'm okay,' I say. They are professional, as am I. They know that what we need to do now is worry about the rest of the mission. This is a mission, where the *Ishiguro* was, what, a jaunt? And I am a scientist, not an action hero. In the old days, there used to be rules: astronauts had to conform to certain physical and mental presets in order to be able to undertake their missions. They had to be psychologically proofed to within an inch of their minds, ready and willing and able to take on whatever challenges would be hurled at them. And when Tomas and I were planning this, we said that our crew would adhere to those rules. You look at the *Ishiguro*, at what went wrong, and they started with their crew. Faces that were too pretty, faces made for television. People with inadequate training – six months, only, where we decided that eighteen was the minimum. And a journalist up there with them, purely so that they could secure more funding. The day that they went, they found out that his wife had killed herself, and still they let him go! It was madness. Tomas was adamant: that sort of thing wouldn't be happening on our voyage. On ours, our crew would be right for the task at hand, multi-disciplinary. The correct people, above all else. When we spoke about it, in my mind, Tomas was the one up here. I assumed, I think, because maybe he seemed to win more coin tosses than I did. But the rest of the crew, in my mind, were to be solid and able. If something went wrong – god forbid, if they lost a pilot, for example, due to whatever – anybody else in the crew could step in and take their place. All of us are expendable, to some extent. I know the research that needs to be done when we reach the anomaly, but if I were to die, Tomas would be able to talk somebody else through it.

They all watch me push away from the bed, even as I squint through the brightness. I flail in the lack of gravity, somehow even less graceful than I was on NISS. Inna takes my hand and pulls me to one side, then puts it onto one of the rails that runs along the side of the room. She folds my fingers over it for me, and then puts her own over mine, putting pressure on it. The confidence of her, telling me that all of this will be all right.

'Hold on,' she says. I clutch onto the rail, and look at my hand, to focus myself. I can't tell if the white is my knuckles or the residue of the spots in my eyes, but it distracts me and I let go. I haven't got control, and I lose my breathing. I feel a hand on my shoulder: Hikaru, steadying me. He smiles.

'Dr Hyvönen,' he says. 'You're okay. It's just a bit of residual whatever. Can't have you ruined before we've even begun.' I cling to him, and I try to make the feeling in my gut die down; I try to think of anything but how easy it would be to spin here, and how tired I am, and the whiteness behind my eyes, which doesn't seem to leaving me no matter how many times I blink, no matter how many times I shut my lids and try to picture nothing but darkness.

Hikaru and Tobi prepare the cockpit. They sit down and they check the pathfinder, the life-support systems, the drag. One of them is to stay here at all times, to ensure that nothing changes suddenly. We are to travel to, and then stop outside, the anomaly, as best we understand it, and take measurements and readings, conduct all of our tests from there. It takes a long time to stop this ship as well: and the force to do it is just as strong as the force it took to get it going. We have to have our wits about us. As they are preparing, they change the cockpit screens to show us behind the ship; and they call us over, both of them smiling. There is the Earth: spinning in the distance, the size of the smallest coin, and getting smaller and smaller as we watch it, as we are moving away from it so quickly that it would be unbelievable if Tomas and I hadn't designed it to be so.

I feel sick, unbelievably sick. Inna takes me to one side and clips me to the safety bars, and she gives me pills to swallow down that will settle my stomach, she says. I know what they do: they settle nothing. Instead, they suppress the brain's ability to feel the stomach churning. I don't say anything, because this is her job. I have no desire to undermine her. The rest of the crew start their checks: Tobi and Hikaru running through every possible fault-point, calling out features of the craft and running analysis on those systems, synchronizing the computers with the ship itself, checking the batteries, reporting back to Tomas to ensure parity of results. Wallace goes off down the corridor, towards the engine rooms, to check efficiency there, to ensure that all readings there are correct; Inna leaves me, patting me on the knee, and then goes round one by one, looking at the crew's eyes, to make sure that there are no burst blood vessels (or, at least, that's what she says, as she looks for signs of stroke or aneurysm); and when he's been checked and okayed, Lennox pulls himself in front of me, smiling.

'You want me to start doing something?' he asks. His accent is bizarre. France by way of Jamaica, delivered with the drive of having studied in London. A proper mélange of an accent. We are kindred spirits in that, if nothing else. 'I'll call up exactly where we are.'

'We know where we are,' I say. The computer does all of that for us. We're useless until we get to the anomaly itself.

'I can set us up. Set your workstation up. Start pinging the anomaly.'

'Fine,' I say.

'You want to check my settings before I begin?'

'I trust you,' I tell him, regardless of whether I do or not.

'Okay.' He pushes backwards, and he somersaults off. He's graceful in a way that I never will be. 'Listen, I just wanted to say: thanks for this opportunity, yeah?' That seems an understatement, but it's not. He's humble. He's a good kid, I suppose. I am too judgmental of ambition. He calls up a screen and starts the procedures, all of which log everything we're going to be looking at. While we're out here, we can do work that would, from Earth, take months. Maybe even years. He checks in with Tomas, and I hear them begin the work together. This is a partnership spread over thousands of miles, over space and time. When Lennox is going, Tomas asks to speak to me. Lennox channels it through to the station nearest me.

'Is everything okay up there?' Tomas asks. The speakers are focused and driven; and voice doesn't carry, not here. Only I can hear him.

'It's fine,' I say. I pause.

'And you're okay?'

'I'm queasy,' I say. 'It happens.'

'Everything looks wonderful from down here. Perfect. I'd say that this has been a triumph, wouldn't you?' He sounds thrilled. I can hear the grin in his voice – big, toothy grin, bending his cheeks, stretching and bending his birthmark. A clap of his hands together. 'So now we've all got a job to do.'

'Yes,' I say. I don't say anything else, and his pause is longer, as if he's waiting for me to.

'I'm going to get some sleep. Go home; it's been a long day. Simpson is taking the post here now, okay? You need anything, you call him.'

'Sure,' I say, but he knows that I won't. I can handle anything that comes up. And then he's gone, and I'm alone again. I'm incredibly tired as well; hearing him saying it does something to me, like the involuntary contagion of a yawn. I shut my eyes, still floating there. Why can I sleep now? Why is it that when I am needed I could drift off and allow myself to be gone? Tobi shouts that she is hungry: I am startled awake. I don't know if I could eat, not feeling like this.

'Our first meal,' she says. 'Feels like we should have some sort of ceremony.' They all float to the table, and I unclip myself. I have to join them, to stress my leadership, my skill here. I need their respect; Tomas and I long debated the importance of respect amongst a crew. I cling to the rail and I pull myself along towards the central dais table. I can feel them staring at me. They are still humouring me, because

44

grace is something innate, that cannot be taught, but I know that I will have to get used to this. I will have to become better at it, in these confined quarters. On the NISS it was one thing; here, I may even have to go outside the ship, and I need to know that I am capable of that. The table divides the central part of the room. The shape, the construct of the room, is a triple loop, like an infinity symbol doubled-up: three circular rooms on top of each other. The cockpit, the table, the beds: all round. Tomas read books on psychology during the interior design stage of the project, and he read that circular rooms could help to offer an artificial sense of camaraderie. No nooks or crannies to hide in. That's why the beds can be darkened and made private: in case we need alone time. There's some wiggle room, but not much. The table has magnets for us to attach our suits to, like everything else. This wasn't our invention. The suits have ten or so of the magnets, heavy duty, and every fixture and fitting in the ship has the other part. You let the two or so of them meet and voilà, you aren't going anywhere. 'Somebody should say something,' Tobi reiterates. We all wait as Wallace comes back down the corridor and sits himself down.

'Everything's fine back there,' he says. He calls down to Simpson, on the ground. 'Temperatures exactly how they should be, working at 97 per cent efficiency. Batteries on 98 per cent.' Better than fine, even: within our optimum parameters.'

'There. Wallace said something,' Hikaru says to Tobi. 'Now we eat?'

'You know what I mean,' Tobi says. 'This is pretty big, right? Being up here?' They all look to me. 'This must be one of the best feelings, to see this actually happen. To come to fruition.'

'It's good,' I say. I don't tell them that my insides are

tumbling and churning, and that I can't balance, and that there's still these fucking white spots blinking in my peripheral vision. I don't tell them all that I think I was awake during the acceleration. I try to be inspiring. 'We've got a huge challenge ahead of us, and we've got a long way to go. Lesser journeys have destroyed people. You have to remember what we're here for.' They're silent. I pause: feeling sick. As if having my mouth open might be my undoing. They're waiting, and I can feel the churn, and I think that I have nothing else to say. But then I hear a voice the same as mine pick up where I left off:

'This isn't something for your CVs, or to tell your grandchildren. This is a mission for the whole human race. There's something out there, and it's our job to find out what it is. This isn't exploration: it's discovery. It's potentially finding the next important thing to push humanity forward. This is Columbus returning to the New World, going back there and saying, This is mine. I found this. Now I'm going to fucking start something.'

I had no idea that Tomas was still there, and listening. He said he was going home, but he didn't. And he doesn't say goodbye; he just falls silent. Tobi unclips and opens a cupboard at the side and brings out a box of meal bars.

'Rub a dub dub, thanks for the grub,' she says.

We worked for the UNSA back before that was what it was even called. Back then it was still a collection of companies and ex-DARPA employees trying to put something new together. We wrote a letter and we spent a summer halfway across the world, suddenly in America, and interning for Gerhardt Singer. It was the summer before he went up in the *Ishiguro* and never came back. Afterwards, we wrote a letter to his partner saying how honoured we were to have met him, to have studied under him. The things that he taught us. I think that's why we started research into the areas that we did, to carry on his work. (We didn't tell him that we thought he played it wrong, and took too many chances. That would have been cruel, I think: he was hampered, and it was not all his fault, the choices that were made.) Dr Singer said to us, before we left him at the end of the summer, that the anomaly was his pet project.

You pick something and stick with it, he had told us. Because, if you focus, there's a chance that it will be important. Some scientists spread themselves too thin, you know? They try lots of different things, go from pillar to post, and they never settle on the one thing. I think it's better to have something that's my life's work – that might be important – than just generalize and leave nothing. He seemed really sad when he spoke about it, as if he might go his whole life and not discover anything. As it turned out, he died, and we don't know if he ever discovered what the anomaly was. That seems such an inglorious way to go: out here, in the emptiness, still asking that question you have always asked and never being able to get an answer.

Inna comes to see me as I sit by myself above the expanse. There is a screen embedded in the floor. When we were young, our mother took us on holiday to Greece, and we went in a boat with a glass floor, and we could see right down into the ocean, and we could see the fish and the water, how deep it was. When we were designing, we took that concept and adapted it. We fitted a camera into the underside-exterior of the ship, and we layered a screen into the floor that could show that camera's feed. Tomas was so

excited by the idea. Think about it! he said. It'll be incredible, to be up there, nothing underneath you. It'll be like
you're floating. It wasn't meant to be me, that You, I suspect:
I suspect he thought it would be him. He wanted to have it
constantly on, a constant hole to space. I said that not everybody would want to see that all the time, want to see that
nothingness. He said, There'll be stars, and I said, Well, they
don't count for that much when they're that far away. I have
seen stars every day from right here. He argued at one point
that it should be glass, even: a clear, unfiltered view. I told
him that was stupid. There was more chance of something
going wrong. Everything that could have been a window is
now a screen, linked to an external camera. We took all glass
out because it was easier. It meant fewer seals, and less chance
of anything going wrong under the pressure we would be
exerting.

Now I can sit here and look down and see everything.
I've called up the trackers, and computer visualizations dart
across the glass, highlighting planets and galaxies. They trace
comets. They assign names, and they tell me distances that
can never – or not in my lifetime, not in this craft and with
this crew – be reached. But it makes it look as though the
galaxy is somehow that much closer. Somehow almost attain-
able. Inna stares at the same things that I do, circling around
me. She puts her hand onto my shoulder, to steady herself.
The skin on her hands – all over her, in fact – it looks younger
than she actually is. I wonder if she's had work done.
Everybody has; I would not judge her. It would be sensible,
probably. It's so hard to tell nowadays. If we didn't have
everybody's details, I wouldn't put her as older than me, not
really. But then, I don't know if I even look my age. I call
up details for the screen for what we're looking at: the age

48

of the stars we're travelling past at such speed. It's guesswork aided by supposition, but some of them – based on their brightness, their distance – some of them we're pretty accurate on, I think.

'It's wonderful,' Inna says. 'This is something I never even dreamed that I'd get to see.' I don't know if this is her way of thanking me for putting her on this trip. She wrote Tomas and me a letter with her application, talking about how excited she would be. How, when she was a girl, she had always dreamed of this, just as Tomas and I had. That's how you appeal to us: you say, I am just like you. I understand you and what you are trying to do.

'Aren't you scared?' I ask her. She shakes her head.

'Not now we are up here. Not in the least.' She dips the tip of her foot at the screen, stretching forward. It focuses on the star nearest her toe-point, and details that system. The name of it, how far it is, when we first logged it as a race. And then it tells how long it would take to get there. She looks at the number, which extends well beyond our lifetimes, and she laughs. 'That's why I'm not scared,' she says. 'You look at this, it's easy to see how big it all is. Much bigger than us. Time is something we have such a limited supply of, and I'd rather do something important with what I have got left.' Everybody wants glory, I do not say to her. It's embedded inside us, entrenched deep down as part of what makes us human. Tomas joked, after we spoke to her the first time, that I was attracted to Inna. He said that I was, and I protested, but he is that way. He will drive a point home, and he will insist, because he always believes that he is right. You don't have a chance, he told me, because she has lived, and she has done so much. She's so worldly, and look at us. We don't have a world: we have a laboratory. I said to him, You've found somebody, and he said, No, we found each other. It's a two-way situation, Mira. She's a baker: her kitchen is as much of a lab as ours is. 'Do you feel pressure?' Inna asks me. 'Do you feel that this is somehow harder, because of what has come before?' The last successful space flight was nearly four decades ago. We're fighting against the odds.

'I don't get pre-occupied with it,' I say.

'But it's there, isn't it? Hanging over our heads.'

'I suppose,' I say.

'Like the sword of Damocles.'

'Yes.' I turn to her. My own foot brushes the screen-floor, and selects a series of planets, sending the data presented into a whirl. 'I try to not worry about these things. We have made this as foolproof as it can be. But then, we fools can try and test that.' I smile. I look for a reaction in her face, to my joke. I am trying these things: I have seen Tomas do them, make jokes and win people that way. He has always been better at that stuff than I have. I am trying.

'It's normal that you would be worried,' she says. 'You have to remember: there's no pressure to succeed. We do the best we can do.' I realize that this isn't the talk that I thought it was. She isn't impressed by me. She is professional. Her timetable says that she will perform Day One psychiatric evaluations of us. This is mine. I feel everything sink inside me. The ache in my insides, that I had forgotten about, it comes back. I do not know what to say to her.

Then I am saved: a shout comes from the back of the ship. It's Wallace's voice, a howl for help, and Inna unclips herself and races off, pushing off with her feet like a swimmer, shooting down the corridor. I fumble with the magnets holding my glove to the rail, and as soon as I am away from the wall I feel myself rock. I feel the bile inside, even through the pills that Inna gave me. I steady myself. I shut my eyes, and I see the white glimmers, the pulsing in my own eyelids.

'The sword of Damocles – you know that she used it wrong, don't you?' Tomas is speaking to me again.

'Yes' I say. Of course I know that. He knows that I know it. 'You're back,' I say, changing the subject. 'Did you sleep?' It doesn't seem as if it can have been long enough. Perhaps it wasn't. Perhaps he couldn't sleep. He ignores my question.

'People just use it to describe any old situation where there's pressure or what have you. But Damocles took the king's place, and then he was the only one on the throne. That's the point of the story: if you're not king, you don't sit on the throne, and the sword will never hurt you.' I know what he's going to say, because he's a fucking shit. 'We're the kings here, Mira. She can say it's hanging over all of them, but you know it's not.'

'I know the point of the bloody story,' I snap. I shut my eyes and I try to breathe more. He hears me, through the earpiece. I pull myself along the railing to the side, and then around the corner, past the table and to the corridor hatch. Tomas is quiet then, and I don't talk to him any more either, but I know he's still listening to everything we are saying. Nothing will slip past him.

Down the corridor, they are all shouting, and I cannot tell what is wrong through the noise. I am the last one to respond, the slowest. I breathe. I try to breathe.

Tobi is pressed against the floor, being held down by Wallace, and Inna is grabbing at her arms as they flap around. She is convulsing, and she is uncontrollable; only pinned down because they are holding her, and it is taking Wallace and Lennox both to manage this. I imagine her breaking free from this, drifting and twitching. I think about the *Ishiguro*, and I pray that she isn't dying. There is no way we would continue. We would be ordered to turn here and head home, because there would be too much at risk. She would jeopardize this all.

'What's wrong?' I ask. I can't see her face properly, because she's moving so much, and her hair – which is short enough anyway, perpetually tied back, as the sensibilities of zero gravity dictate – her hair is mussed all over her face. I catch a glimpse of one of her eyes, and it looks all white, but I cannot tell if that is true or if it is me: the after-images still dance in my own vision. Then she turns her head on a convulsion, as Inna tries to prep a needle for her, and I see that her other eye is dark red. Just the eye, not running down her face: a thick blood-colour in the eyeball itself.

'Please,' Inna says, and Wallace and Lennox hold her extra tightly, really struggling for that second. Inna reaches in and presses the hypodermic to her neck and it only takes a second before Tobi goes limp. Lennox and Wallace let go and she starts to drift; her limbs all loose, her back arched. I think of my mother, and her angels: this is, for a second, as if Tobi is ascending. I stare, and Wallace and Lennox pat each other, checking they're all right.

'She's fine,' Inna says to me, as if she knew that I was about to ask. 'It's a subconjunctival haemorrhage. Bleeds can happen when the body is this stressed. Does she have a history of seizures?'

'I don't think so,' I say. 'Tomas approved the medical checks, in the, uh, the personnel files.' We split the tasks up:

he took some approvals, I took others. We shared everything, but his memory of these things will be better than mine, I am sure.

He interrupts. 'No history, doctor,' he says. His voice comes over the intercom, filling the corridor. It's jarring: how sometimes he is only in my ear, and sometimes all around us.

Wallace pulls Tobi towards him and folds her up slightly in his arms.

'Where shall I take her?' he asks Inna. He holds her like you would a child, maybe, carrying them to bed. He has daughters; I wonder if he carries them like this as well. She convulses slightly still, and her eyelids flicker. I imagine, under them, her one red eye darting left to right. I think that she could shake like this even if she was dead; when we were children, my mother kept chickens: I have seen them killed, their wings beating their sides long after their heads have been taken.

'We should get her to her bed,' Inna says. 'We can secure her there. She'll be fine when she wakes up.' So Wallace carries Tobi past us all, and Lennox and Inna follow them. I pull myself along the rail behind. They are like swimmers. This is what it was likened to, in the early lessons. Push off, use your arms to steer and guide yourself, like rudders; use the environment to control your trajectory. That was the first lesson. I didn't attend the others: there were better uses for my time. Hikaru cranes his neck and looks back from the cockpit section, and he asks how she is.

'She's okay,' I say, and he nods. I feel as if I need to control this more. Otherwise, it could all be in danger of running away from me. We – they – strap her down, fastening her into the bed. Inna checks Tobi's eye properly while she's out, looking behind it, then scans her skull. We all stare at the results on the screens, and we're relieved to hear that she's clear. Inna tells us that it's stress, pressure and stress that caused what happened, and nothing else. She opens the other beds up, and she floats above them.

'This is as good a time as any,' she says. 'The rest of you should get some sleep as well. I'll stay up with Hikaru, keep him company.' She means: interview him. Take her time talking about who he is, how he feels about this mission. Check he's okay, because now he might be the only pilot for a while.

'I can stay awake as well,' I say. 'I'm not tired.'

'Liar.' She opens the lid of my bed and darkens the glass. 'You need to sleep. You look like hell.' That hurts, to hear her saying that. She leans in close to me, so that the others can't hear. 'If you truly didn't sleep when we launched, you will need to now. Don't argue with me, and go to bed.' She takes my hand, or the end of my arm, and she drags me off the rail and towards the centre of the room. I let her.

'Wake me if anything changes,' I say.

'We're in the middle of nothingness, Mira. What's going to change?' I lie down and she links the magnets for me, then lowers the bed lid. She watches me until I can't see her through the dark glass.

'How long do I sleep for?' I ask her, through the lid, but she doesn't answer, and I can't see out. I don't like how little I can move in this thing. At home, I sleep on my side. It's how I'm most comfortable: facing the wall, my back to the expanse of the room. Here, you are forced to lie on your back; and the hardness of the plastic now jars, it all seeming less comfortable than it could be; and the oxygen supply in these things runs slightly too cold. It regulates itself, because we didn't want blankets or the opportunity to trap yourself in a sweatbox. It regulates itself: another way we have stream-lined this whole process. Innovation through automation.

'She's forceful,' Tomas says in my ear. I had forgotten that he was there.

'I don't need to sleep,' I say.

'Of course you do, Brother.'

'You didn't. You said you were going to bed, but then you were back again. You didn't even leave.'

'I did,' he says. 'I slept in the room here. Four hours, that's all I need.'

'Every night?'

'Nowadays, sure. Sometimes it's less. Sometimes more.'

'Okay,' I say. I think about talking to him more, but then it strikes me that he is already gone: that the slight hiss on the connection when he is listening to me is no longer there, and that in this bed I am all alone. So I talk to myself. We used to talk in bed, as children: every night before we went to sleep we would lie there, in the darkness, and we would go through what had happened. I don't know when or why it began, but it was a habit. An addiction. It was something we always did. Our mother used to say that we jabbered ourselves to sleep. It wasn't until we were sixteen and we moved into a new house in the city, away from the farm that we grew up on, that we were given separate rooms. I felt the space there, so I carried on talking into the darkness. It was only then that I realized it had always been that way. It wasn't a conversation. We told each other what had happened, but we were actually talking to ourselves. Without him it was the same. I told myself what had happened, and I told myself what was going to happen on the next day. Look back, then peer forward. As an adult, speaking to myself, I pictured myself as a scientist, in a white coat, standing at the front delivering a lecture or a sermon. Increasingly, I could feel the pull of becoming somebody great. I wonder if he still does it now, with his baker lying next to him: if he mumbles to himself as I do, barely comprehensible but understandable by my own ears.

Here and now, I talk to myself. I tell myself what happened in the day that has just been, and before that, back to the last time I remember sleep as it is here: in a bed, and of my own volition.

4

I sleep, and there are dreams, but I do not remember them. I suppose that's better, sometimes: to not have that looseness concerning their reality. When I wake up, I forget where I am for a second, because I could be anywhere but here. I push the lid of the bed and it opens upwards, and I see that they are all crowded around Tobi's bed: I can see the back of her head, and I can see Inna peering into her eye, shining a light in there. I am selfish. I worry about my own being first, checking myself before asking about her. The white spots in my vision are gone, but my gut still creaks, and my body hurts. I do not know how long I slept for, because there is only a constant darkness outside to judge it from, and there are no clocks visible from here. I unclip myself and push up, turning to look at them. Wallace is here looking at Tobi with Inna, and he nods at me in that way that comfortable men do: dipping his head, no smile on his face. This is my good morning.

'How is she?' I ask.

'I'm fine,' Tobi says. 'Freaked out, maybe.' She nods at

Inna, who lifts a screen to Tobi's face. It mirrors Tobi's eye back at her. I can see it from here as well: the sclera completely red, the cornea and pupil a muddy brown, floating in the midst of the bloody mess. I can see Tobi struggle to hold it together, her eyelid twitching, but she manages. 'How did it happen?' she asks. Her voice sounds dulled and slow, and somehow using a slightly lower register than usual. Perhaps she is still sedated, or the effects are wearing off: I can imagine Inna wanting to ease her into this, in case the shock causes a relapse of whatever her fit before was.

'It's nothing to be scared of. Sometimes, bleeds can happen in the eye. They're as full of veins as the rest of you, and they're tiny. It was most likely the pressure up here.' She says that as if there's a direction. So curious: we call space Up, and yet we're just as likely to be below where we started at any given time. Up makes it easier to understand, I suppose. 'It'll pass. I've checked that it's nothing insidious, and it's not. It's just a bloody vein. Like a cut, but it shouldn't even hurt. Does it hurt?'

'No,' Tobi says.

'And it won't affect your vision. It's just a bleed. You'll be fine, honestly.'

'Just a bleed,' Tobi repeats. She pulls on her cheek, pulling it down so that she can see as much of her eye as possible. She looks from left to right, and she blinks, as if that might suddenly fix it. 'I thought I was dying,' she says. According to her file she's survived two plane crashes. Maybe that was different. She rolls the eye around, looking to see if the red ends anywhere. 'Is it a bad one?'

'It's nothing,' Inna says. 'I'm more worried about the fitting. You've had that before?'

'When I was younger,' Tobi says.

'It wasn't on your records,' Inna says.

'It nearly stopped me getting into the air force. But I was tested. I was cleared.'

'Must be the pressure up here,' Inna says. 'Don't worry about it. We can keep it under control.' She smiles at Tobi: this isn't her fault. 'I'll be back,' she says, and she leaves Tobi magnetically clipped to the bed. Inna pulls herself over to me, smiling, but I can tell that she doesn't mean the curves at the edge of her mouth.

'You slept well?' she asks.

'Fine,' I say.

'Sunspots gone?'

'Gone,' I tell her. I blink a few times, to check, but my vision's clear. Tobi has taken my cross. 'She's okay?'

'Did you know that she was ill when she was a child?'

'No, Tomas did the medical checks. Wait,' I say. I call him, but Simpson answers. He asks what's wrong, and I tell him nothing. I tell him I'll call back later, as if he is just down the road, as if this is all meaningless. 'Is she okay? Can she perform her duties?' I ask.

'Yes,' Inna says. 'But I didn't have it logged. I am meant to know if there's something could go wrong.'

'I'm sorry,' I say.

'Don't you know any of the medical conditions on this ship?' she asks.

'Tomas did it all,' I say again. 'I focused on the technical side. I am more like that, I think.' She is quiet. She looks into my eyes, examining me, checking that I'm okay. 'My gut is still churning,' I say.

'You're probably hungry,' she says. 'You should eat something. We've eaten without you. We thought we should leave you to sleep. We asked Tomas, and he agreed.' I was cut out of the loop, I think. I was, for a second, useless to them.

'Did you sleep as well?' I ask. I don't want to be the only one who is struggling. I want them all to be crumbling, and I will be the glue.

'For a few hours,' she says, but I think that she's lying. I detach myself and she reaches out her hand. She pulls me to the side, to the bar, as if I need her help. I cling on, and try to stretch out – back pushed forward, feet pointed, arms reaching for the side. I wonder if I look as ungraceful as I feel. 'You'll get used to this,' she says, meaning everything, not just the lack of gravity.

'I'm no good at it,' I say.

'You're getting there,' she lies again. I wonder if it's something she does a lot: professional falsity. Or, maybe, it's something she does with me, to make me feel better. A happy leader is a successful leader.

'I am useless. I have never been one of those people with balance.' This hurts more than I thought it would, because I am tensing all my muscles. I let go of the side-rail and drift out, and I crane my whole body around, trying to turn. If I can turn I can control this better, I think. I see Tobi, still there on her bed. Her eye is as if she's been shot. Wallace is with her, consoling her. He is making her laugh, or he is laughing and she is watching him, but she is moving on. Rallying herself. I get distracted, and suddenly I'm not near the rail. Inna's hand grabs me and pulls me back.

'Easy to get adrift. No walks until you're steady with this, okay?'

'Like you could stop me,' I say.

'Try me.' I feel more stirring; my gut, my groin. My entire body, reaching out for something more than I currently have.

60

I look away, towards the cockpit, where Hikaru is either still on duty or back on duty, and Lennox is keeping him company. They are not talking, though: instead they are running the tests. It's constant, testing. This is the difference between our mission and whatever it was they were doing on the *Ishiguro*.

'I should see if they're all right,' I tell Inna.

'Want a push over there?' She is playful with it, but I am too uneasy, still. I have no desire to make a fool of myself any more than I already have.

'No,' I say. 'I'll crawl.' She pulls her hands back and swats them together, as if washing them clean of me, and she pushes off, back towards Tobi. She puts her hand on Tobi's back to console her, and Tobi looks at her with her one bloody eye, and she pulls a face: resilient and powerful. I cling on for what feels like minutes, and then wonder if I can't move on.

This is a mission. It has always been clear to us, to Tomas and myself, that it is, and that it should be treated with the utmost seriousness. It may not be glorious, not yet, but there has never been an actual mission to space. Before this, everything was simply to see if we could do it. It was a desire, a proving of ourselves as a collective people. Breaking Earth's atmosphere? We can reach it. The moon? We can land on it. It was showing off, puffing out our chests, planting flags. This time, there is a reason to be here. The *Ishiguro* was the most selfish, vainglorious expedition. Dr Singer's research was only an afterthought, a bonus thing that he could do while they were up there. It didn't matter, because what mattered was how shiny the crew were, how beautiful, how unstable.

We have a task, and it's hugely important. I look at the results of the anomaly while we are up here, and I think that we do not know what this is: that it is so far beyond our comprehension that this discovery, this mission, it could change everything. It could be the thing that realizes our position in the universe. People search their entire lives for an answer, and maybe this is it: maybe this anomaly might give us a clue as to our beginnings. It will not be showy, and it will not be glorious, but it might be an answer.

A scientist wants nothing more.

We spend the day running tests. One of the things that we can do, as we get closer to the anomaly, is to discover its span: to see how wide it is, what expanse of space it actually covers. We have measured it from Earth, of course, plotting the space that it doesn't fill, but from here we can be exact. Accuracy is easier up close. Wallace and Lennox and myself establish the equipment and run the software. The ship will do everything once the programs start running. We have scanners on here, deep-range systems that will be able to search further than anyone has ever searched. It's a grab bag, a huge potluck of whether you get anything useful or not. When the software is running, Wallace shows myself and Lennox how it works, even though I already know. I helped design it. There is a room dedicated to my work: the lab, I called it in the early days of development. A room off the corridor, opposite the changing rooms and the airlock, and small, but enough space for the screens that I will need. Above all it is somewhere quiet for me to work. When the software is running, both Wallace and Lennox go to get some sleep. I stay here alone and attach myself to the bench in front of the console. I bring up the screens: 3D visualizations of the results from the pings being sent out, a map of the area of space we're charting being drawn and constructed in real-time, and I'm able to zoom and pan and focus and highlight it as much as I like. I see the outline of the anomaly starting to be drawn: a patch of nothingness amongst the stars in the distance, surrounded by space. I spin the scene with my fingers, look at it from every angle, and I call Tomas.

'This is incredible,' I say to him.

'I know,' he says. He has an exact replica of my screens on Earth, showing him real-time – or as close to real-time as the lag will allow – what I am looking at.

'Did you know about Tobi?' I ask.

'Yes,' he says. 'It wasn't important, I didn't think. It was a long time ago. We certainly didn't expect it again.'

'I would have thought it enough to not let her up here.' I can trace each ping from here, and watch them: little orange dotted lines, pushing out like digital ticker-tape. They disappear, and another part of the anomaly is confirmed: an area of space that we cannot see, that barely exists. 'But you made the call.'

'Yes,' he says. 'She was the best person for the job. I don't mind there being something wrong with you if you're the best person for that particular job. I honestly never thought that it would be a problem, Mira.' He is silent. I imagine him leaning over his computer, bent towards the screen, examining the visualization of this. Watching the pings that I watched fifteen seconds before, as the data reaches him. 'You'll have to deal with it.'

'It's fine,' I say. 'Is there anything else I need to know about any of the others?'

'Nothing,' he says. 'Would it matter if there was?'

'What if she had died?' I ask. An orange line flies past the anomaly and carries on into the distance: traced away, so small that I will never see it. The result of what it finds will return to us when it does: eventually it will stop. Maybe it will stop so far away that we will no longer even be receiving data when it sends itself back. That we, humanity, will no longer even be alive.

'Well, she didn't,' Tomas says. 'She is fine. Bruised and embarrassed, but she's fine.'

'Okay,' I say. I spin the anomaly again. We have no way of knowing how deep it is, because we have to imagine that it is a wall, and there is no way of seeing what's behind it. 'Does it scare you?' I ask. 'This anomaly? Whatever it is.' I wait for a reply, but one doesn't come. 'Are you there?' I ask, but nobody answers, not even Simpson; which means that Tomas is still sitting at his desk, still at the computer, but he's simply choosing to stay quiet.

I stay and watch the lines. This is such a process: like tracing the outline of a planet with the ends of strings of thread. Tomas and I wrote an algorithm to plot the pinging of this thing. The intention was, it would find likely areas and match them, following lines and trying to extrapolate the size of it that much faster. There is a game you play when you are children, Battleship: you pick a place that your opponent might have placed their ship, a number on a grid that you cannot see, and you hope that you will somehow pick the right space. If you do, you extrapolate the rest of the ship based on that: moving up or down or left or right, assuming the likely choice that they have made, hoping for another hit and to sink their ship. We played it a lot, Tomas and I. It was the perfect way for us to test how much we thought alike: how much we had to work to outfox the other. I imagine him, watching these with me, or slightly delayed; or maybe not. Maybe gone from the lab, finally heading home to his baker, to spend time with her. Forgetting about me, about this, about us, for an evening. Thinking of this as work, not what it actually is.

I switch the screens off. I don't need to watch this. If he is still with me, so be it. I detach myself and push off, and I struggle at the ceiling, but then I push myself through to the corridor, and then down to the living quarters. The ship is quiet. Four of the bed lids are down and darkened, and only Tobi is still awake. I drag myself through, trying to make as little noise as possible, and she turns her head to watch me gracelessly approach. I settle in the seat next to her and clip myself in. She yawns and nods at me. I feel secure for a second. It's nice, after the chaos of floating, to have this security. She is confident, and taking back control.

'How long do you reckon we've been up here now?' she asks. She puts her hand over the clock on the screen and looks at me. 'No cheating, take a guess,' she says.

'What?'

'See if you can guess. I couldn't. I can't tell if it's only been a day, or if it's longer. Everything becomes loose here, you know? Without the sunrise, without the sunset. Without defined bedtimes. And I feel tired all the time, whatever I'm doing. And that's not my eye or whatever. Even just sitting here, that feels tiring.' She turns back and looks at the screen, focusing on the expanse of nothing that's in front of us. The view that offers precious little sensation that we're even moving, so large is space and so small are we. She reveals the clock.

'We should try to think of it in terms of hours here, hour to hour, rather than concentrating on the days. Back home, that's where they need days,' I say to her.

'Yeah, maybe. Maybe.' She yawns again. 'But everything is looser. Time, speed, place. Everything. If you focus on a star you can see it move, if you stare at it. Or, you know, you can see us moving.' I do as she says. I pick one – Algol, in Perseus – and I stare at it. I plot where it is in relation to the rest, and to the console and the frame of the window, and then I keep staring. Over time, and I have no idea how long that time is, it shifts, or we do. Such an infinitesimally small amount, barely perceptible. Barely registering. 'It's humbling, I think,' Tobi says. 'But at least we're definitely moving.'

'You walked away from two crashes,' I say.

'I did.'

'Were you scared? How did you do it?'

'What do you mean?' she asks.

'You were scared, with your eye,' I say. She reaches up and touches it. 'But back then.'

'Well, now. See, I couldn't do anything about the eye. If something had gone inside me, that's not a thing I alter myself. If I was dying, not like I could change that. If I was dying then, that was it. Boom, dead.' She rubs it, as if she can feel the wound. 'With the crashes, that was in my own hands. All I could do was try to save myself.'

I stay sitting next to her. Neither of us talks after that.

Wallace, when he wakes up, asks me to go to the engines with him. He is proud of them. They are one of the few parts of the *Lära* that we avoided directly working on, once we had told him our brief. We helped him assemble his team and they designed them. There were stipulations – cost, consumption, having to work alongside the piezoelectric life-support systems – but they had carte blanche after that. He shows me them, because he wants my approval. He wants me to see how impressive they are, and how well they have worked. He waits by them, and he runs diagnostics.

Now, they're doing nothing: our plan is that we will not stop until we reach the anomaly, and we're coasting off the momentum that we established with the initial acceleration. The boosters stop us accelerating any more – or, at least, stop us moving out of our allotted safety zone of acceleration – so, for the most part, the engines spin quietly. They are ready to stop us, when needed, but now he can run checks and tests, and, as he tells me, try to optimize them out here, to do real-world work on them that was impossible back on Earth.

'It's good,' I tell him. 'You do what you want to, okay? I trust you on this.'

'Excellent,' he says. 'Appreciate it.' But he doesn't look away, and he doesn't ready himself with work. 'Look, I have a favour to ask,' he says. 'I'm missing my girls.'

'Okay,' I say.

'Would it be all right if I called them?' He has a wife and two daughters. They live in a house in Orlando. His wife is a teacher and his daughters are both at the school she now works at. I try to remember any other facts from his file. 'It's Karly's birthday tomorrow. On the eighteenth. I just wanted to give her a call, say hello to them all.'

'I, uh. Listen,' I say. We have rules. They are allowed to pass on messages or have messages passed by Tomas or the ground crew, because that's the only approval for bandwidth we have. He knows that. I don't want to have to say it.

'No, sure, it's okay.' He is saving me from having to. He is lost, for a second, not making eye contact with me. 'I know, you let me, you'll have to let them.'

'You know how it is,' I say. I cannot stand this. I cannot abide this conversation: not just the favour he's asked, but the very being part of it. I want out. 'I have to get back and check on the others,' I say, and he nods, so I go. I move down the corridor and I leave him there by himself.

'Problem?' Tomas asks. He has been listening in. I want to tell him to stop, but we designed the system so that he could; so that, were it me down there, I could, if I wanted to. Complete mission parity. Completely open.

'No,' I say. 'He's lonely.'

'Aren't we all,' Tomas says. I picture him with his baker. I do not say what I am thinking.

I want to sleep, but I cannot. I lie there and I think about what this means, and the pressure. There is always something coming, here. I have to be at my best, and that is my worry: if I do not sleep, I will function at some percentage of my absolute ability, and I could ruin everything. I get out of bed, and nobody is looking, and I contemplate staying awake; but there is another option. In the medical cupboard, the hypos with the sedative. We have so many shots, delivered in tiny liquid capsules which are then injected into the neck before dissolving; and they are harmless, non-addictive. Before, Inna administered them, but, I reason, how hard can it be? I am not scared of needles. Needles are a necessary evil. I load one into the hypo and try to find the spot she pushed it into my neck before, where there is still a pock-mark on the skin; and I hold the injector there and push the button. When I have done the first I make a choice: to take another, straight away. Two to settle me, to ensure that I am down. I inject it into the same spot; this one stings a little more. I get back to my bed and I begin to count, and I am gone. This works. This has really worked, and I can sleep, and be safe.

* * *

'Wake up, Brother,' Tomas says. 'We've found something you're going to want to see.' He opens the bed for me, and I'm alone in the sleeping area. 'Come to the lab,' he says, which means it's something related to the anomaly. He was meant to wake me first, before anything was announced, before any decisions were made. We were both meant to be there at the start of these things.

I have an erection, so I dress myself, pulling on the thick trousers designed to regulate our temperatures, and I desperately need to piss but that can wait, because I've obviously already missed something that he thinks is important. Down the corridor, all their voices coo as I float down, clinging to the bars. I think of myself as a trainee ballerina. Pointe. Demi something. Stupid. I should have been here.

I wonder if Tomas has done this on purpose.

One of the screens has been extended to fill the length of the wall, and they're all peering at it. It looks like nothing at first; as if it's been switched off. But then Inna turns to me, and smiles. She holds her hand out to usher me to the front.

'Isn't it beautiful?' she asks. I peer at it, and then I see it.

It's the anomaly. I can't tell the scale, so I shift the screen to a more scientific view – and they groan as the grid pulls itself over the image, a scientific sheen over this thing of natural beauty, but then I can see how far away it is, and still how large, even at this immense distance – and then I see the edges of it. It's like a sheet of something that sits in the middle of the nothing: a pulled, taut sheet, where the corners and edges ripple like waves. And the texture – admittedly we're far out, and this resolution, as much as we can see, isn't going to be entirely trustworthy – but it's like oil, somehow. It's black, but not like the colour of space. Space isn't true black. When you look at it, sure, that's what it seems. But when you examine it, it's got colour and light bouncing around inside it. It's lit, and the blackness you can see is just a temporary absence of light. This is a different sort of black, painted or created, but I've never seen anything darker. I've never seen anything this pure before.

'This is from the bounce?' I ask. We have a chain of satellites between us and the anomaly. Tomas and I spent a year setting them up, sending them out and getting them roughly where we wanted them to be. They bounce visual data, downscaling it at each choke-point. The bounce is how I can talk to Tomas from here; and now we are finally close enough to see this in a resolution that lets us make out details.

'It is,' Tomas says. 'We are finally close enough.' Any chance of this being as incredible as I know it is – because it's never been seen on a live feed, not like this; and that fact alone essentially means it's never been truly seen full stop, as that's how humans work – is diminished by seeing this last. It is, to me, like being told the ending at the start of the story.

'We couldn't sit on our hands while you slept,' Tomas replies. I wonder how this reads to the rest of the crew. How antagonistic they think he is, or I am.

'No,' I say, but I can taste the lie in my own mouth, and feel myself brimming with anger. 'Of course not. You were right to continue.'

'We woke you up as soon as we were close enough to see this thing, and when we had processed the picture properly. We had to be sure.' Of course you were sure. Of course you waited. I call up the readings from the ping, try to compare it to the pictures we have received from the satellites. The ping is working, giving us something resembling an edge, numbers, an outline. I examine the readings concerning the scale of it, the approximations of how large it is. I check the numbers against what's in my head, and then call up the old measurements – Dr Singer's best guesses, the estimates that he worked on his entire life. They are wrong, and I can tell that. It's obvious to anybody even glancing at a comparison. While it's possible that Dr Singer was wrong, it's unlikely. 'The scale of this thing,' I say. 'Were we off?'

'It's definitely larger,' Tomas says. 'It's grown.'

'Or it's closer.'

'Either way it's closer, surely? Whether it has physically grown or hasn't.' He is explaining the basics of physics to me. I am grateful that he cannot see me.

'How far away are we?' I ask. I can hear the shake in my own voice.

'Ten days,' Tobi says. 'Somewhere between ten and eleven. We'll have an exact number of hours soon.'

'That close?'

'That close.'

I peer into it as much as I can. I know that Tomas will be doing the same: standing close enough to smell the holo-screen he has fitted down there, the vague waft of the chemical processes that give it capacitive abilities. He will be trying to find something else before I can. And to think: he said that he wasn't jealous of my being up here, and him being down there.

The crew filter off, back to their jobs. Apart from Inna: she stays in the doorway. She leans back and becomes a sudden distraction: I notice her there. She leans back as far as she can. Almost like a stretch.

'It's incredible,' she says.

'It will be,' I say. I wonder if Tomas is still listening. 'Soon, we might know exactly what it is that we're looking at. Then it will be truly incredible.'

'That doesn't change the fact of seeing it, does it?'

'What?' I try and soften the question, which I know comes out far too hard. 'It has to change it, surely?'

'Why?'

'Because we don't understand it. That's human nature, isn't it? To understand.'

'Human nature', she says, 'is to be there and watch as everything unravels.' She says it so lightly and gently, as if she's leading me to a concept that I might not otherwise understand. 'That's what you're really doing, isn't it?' she asks, and then she pushes away from the wall and pirouettes. I don't understand what she's saying. I don't.

'Wait,' I say, but she has gone down the corridor, disappeared into the living quarters. I turn back to the screen and watch the anomaly: as the edge curls and the light runs down it. I try to find the beauty in it; I try to appreciate it for what it is. To see it as nothing more, not anything that runs deeper. It is something we do not understand, and that has to be appealing. We are here, and so is the anomaly, and it is as real as anything else I have ever seen. That has to be enough, I tell myself.

'Careful,' I hear Tomas say. I decide to not ask what he is talking about, and instead I pull the picture apart with my hands, zooming in as much as I can, until it's a blurry black grain. There are specks in it: miniatures here and there. Nothing, probably: asteroids, detritus, scree. I make a note to myself to track them, to aid us plotting our course or in case they do anything interesting. I don't say anything to Tomas about them, because then he'll watch them as well, and that can be one more thing that he can keep from me, that he can let me sleep through. Instead they can be mine: something that I have discovered by myself.

The rest of them work silently. Ten days, is what Tobi said.

Ten days. When we were kids, we counted everything down in sleeps. Here, there's not much guarantee of that meaning anything.

5

The first few days are incongruous, and they pass without incident, and without crisis. We do not sleep with any uniformity, but this suits me, as I do not want to. There's no set time for bed, no set concept that we should lie down when we are told to, and shut the beds and try to shut our eyes. All we know is that at least two people have to be awake at any given time, preferably one of them a pilot. We've decided that there should always be somebody watching and guiding us. Another flaw of previous attempts at excursions this deep was in their attempts to take control away from the real people on the ship. Human fallibility is one thing, the failings of a computer quite another. When the *Ishiguro* didn't come home, the good people at DARPA – wealthy parents sending their privately tutored child out into the world before being surprised that it could fail when forced to react to the realities of life – examined where they felt everything had gone wrong. It was in the computers, they said. We put too much faith in automated processes. They bullshitted, said that they could trace that back to programmers, clearly, and still blame humans, but it was blame through a proxy. We don't want that. Processes may be automated on a base level, but the enacting of them is still dictated by humans. Even though there were people coming to us with their software solutions, trying to get us to take them on, to trial them even, Tomas and I knew that they were not right. We knew that real brains, real minds: they were what was needed here. The *Ishiguro* failed because there was a lack of trust: not in the machines, but in the people on board. They had two pilots whose job was to sit and watch the stars go by.

So, here, Hikaru relieves Tobi or vice versa, and one gets dressed as the other sleeps. Tobi insists on doing more than she should, because she's proving something. That her eye – which is still red and dark and hard to look at – isn't hampering her. (Though she blinks too much, and you catch her looking at it: peering into a mirror, or anything even slightly reflective. We, the rest of us, have stopped noticing it. She will not until it is gone, and her eye is white again: normality resumed.) Her behaviour says that the panic, the eye and the fit, they have only made her stronger. This is a lie, which means that Inna spends a lot of time watching her. Inna insists on us eating together as much as possible, for the solidarity that it provides: she's even started preparing the food, unwrapping the bars and presenting them to us as if they were somehow a proper home-cooked meal. Wallace hates that, but he puts up with it. Inna has a way with people: she can make them do whatever she wants, somehow. She has an authority here that is natural and unforced.

After we've eaten we set about our jobs.

Wallace runs diagnostics. Ninety per cent of his job is ensuring efficiency. The *Ishiguro* burned fuel constantly, stopping and starting in ways that should not have been possible, that were engineered to be unrealistic and false. We saw pictures of the inside, their big button to stop and start the engine like they were children. Artificial gravity generators, constantly switching on, keeping them grounded, retaining their humanity, that was the logic. Everything a waste of time and resources. We are not like that, not even slightly. We have a gravity generator, but we will never use it. It has been built into the hull for emergencies: in case an operation needed doing, in case somebody died. These are exceptional circumstances that every other failsafe, every other system is designed to prevent. So Wallace runs diagnostics, over and over. These things are his, and when we need them, we will need them to work. You need to keep an engine ticking over, he says. When he isn't running diagnostics, he sits and speaks with Inna, and she listens to him. She puts an arm around him while he talks about his family – I can hear their names mentioned, and his face droops, and his shoulders slump – and she consoles him. I find myself jealous at this. And when that's done, and he has stopped feeling sorry for himself, he talks to Tobi and Lennox, and he acts like a younger man. As if they – sans families, sans ties, footloose and fancy free – are like him. They are not.

Lennox talks to me about his life while we're working, mapping the anomaly, charting issues, and he tells me stories about who he is. He is young, still. I hear the stories, and they make me think of my life when I was his age; the conversations that I had with Tomas. Lennox sits with me for a good portion of each day as I examine the anomaly, and he's another pair of eyes. And his eyes are less tired than mine, I would warrant. He logs everything that we discover, a manual backup of facts – one of the places that we are inefficient, failing to resort to computers, and all the better for it – and he works on direct comparisons of scale, as well as being in charge of distance-pinging anything else that we pass. One of the ways we can use this mission is to help plot parts of space we are further from. We are going to be closer to some of these stars than ever before. We might be able to get something out of this. He's dedicated, as well, and he wants discoveries of his own. That's a difference between him and many of the other people we saw for his position. They liked the principle but not the practicalities of this. He knows that this is learning and it's vital. In twenty years, I tell him, he could be me. He could be discovering things, a scientist who does work for the good of mankind.

Inna is unfaltering, it seems. She doesn't rest. I barely see her sleep; or she sleeps at the same time as I do, lying down after me, rising before I do. She walks – I cannot get used to verbs like this, when they require modifiers based on a lack of gravity – she goes from room to room and talks to every single member of the crew about what's happening. She asks them how they're feeling and she tells them the best ways to deal with this situation. I hear nothing of their private conversations, but I can tell. There is sympathetic nodding, hands on shoulders. She's a doctor, but psychiatrist by proxy. If nothing else happens, this will be all: checking that we don't succumb to some temporary insanity, and ensuring that we are all safe around each other. That we have everything we need. (She has asked me about Wallace's request, and whether it might not make sense to allow him, and I have denied it again. Because, as I have repeated, once the floodgates open, they never shut. They all know the rules. She has said it will be good for him. I say, We are all missing things. We cannot take these things for granted. She didn't look angry with me; she told me that she understood. You do what you must do, she said.)

Unless somebody is asleep, we eat our meals collectively. Lunch is protein bars that taste of sandwiches, meatballs and tuna and BLT and chicken mayo only without any of the textures of the sandwich itself. They are intricately processed. If they didn't softly crumble in your mouth, you could swear that they were the real thing. Dinner is roast meals and hamburgers and fried chicken and fish and chips, only turned into slightly larger bars that we heat in what amounts to a complicated descendant of the microwave. When you eat, you shut your eyes and think of home. You imagine walking into a bakery and buying a fresh, warm-bread sandwich from the counter and then eating it, bite after bite. Meals are a moment, hinging on socialization, on feeling part of something. Inna insists on them: she says that the psychological effects of being together for occasions such as these can be enormous.

In the afternoon we repeat everything: we check that everything we did in the morning is correct. Aspects are checked and double-checked. When Tomas and I worked with the engineers to design this trip, every single component of every single part of the trip was torn apart and rebuilt. We tested individual spring coils when they came in to ensure that their kinetic power loss was as low as we were comfortable using. We would rather spend the money to build custom parts, we said, than use something that was less than perfect, and thus liable to fail. Each component was built in duplicate, even the ship's hull itself, because if you're going to stretch to the cost of one, and something goes wrong, it's less expensive to have a second ready and waiting to pick up the slack, ready to go on a second launch pad. Less expensive certainly than having to back to the drawing board or the designs and rebuild it all, especially where the custom parts are concerned. Two of everything, we said. Tomas and I enjoyed that synchronicity.

For his part, he is omnipresent. He drifts in and out of conversations, and he imparts his wisdom and he tries to not miss anything. He is controlling: even just as a voice from nothingness they all listen to him. I listen to him, because I don't want to be the cause of dissent. Once that happens, we will struggle to maintain control, and we haven't worked as hard as we have for so long for that to happen. The lag is up to a fair few seconds now, long enough that a conversation can become irritating, and we've taken to shouting as trickles of static start to settle into the broadcasts. (I quite like the lag. I like knowing that I'll get to see everything before him; that even if the scanners pick something up and we have a breakthrough, it'll be a few seconds where I explicitly know something that he doesn't, and if the rest of the crew aren't there, it will be a discovery that's mine. Solely and entirely mine, just for those few seconds it takes for the information to make its way through the ether.)

We spend the evenings in conversation, and we never stop working. I learn details about the crew: Lennox trained to be a lawyer, in his youth. That was his father's plan for him. He let him down, because he was more concerned with this stuff, as he calls it: with the larger, the greater. The incredible. This explains his goggle-eyed amazement and his dropped jaw. It's worth this to him. Tobi was on a television show, a reality thing, when she was in military school. She says that there are clips of her on the net, and I threaten to pull them up from here and watch them, waste our bandwidth for the sake of a funny time, but she scowls and starts to look genuinely concerned at the prospect so I stop. Inna looks horrified when I suggest it: the boundaries that it would cross. Hikaru talks about his religion, his obsession with his food. We listen, and nod, but do not comment or judge. That is a minefield that I have no desire to enter. I know about Wallace's children and wife already, but he talks incessantly when you get him going: about how he doesn't spend the time with them that he should; and how he's lonely even when he's at home; and how he feels that he owes them all something, more of himself than he's able to give. His words. And tonight we ask Inna questions: the last to speak, the last to tell all.

She sighs and looks away, and she protests but only a little. 'Tell us about yourself!' Tobi says. She's on duty, sitting in the cockpit, but turned around enough to see us all. Finally, and through her fringe, which covers so much of her eyes, Inna tells us. She lists the information, pulling her fingers back as she does, as if she is counting how much she is willing to tell us all about herself.

She's older than she looks, she says. (I know how old she is, thanks to the files, and she is not wrong.) The others ask her age exactly, and she bats away their questions.

She's more selfish than she would like. 'Single-minded,' she says. 'When I want something . . .'

She has been married four times. 'Each time', she says, 'worse than the last. In my profession, you'd think I would learn. You'd think that I would be able to smell them a mile away. But they were all the same sort of man. All brilliant. All failures, even though they didn't know it.'

She talks about the village that she grew up in as a place that's torn out of time: where they concern themselves with the Cold War of the 1980s as if it's something that they should still be concerned with, rather than something that only affected them as children, or when their parents were children; where they wouldn't have let her do the job that she became trained to do. She explains that this is why she left.

We sleep: or they do, all in their beds. I try to stay up later than the others, but we have broken all semblance of a cycle, of sleeping together; and because I do not want to sleep, because I cannot, for the worry of the following day, I spend time in the lab. I watch the pings drawing the trace outline. I watch the anomaly get bigger still, or seem to, as we draw closer to it. I try to see more of what it is, as the picture becomes more focused, as the resolution improves and the image suffers from fewer artifacts; but that feels like a folly, as I see the nothingness there, the expanse of emptiness, and I try to give it form in my mind. I try to make it something, so that I discover what it is. Each day it grows bigger. Each day the pings disappear into it, or fly past it. I see the edge of it, on the picture: because this is where the anomaly ends and space begins. The folds of it become clearer along the fringes. They're like the pages of a book, peeling back to show the page underneath. Giving away all the secrets. And then there are the whatever-they-ares inside the anomaly itself. They get closer, and they're no longer specks. Now they're lumps. I worry, constantly, that I will sleep through their discovery. I have started to imagine that they might be important in and of themselves: that maybe, in this quest for answers – what is science if not that – I will miss something important because I am too tired, and because I am lazy. I think of solutions. One is to not sleep. Another is to sleep as little as possible. A third is to rely on Tomas to wake me up, but he has proven himself the most unreliable option of the three.

During my own definition of night, when I lie in my bed to rest my body, I talk to Tomas.

'It's like sifting for gold,' he says. 'You know in movies, when they bring the pan out of the water?'

'I know what you're talking about,' I say.

'Right. It's like that: seeing the glinting specks on the bottom of the stream.'

'Okay,' I say. The pause is close to ten seconds now. Conversations start to feel the lag, and they're like treacle. You can monologue and stop him getting a word in edgewise; but I don't. 'How are you?' I ask him.

'I'm fine,' he says.

'Good. Good. It should be even clearer to look at tomorrow,' I say.

'It has been every day so far,' he replies.

I wonder if Tomas has the same trouble sleeping as I have. His patterns are impossible to track, because he is seemingly always awake and yet somehow managing his life at the same time. I haven't mentioned to him how improbable I find it all: the way that he can balance his relationship and his work. I reason that one must be suffering, and I pray that it is not our mission. I can tell, in myself, which I would choose: this is everything to us. This was what we always wanted, what we dreamed of. It was a future that made perfect sense to us, and we never wanted to jeopardize it. Back then, we knew our priorities.

The body only needs three hours of sleep a night. Famous leaders throughout history have survived – thrived – on less, but theirs is a story twisted by myth. Three is enough to, in theory, enter and complete a REM cycle: solid, deep sleep for that amount of time is easily sustainable with no loss of faculties. It brings about a state with its own set of challenges. One, how to ensure that the sleep happens during the allotted time and doesn't either overspill or intrude into the rest of the day. Two, how to ensure that one works at maximum when awake. I do not want anybody to suggest that I take more sleep, or start to question my abilities. Three, to ensure that it doesn't affect me in any real way over a long term. I read about sleep deprivation when the others aren't looking: attached to my chair in the lab, the anomaly drawing itself in behind me, and here I am, reading about the chemicals that the body produces, and ways to stimulate and replace them. Nowadays, in theory, we could stop sleeping. We have the supplements and drugs to replace the sleep itself with minimal damage caused. I am worried that Tomas will know, because we linked the keypresses from up here with the ground, but I can't imagine Tomas trawling through the logs to see what I have been reading about when I am alone. I ask myself if I would, were our places reversed, but I cannot tell: the situation is so different. We have diverged, maybe.

Everything points me to the pills we have. Drugs are incredible: those aspects that once hindered us using them with anything resembling real regularity ironed out. Non-addictive, non-intrusive, working instantly. Everything that they used to be rendered so archaic. As we get closer to the anomaly, I need to be here all the time. Discoveries are made in seconds, and my name – our names, Tomas and myself, Tomas and Mira Hyvönen – will be the ones underneath the discovery in the history books. There is a cupboard full of pills, and I find what I need, and I take them. I stocked this ship. To some extent they are mine anyway.

So: I stop even attempting to sleep, and I become powered by pills.

*   *   *

83

Hikaru is on his shift, and the rest of them have been down for how long I cannot say, because they wake when they wake, and that is how we run it in these early days. Hikaru and I are in different rooms, but he calls me through and asks me to sit with him in the cockpit. I do, because I have no reason to not. My work here is watching something happen, increasingly. There will be more to it, when we reach the anomaly, but here and now the technology is doing this for me. Tomas and I designed it this way: I am a creator, watching my creations work. Any problems with the software, Tomas and the ground team tweak it.

Hikaru doesn't want to talk, not really: it simply feels so lonely on the ship when everybody else is asleep.

'You not sleeping?' he asks.

'I am too excited for sleep,' I say. He nods.

'I hear you. This is your life's work, I guess. It's a really big deal.' He has a stash of his nougat bars up here with him, and he unwraps and eats one. It's pure whiteness in a chewy bar, and I watch him pulling it apart with his equally white teeth. The teeth look as if they have been grown: an absolutely perfect bite, better than implants even. I don't like to ask: I run my tongue over my own, which are less than perfect, slightly crooked even in places. Tomas and I have forgone any genetic tinkerings or after-surgeries. Even Tomas' birthmark, which they could have taken away so easily from him: he decided that it was distinctive. Tomas always said, Something like this can be defining, and you have to own it. At least they will always be able to tell us apart. Hikaru passes me a bar, and I eat one; it's tasteless and bland, but I wonder if some of that is psychological. It looks thus; thus it must be. 'What do you think it is?' Hikaru asks me. He sighs mid-sentence, as if the very act of gasping the words

84

out is somehow difficult for him. I am chewing, the nougat stuck to my teeth, and I make him wait as I struggle to swallow.

'The anomaly?' I finally say.

'Yeah. Somebody said that it could be a wormhole.'

'Who said that?'

'I forget. Tobi, maybe.'

'It's not a wormhole,' I say.

'Right.' He leaves space in the sentence; he wants an answer.

'I have a few theories,' I tell him. The theories are, in actuality, mine and Tomas'. They are shared, the product of both minds working together. I look at the clock and know that Tomas will be asleep. I picture him, for a brief flash: with his baker, curled up and naked. Almost as if he's taunting me. 'I don't want to jump the gun and make a guess that turns out to be wrong.'

'Something we haven't seen before?'

'It has to be.'

'Why's it getting closer?'

'Who knows?' I say. 'Maybe it's just drifting. Or maybe it's like a wave.'

'Strange, finding something new. You always wonder what it means.'

'Remember dark matter? That question? This might be the new equivalent,' I say. 'Maybe we won't know what it is we find. But we can know more about it, certainly.' I sit back, because it feels like a cap to the conversation. He doesn't ask anything else, and after a while I excuse myself. He thinks I'm going to bed, but I don't. I go to the lab. I sit and watch the anomaly being drawn, and then I bring up the visual image from the bounce, match the two up again. I make it full-wall. I stretch it out. I turn it 3D, projecting it with an approximation of depth. I stand inside it and I spin it around me. I make it swell into every inch of the room, until it covers the table and the shelving units and the walls. I get as close to it as I can. In this resolution the colours on the edge are somehow duller – this close they look like a flatter version, when they're not so nudged up against each other. Like the aurora borealis, that's what they remind me of: that sense of colours dancing and brushing up against each other.

I pull it right apart, until the resolution is breaking at the seams. And then I see it: one of the smaller glints in the space, one of the things that I have been tracking, is moving. I drop a virtual pin onto it to note where it is now, and there it goes, sure enough. It tracks slightly, moving away from the pin with an almost crippling, crawling slowness; but it is moving nonetheless.

I stay there, as still as I can in this infernal lack of gravity, and I watch it. It creeps forward. I think about waking up Tomas, but then I do not: I do not call him, or the ground. I keep this for myself. When I feel myself lagging, I go to the medical cupboards. In there, we have packets of stims, designed to help you stay awake, to perform to the best of your ability even when at your most tired. I do not even check them; I pop them from the blister pack and swallow them down. I have always dry swallowed. On the packet there is a promise of upwards of sixteen extra hours of 'pure thought clarity' after the user takes the pill. The stims make everything seem faster for the first few seconds, as they kick in – they make every frame of vision twice as clear, as if I'm seeing in a far more extreme frame-rate than usual – but the thing on the screen is still crawling. It passes every pin I drop, constantly going forward in a straight line. It is headed towards the same point

86

of the anomaly that we are, curiously. It's much slower than us, however. We can catch it, whatever it is.

I wipe the pins from the memory in case Tomas wakes up and looks to see what I have been doing, and I set the resolution back to almost nothing, in case he's set his display to show what I'm seeing. When the announcement is made that this is something we should pay attention to, I want it to be clear that I found it.

This is mine.

When I am ready, when I know that Tomas is awake and the crew are all readying themselves for a day, before Hikaru goes to bed, I assemble them all together. All day I have watched it, with my naked eyes: a speck of dust making almost imperceptible movements. I tell the crew that it's important: that this might be crucial to our mission.

'What's this all about, Mira?' Tomas asks. I imagine him down there, desperately trying to preempt me. Wanting to find this before I can announce it. He hates being second; playing any sort of catch-up. I am up here, though; and he is always behind the lag, now.

'You'll see,' I say. I lead them all through to the lab and tell them to crowd in. They float and watch, most of them in their underwear, all bleary-eyed still. I am not like them. The effects of the stims are still there, not even threatening to wear off yet. 'So,' I say, and I explain it all as they listen. I pull the screen large again, to demonstrate, and I pop a pin in and let them all see it. They lean in, some of them, as close as they can, pulling the speck out until it's the size of a low-resolution beetle, a silvery shimmer of boxy pixels.

'Jesus,' Wallace says. 'Huh.'

'Good find,' Tomas says.

'Oh my God,' Lennox says. He gets closer, almost past me. It's infectious, his enthusiasm. Makes me feel justified in my own excitement, such as it is. I like him more and more, when he is like this.

'What do you think it is?' Tobi asks.

'I have no idea,' Tomas says, before I can. 'Mira?'

'I don't know yet,' I say.

'A comet or something,' Tobi says.

'Inside the anomaly!' Lennox says. He is working this out. 'What the hell can it be?'

'It has to be something,' I say.

'It's definitely not nothing.' Tomas sounds weary. Like he knew that this was coming. 'But we should be loath to declare it a something yet.'

'Tomas,' I say, 'it's moving. It's got velocity, and a trajectory that seems to almost match ours. We can assume that this is not a coincidence.'

'And yet space is made up of the things,' Tomas says. I can hear him shrug. And he speaks with his mouth full of something or other: 'Being out there, you're just one in a chain of them. Let's wait until you're closer and we can make out what it is.' I picture him there in the safety and comfort of his stupid fucking launch control room, in that suit of his that he persists in wearing, his pressed black suit trousers and his white shirt and his slicked-back hair, like he's there in 1969, recreating that schtick, that feeling; and whatever he's eating, it's no doubt a gift from his baker, some doughy hand-made pastry. Everything about him is superiority: not just over everybody else, but over me, even though I am his equal in every single way. I know it, and because I know it he must also know it. 'Let's come back in twenty-four hours and look at it again,' he says, and that is that. I know that he won't take his eyes off it until then; I know that he'll examine it as closely as I will. For the good of mankind we discover; and yet.

They listen to him. He dampens the crew's enthusiasm, even though this is something so important. They leave, back into the main body of the ship and their jobs or their sleep, and Inna squeezes my arm, as if to congratulate me for a job well done, and then she watches me from the doorway for a second as I hover in the centre of the room and I stretch the thing out like it was when I was alone. I know that Tomas will be doing the same: strutting around his room, ordering the people desperate to please him to get him coffee, to help him analyse what it is that I have found. He can say that it's unimportant all he likes: I do not believe him. I have found this. I have. I put a pin in the object. I fold a chair down from the wall and clip myself to it, and I watch the pin, and the whatever it is move away from it. After an hour I move the pin, tracking it, plotting it. I want to be here when the resolution finally clears up enough that we can see what this thing is.

We eat lunch, and I sigh when Inna tells me that I must join them, because it means taking my eyes off the image. Tobi thought that it would be entertaining to eat Hikaru's food for a meal. She is more herself again: there is a spark in her. It's the sort of thing that is attractive to people, and she has it. It's behind her eyes, so we give her this. Her eye is still red, but we have stopped noticing. She has stopped looking at it as well. We are all moving onwards.

'White lunch,' she says as she puts the protein bars into our hands. They taste as they look, and we each tear into them knowing that we need the nutrients.

'Jesus wept,' Wallace says. 'This is what you eat?'

'You wouldn't believe how good it is for you, for your guts. Your digestive system. So good for your insides.' Hikaru relishes this. His bar is half gone even as the rest of us are only single bites down.

'It would have to be, tasting like this.' He eats it regardless. We don't talk about the anomaly, but I know that they're thinking about it, and me. I don't say a word over lunch, and they keep looking at me. As if I'm about to announce something. As soon as we've eaten I unclip myself.

'I'm going back to the lab,' I say.

'Okay,' Inna says, as if she is giving me permission to leave the table. I push myself back to the corridor and then down to the lab, still clinging to the walls, hopelessly behind the rest of them in my aerial acrobatics – they can spin and twirl and somersault as part of their movement, and still somehow end up where they want to be – and then, in the lab itself, I cling to the console desk and it takes me a few seconds to notice, but the pin that I laid before lunch is still exactly where the thing is: sitting right on top of it. The object hasn't moved. Whatever it is, it has totally stopped; not even a tiny bit of drift away from the last point it was set at.

'Refresh the image,' I say, which the computer does, and it's still there. I wait, on the highest resolution, to see if it moves again. It doesn't. I call Tomas, and he answers, tired and lazy-sounding. He is not here: and he is fifteen, thirty seconds behind me in seeing what exactly it is that I am looking at.

'It's a ship,' I say. 'Inside the anomaly, Tomas. It's another ship.'

We all watch it. Not one of us takes their eyes off it. In the cockpit, even, the image is stretched across the front windows, and we are all awake. In the living areas, it's stretched across the screen that we use to show the expanse below: suddenly more impressive than the vastness of space itself. I stay in the lab, because here I can see it all, and I pull up multiple screens showing every aspect. Lennox is working on trying to ping the ship – I call it that, still partially guessing, but this is how we must work – and trying to see if we can get an idea of how deep in the anomaly it actually is.

'You're sure about this?' he asks. Tomas is listening but doesn't chime in. He'll have his own people on this. They are working with the lag against them, which is a disadvantage for him.

'It has to be a ship,' I say. I feel like I only talk in vagaries, not absolutes. The mark of a good scientist, Tomas used to say, is in the absolutes, though even he is lost here. I can tell because he is silent. For the first time, he is as preoccupied as I am.

'Could it be aliens?' Lennox asks.

'Don't say that word.'

He laughs. 'Fine, it has to be something else, then. That's only logical, right?' I know exactly what he's talking about. We all know, all of us. There are very few options, and one of them is that it is the *Ishiguro*. That would mean that it has been out here for over twenty years. It would mean that it is a freak, a fluke. Something that should not be. To see it still moving, and still with power, after so long? And the fact that it has stopped, now, would suggest that it's crewed still. That cannot be right. The crew would have succumbed long ago. They would have given up, gone insane, run out of food, their muscles and bones atrophied and worn down. No way they're running off their own batteries – that's true perpetual energy, there is no way that it can be that

91

– and there is no way that they've found fuel. So it's not crewed, because there will be no life support. But there's fuel? Perhaps it's set to a cycle? Back then, the system was entirely run by computer, by a programmed set of instructions designed to be foolproof. There was barely any need for a pilot. It was a totally flawed idea, totally and utterly flawed. You can't test code in the field like that, not when there're lives at stake. Not when there're a mission to be done.

Lennox has raised another screen, a smaller one, and he's called up an image of the *Ishiguro*. We drag the picture of the ship itself across to the bigger screen, compress it to the right size and lie it on top of the unrecognizable thing, and it's a perfect fit for the general shape and colour, but other than that we can't tell. When he isn't looking, I take another stim, and there's that rush of a faster frame-rate when I feel like I could do anything, but that fades, and I am still left looking at the same shapes, trying to make them fit.

In the middle of the night, with the rest of the crew asleep, I drift to the cockpit and cradle myself into the seat there, attach the magnets to stop me drifting. It's Tobi's shift. She looks over at me, and then reaches into her pocket.

'Wait,' she says. She fiddles with her face, and then she pulls back, and I see that she is wearing a patch across it: like a pirate. She laughs out loud, a sudden exclamation of her own amusement. I do not. 'I found it in the medical stores,' she says. 'You like it?'

'Yes,' I say. I don't know if I say it wrong, but she reads it as a lack of amusement, and she turns professional.

'You need something?' she asks.

'We have to change our destination,' I say. 'Only slightly, but we have to.'

'Where to?' We've had a course decided for years now: into the centre of what we understand to be the anomaly. But the ship we've found has changed everything: it's higher, in the scale of things, based on how far we think the anomaly stretches. Still the anomaly. Still our mission, not forgoing that for even a second, but it's something else. Two birds with one stone, I think. It could be. If it is the *Ishiguro*, if it is inside the anomaly, if it has been for the past two decades, think of what we could learn from it. Think of the things that its sensors could tell us.

'Plot a course for it.'

'The other ship?'

'Yes.'

'Everybody signed off on it?' She means Tomas.

'Yes,' I say. He hasn't, but he will. He would. She nods, and she starts typing onto her keyboard, changing what she needs to. She can tweak the trajectory with the boosters; such a subtle change, enacted over the next few hundred miles. Easy as anything. 'Thank you,' I say.

'It's fine,' she says. I start to unclip myself, but she stops me. She puts her hand out, blocking me. 'I have a favour,' she says.

'Oh?' I say. I am thinking about the ship: the screens here are now full of her calculations, and I can't see it. It could have changed. This could all have changed while I am sitting here, getting away from me, the situation developing.

'Wallace's family,' she says. 'He really wants to speak to them. Can you let him call them?' She doesn't make eye contact with me. She keeps working. She is showing me how diligent she is. This is like a trade for her; even with her ailment, she is working hard. They are all working hard.

'He has already asked me that himself,' I say.

'I know.'

'So I have to give the same answer.' She doesn't look at me. She types. 'You know what it will cost to let him do that.'

'I know,' she says. 'But, Jesus. Come on.'

'I'm sorry,' I say. I drift upwards and turn and kick off, back towards the lab. When I am at my console I take another stim. The image is getting slightly clearer. I'm there watching the pin and the ship as a tiny burst of light, no more than a few pixels wide, comes from the rear of the thing – of the ship – and the ship starts moving again.

'Tomas,' I say. 'Tomas.' He's still asleep. That's the difference between him and me: how far we're willing to go.

6

Somehow, I am asleep; and somehow, I have a dream about Inna.

I cannot really see her: only a shimmer of her flesh as I chase her through the corridors. I have skills that I don't have in real life, the ability to dance through this lack of gravity as if I was born in it. I catch glimpses of Inna's tattoos as I chase her: the head of that bird, and in my dream, the way it coils around her body, turning into chimera, bird and snake and lion, all drawn around her body. She stops and turns, and the tattoos shift around her, like a story come to life. The lion eats the bird. The bird eats the snake. The snake somehow consumes the lion, slackening and dropping its jaws and taking it all in. This is all I can see: the swirling colours of the animals, so bright and crisp and deadly.

I wake up and I am at the console, and I am drifting slightly upwards, my body slack. It's scary, this feeling; and my mouth is dry, and my neck throbs and aches. 'It's definitely the

Ishiguro,' Tomas says over the speakers, and that is what wakes me. I look at a clock: I have been asleep for three hours, as best I can tell. I don't know how it happened. I must have passed out when the last lot of pills ran their course, and my body did the rest. I had been awake for a long time before that. Hours and hours.

'I can see it,' I say, but my voice croaks. I find the stims and the water and I wash one down with the other, and I feel so much better for a second, and then slip into normality. I peer in at the ship. The distinctive hull shape. The fringe of colours that runs the rim. The distinctive stamp of the name on the side, as they used to do with galleons. Curlicued and delicate writing, at odds with the presentation of the rest of the ship. It's a blur, and still slightly pixelated, like some old video game from a museum: constructed of the individual blocks. 'That's confirmation.'

'It is.'

'I've already told Tobi to change course and head towards it.'

'She told me.' She double-checked with him. My word was not enough.

'Have you told anybody else?' I ask. He knows what I mean: the UNSA, who will, in turn, tell the press. The funding opportunities for this trip, which were tight before, would be boundless if the world knew what we had found. The world was, once upon a time, united in their grief for the *Ishiguro*. To find it now would have implications.

'Nobody else knows yet,' he says. 'Doesn't make sense to cause questions to be asked before we even know the answers. You should tell the crew, though,' he says. This is his gift to me. This is a give: a way for me to get a win, for them to see me as a real leader. This is a farce, the way that we are.

He probably wants me to thank him. 'You should do it soon,' he says. 'They'll be wondering. You should confirm it with them.' He sounds distant, as if this isn't where his focus is.

'Okay,' I say, and I pull myself to the corridor. They are waiting and watching, because they know that something important is about to happen. When they see me it is permission, and they come and they gasp, and I cling to the wall at the back of the room. Tomas talks them through what I have found, and they coo and speculate out loud, and they ask questions: but he answers them all, even though neither of us has any of the answers.

My brother's full and complete name was printed first on our initial funding pitch: Tomas Johannes Hyvönen, named after both grandfather and great-grandfather, the two most important male names in my mother's life, both claimed and consumed before I even squeezed my way out of her. He was the one with the previous positive funding experience; it was easiest to go with what you know, I granted him that. Dr Tomas and Dr Mirakel, my full name because the funding committees needed to be able to look us up. (He said once, Why not change your name? Legally, pick a new one that sounds better. This was after our mother had died, and I said, It seems wrong. This is the only part that's left, and she loved it. So it stays. He even suggested alternatives. John. James. Boring biblical names, dull names. Is it better to be a joke than to be staid?) So after that his was the name that the board wrote to, to tell him of our successful pitch. He had the letter arrive at his house, read it before me, and he called me up and sent a scan of it across for me to look at. He framed it, the original, and hung it in his office. That was the precedent: they called him when they had issues, and he was the first port of call for interviews and articles. In photographs, he was placed in front, because the birth mark – a crutch in a time where genetics couldn't be modified willy-nilly, but now, for us, something to flaunt, a statement – singled him out and sold issues of magazines and newspapers. It made him a spokesman, and I his parrot, sitting behind his shoulder, repeating that which he had already said. One interview for a television show, as we headed towards the process where we would start to pick the crew, was taken by him alone. They explained that there wasn't enough room on the sofa – next to the presenters and the other guests – for two. He spoke about the mission in singular absolutes – I, Me, Mine – and then tasted food designed to be eaten in space, freeze-dried but created by a celebrity chef, and then he laughed at a comedian who joked about motorways and the inherent dangers of them versus space travel. I watched from the green room, on a small monitor, and I ate biscuits and drank weak lemon tea.

And when we went on television to announce the date of the launch, it was Tomas who spoke. He told them and he took the applause, and I sat quietly by his side. Scalded, almost.

I take another stim and miss another sleep, which is fine, because it means I do not have to worry: about sleep, or the day to come, or anything. Instead I sit in the lab and watch the ship get clearer and clearer. It stops again, only briefly this time, and then continues on its way. I don't speak to Tomas, even though I hear him talking to the rest of the crew as they wake up. I don't even bother to eavesdrop, because it's immaterial what they're saying. Tobi says it's only another twenty-four hours until we're close enough to see the ship better. Now, it's the size of a fingernail. By then it might well be the size of a fist.

Inna tells me that I should sleep, or rest. She stands in the doorway. She has mastered, in her graceful ways of movement, a manoeuvre where she touches the floor with the tips of her feet, letting them drag slightly along the plastic as she moves. From behind it looks as though she's balancing on them, creeping on tiptoes so pointed that they suggest a ballerina who has managed to break the laws of physics. Now she floats in front of me. I try to pay attention to her, but the ship is still there.

'Come on,' she says. 'You must have been awake for hours.'

'I won't be much longer,' I say. I remember my dream again; and her tattoo. 'I have work to do. Not too much. I'll sleep soon.'

'Or you'll sleep now,' she says. 'Do I have to come over there and force you?' I don't answer, or move. She sighs and sinks towards me. 'Mirakel, you have to sleep. We need you at your best.'

'You used my full name,' I say.

'I shouldn't?'

'No,' I say. I do not say: it forces people to take me less seriously. They mistake me for a fool. They think that I am temporary, or somehow worthless. They treat me as a child, as somebody that needs their assistance. Mirakel is a different person: I left him when I stopped being a child. 'I prefer Mira, honestly.'

'I'm sorry,' she says. She reaches out for me, and she takes my arm, holding my hand at the wrist.

'It's no matter.'

'But my point stands,' she says. 'I am tired. You are tired.

We are all tired. Being here, it's one of the most tiring things you can do. Your body isn't meant for this, and you have to deal with it properly. So, sleep, and then tomorrow you'll do some exercise.' I unclip myself and allow her to pull me away from the console, and she pushes off the wall and into the corridor, putting her weight into it. It's easier this way. To let her lead. Her hand is warm. Here, we keep the air cool. You don't want to get hot here, no sweat peeling itself off your forehead into globules that drift and threaten to collide with others. Far better to be nice and cool. But her hand is still so warm, warmer than I'm used to. I don't remark on it, but it's nice. She takes me down the corridor and to the living quarters, where the others ready themselves for bed. She doesn't know about the stim I took only a few hours ago. She grabs the lid of my bed and grips it, as if she is holding it open for me. As if the entire apparatus isn't automated. 'Okay,' she says. She watches me climb in and strap myself down, and then she smiles and shuts the lid to the bed and I lie there in the dark and don't sleep. I listen as much as I can, through the seal, and the others gradually shut their own beds. The one next to me, Inna's, I listen for that seal, and as soon as it hisses I count to a hundred – eyes pinned open by the stims, no chance of me accidentally drifting anywhere in this thing – and then crack the lid. The ship is quiet; Tobi is in the cockpit. I don't say anything to her. It is none of her business how much I sleep.

I watch the *Ishiguro* on the screens in the lab. It moves. It gets larger, slowly, bit by bit, as if it is swelling.

Because I never leave its side, or because I am here almost the entire time, there is no danger of me missing the developments. Now, I see it stop again: once more it slowly grinds to a halt.

I imagine them inside: their artificial gravity generator doing its work, ruining the experience of this: making them feel as if they are on a train, travelling forward on a path, no bumps or variation. I don't know if I am imagining them now or then: what they would be like now, twenty years after the fact. I have so many questions for them. I want to know what they have seen. I want to know what happened. I want to know why they have not made it home. In my worst daydreams, the starting and stopping is a malfunction of the computers, degraded and useless; and the ship is full of their corpses; and there are no answers to be gained from this, only a husk of metal that doesn't belong out here. We have the image stretched as large as we can, but it's not enough. I want more. I lean in, so close that the vapours of the holo are almost overpowering, but it's what I need to do. I need to see this. I can see the plating, and I can see the engines, and I can almost see details in them, that's how close we are. It is deceptive: we are still four days away. Through the use of the bounce, we have a camera so powerful and important that we can almost see into the future, and here I am, watching a ship from the past, stopped still in the expanse.

Then I see it: something else. A speck, a dot, circling the ship. Only a few pixels, even at this resolution. It is small and it is white, and it seems to float and then cling to the side of the *Ishiguro*, and I can only just make it out: arms and legs and the solid lump of a body holding them all together.

'There's somebody alive out there,' I tell Tomas. I send the message across space to him, but I don't leave the channel open to wait for a reply, and he doesn't try to instigate one. I heave myself to the living quarters and hammer my fists on the lid of Lennox's bed, and Wallace's, and they all wake up one by one, an hour before they're meant to. I'm telling

Tobi what I found as they blearily join the conversation, and I have to repeat myself four or five times, over and over, but I never get tired to saying it. 'Come on,' I say, and I lead them, like the Pied Piper, to the observation lab.

We watch him, her, it, whatever, dance around the outside of the ship. It's brief. I record it, and then we watch it again: somebody is outside the ship, still alive, and then they get back into the ship and the engines start, and they move off.

We don't talk, any of us. We don't know what this means. We are travelling as fast as we can.

'It has to be Dr Singer,' Tomas tells me later that day. We're both sitting in our respective labs as everybody else readies themselves for the evening: whether that means home and families for those around him; bleached-white protein bars and idle speculation for mine. He's drinking, I can tell. There's a slur in his voice, a slur that I absolutely recognize. I do not drink, not really, because I cannot stand the lack of control. I cannot stand feeling that loose. I think that that is why Tomas likes it. He will be there, drink in hand, fashioned from the ingredients that he keeps in his desk, the different bottles. He has those little plastic sticks to mix the drinks. Maybe he is even smoking a cigarette. A period costume for performing this very particular type of science. 'He's the only one who would even think of heading outside by himself, I suspect.'

'Why aren't they still sending results?'

'It must be the anomaly,' he says, as if that's enough to excuse and explain anything that doesn't make sense. We haven't asked each other how Dr Singer would have survived this long; what he must have done to have found food, to have eked out an existence out here. It seems almost gauche. Soon he can tell us those things himself. 'I'm going home,'

Tomas tells me. He pauses, then: 'Good work today, Mira.' Patting me on the head.

'Go back to your baker,' I say. I try to make it sound light-hearted. He laughs, so I think it worked.

'Goodnight, Baby Brother,' he says. I hear the click of his severing the connection. I feel uneasy: we never say goodnight. We never say goodbye.

I pull the image back from the *Ishiguro*, spin it, examine other parts of the anomaly. Not that we have forgotten it, but we have been preoccupied. The pings are still drawing the outline, and there is a shape forming: here, with the orange trace lines, it is almost the fruit of the same name, this shape, nearly round. Not perfect edges. They will be discovered, as the pings keep being sent and the results keep being recorded. There is nothing as black as the anomaly. No stars; no planets in the long distance, even though they should be there, but they're hidden behind the sheet of blackness; nothing apart from the *Ishiguro*, now, and lumps of rock in other quadrants, floating as if they're caught in a tide. I pull the camera to the edges of the anomaly, where it looks like the aurora borealis, folds and lines of colour along the rim. I trace the line of the thing as best I can: I overlay the pings, and I stare at it. 'What are you?' I ask it. I watch it for hours more. When I start to falter, during the night, I take another stim. The next thing I know, I've been looking at it all night; and then Inna is behind me, hand on my shoulder, asking me how much sleep I had, but I do not answer. She says that they're all going to eat breakfast together. She wants me to be a part of this.

'Come on,' she says.

*   *   *

Soon the *Ishiguro* is bigger still: a whole hand with fingers splayed. By the start of the next day it's like a remote-control toy spaceship, floating across the room. It stops and we marvel at it. Even with the anomaly, this is the most impressive thing here: we're not strangers, and we're not even alone out here any more.

Tomas concentrates on the anomaly. We spoke about it and agreed: he would do the research on the thing that doesn't change, that is immutable, and I would deal with the ship. With the lag, he is now thirty seconds behind, and he cannot see the picture as well as we can. Besides which, I am happy with that arrangement. The *Ishiguro* being here is unexplainable, and it might be inspiring, or important. The anomaly is almost a trick of the light that can barely be described as existing, if our readings are correct; the *Ishiguro* is solid, real, tangible, a picture of human triumph and failure both. It is a capsule of us as a people. When the Indian launch failed, when the ship collapsed out of orbit, the world knew that it was human failure. The crew's deaths were caused by their own desire to get into space, a rush and a push to prove themselves. When the *Ishiguro* went missing, however, it was something else entirely. It was man losing to nature: science failing. But I can prove something else, something different. I can give it an ending where science wins: because here is the ship, decades later, still working, still going. Inside it, a man who will surely have discovered something; because, otherwise, why would he still be here? Why would he not have come home?

It stops more frequently as we get closer. Once a day, maybe. I wonder why, and I picture Dr Singer – Gerhardt, Guy, the great discoverer who almost never was, lost to everything and space and nothing – taking his readings still.

A scientist to the very end. What has he found? To have stayed out here this long, riding in the darkness occupied by this anomaly, it must be something truly incredible. The energy used to stop and start, with their utterly fallible, near-broken systems. He found the anomaly in the first instance, so many years ago, back when it was only a speck of nothing in the distance, a vague blur, thought to be something else entirely; and that glory can be his. (If, indeed, it is a glory. We scientists are notable for finding fascination in things that the layman may find tedious. The public, they can relish his return, the conquering hero; we in the science community can relish the results, the numbers, the facts that he will bring with him.)

I have no imagination, I have always been told. I have always struggled to picture that which doesn't exist: instead, bloody-minded focus, a stubborn singularity in my mind. But this mission, it has done something to me: I am imagining, I think. I think of my dream of Inna, when I never dream like that; and how maybe it was somehow a catalyst. And Dr Singer now, dreaming of what he might be: it isn't real, not yet, but I desperately want it to be so.

I call up the files on the *Ishiguro*'s crew on the computer and read about them, information I obsessed over as a younger man, when the trip was announced: jealous, desperate to be involved. I postulate their ages now. Older men and women, and they won't have the medicines that we do, and none of them will have had the surgery afforded to the elderly back home. They will have suffered bone loss. They will find it hard to adjust to life back on Earth. I do not know how many of them might be alive, or how many dead. I do not know how they have survived. But it is that ship. Out of this

we will garner unassailable facts, and we will know things
that we did not know before.

'The *Ishiguro*'s inside the anomaly,' I say to Tomas. 'I wonder
what is inside there. What Dr Singer has found.' Tomas only
slightly listens. He is working, as I am. This is how it was
always meant to be, and we are almost back to back, if not
separated by such a distance.

7

Deceleration is a process that can hurt. It's not as violent as when we left the NISS, but it's close. Parts of the ship's systems have been slowing us slightly ever since we reached peak velocity, so that it wouldn't be as extreme; but it's still violent, and we still have to be in the beds, still have to be asleep. Tobi gives us a warning when we are an hour out from the anomaly, from the *Ishiguro*. She tells us that we have to lie down and seal the beds, so we prepare. I tell Inna that I will do my own injection, and I take three of the sedatives and pop them into the hypo and then fire them into my neck. I need to counteract anything that might remain from my last stim. As I get into my bed I can already feel that it will not be like the last time. I talk to myself as I go to sleep; or maybe I am talking to Tomas. I do not know if he talks back.

We wake up, all of us, at the same time. We cannot be left to sleep: there is too much to be done on the ship, in the here and now. He could control this from the Earth, of course, and then when we wake tell us that we have missed it, that the mystery is gone and the puzzle solved and the mission over, turn around and head for home: but he knows that he needs us. This is why we are still manned and crewed. There was a logic a few decades ago that we could do space travel with robots, with a man controlling them from a shuttle or a base somewhere. This is how, the theory went, we can conquer Mars. They were wrong, of course, because everything will go wrong. And we have still not conquered Mars. In reality, we have decided to abandon that plan for now. For now, there are more interesting concerns than a cold, dead planet we do not need to conquer yet.

So now we wake, and we rub our eyes, and we detach ourselves. I feel dismal. I feel as though I could stay there, but the bleating from the alarm that Tomas has employed is too loud, and I know that there is work to do. I fumble from my bed and to the medicine cupboard, and I take a stim. I am not the only one: behind me, Wallace asks if he can have one as well. I nod and pass it to him, but I miss, and the pill hangs there between us for a second, drifting. I look at him. His face is different. It is grey. He hasn't taken to being up here, I don't think. We said, at the start, that this is not for everybody. In a capsule, out here, you are so isolated. They used to worry about submarine crews in the last century. What might happen in one of them if the person lost control of their faculties. Wallace takes the pill and swallows it, and he looks at me, but not eye contact: instead staring at my cheeks, just underneath my eyes.

'Thanks,' he says.

'It's fine,' I reply. I have to say something, I feel. The others are ready before us, rushing to positions. Tomas speaks to them, but I can't even hear what he is saying: as my own pill kicks in, and the sleep rushes away, and for a second I am not even where I am.

'We've got it on the screen, right in front of us,' Tobi says, and that's enough to bring me back. That is all.

Even though we have screens throughout the ship; even though it's the same video feed as you would see anywhere else; even though we had seen it like this from a distance before we even went to sleep: we all crowd into the cockpit as we approach the anomaly, and the *Ishiguro*. The anomaly has become a second part in this, the thing that will be dealt with after the excitement of the immediacy of the other ship. The anomaly isn't going anywhere. Yet this is the only other ship in the entire solar system, the only other travellers that we'll see this entire journey, and they have been missing for decades. The things that they will have seen. Hikaru is piloting. Tobi sits next to him, eye patch covering her bad eye ('I figure I can make first contact,' she jokes, 'pretend I'm a pirate and try and to get them to bug the hell out.'); Wallace behind Hikaru, though I would swear, looking at him, that he isn't watching this, that his mind is somewhere else; Lennox floating a few feet back, lodged near the ceiling to get a view; and then myself and Inna, at the edge of the scene, our sides touching. She is close to me; she puts her hand on my arm to hold me steady, then pinches the fabric, and, by default, the flesh it covers, and she asks me how it feels: to have seen this through.

'I don't know,' I say. 'I cannot tell yet.'

The *Ishiguro* begins as a speck in our real view, not enhanced, not zoomed. I tell Hikaru to pull us towards it. It sits against the anomaly, or inside it – there is a fine line, and from here it is hard to tell – so it's surrounded by black-ness. Nothing inside, and it looks as if it isn't real. But the

Ishiguro is. We try making contact on the radio frequencies that it used to have, the same ones that were once used to send updates back to Earth, but there's no answer. They didn't have the external cameras that we do, or any sort of radar. They were never expecting to encounter anything else out here. Certainly not another ship. We have to alert them, because we don't know how they might react, otherwise. Hikaru uses the boosters to push us forward, but it's a slow crawl. We cannot risk touching the other ship. We didn't contemplate anything colliding with us, not something like that. The metal of the outside is strong enough to let any debris bounce off, but not a whole ship. These are not cars; this is not something we could have foreseen, or tested. Haruki is cautious, therefore. Not too fast. But, there, in the flesh: the metal, the construction.

There is no way of hailing them, so we have to get their attention some other way. We have the ship itself. We formulate a plan, there and then, Tomas and Hikaru and Tobi jabbering at each other. We will push ahead of it, external lights on, and we will make our way in front of it, while staying outside the anomaly: and then they can't not see us. Dr Singer will see us. It is an easy solution.

We will have our reunion then, is the hope.

The anomaly itself is like a wall, here. We can see a shimmer, a shine on it. Something that makes the inside darker, like looking at the *Ishiguro* through glass: the way it slightly warps the light. Everything is dark inside the anomaly except the *Ishiguro*; a run of almost insignificantly small white lights along the stretch of its hull illuminating it, giving it shape and form, letting us see it. There is no light from the sun in there; nothing backlit. They designed the ship to shine, to sparkle: again, such a waste. Tomas tells us that we should not go inside the anomaly,

110

that we should not even get close enough to touch it, not until we know more about it. I agree. Even though we can see the ship, and it's perfectly healthy. Even though it is still somehow running.

Hikaru draws us closer. We can see the plating on the side of the ship: almost perfect. As if it's been out here no time at all. Closer still means hundreds of metres, at this scale. Inna's fingers clasp tighter. Tobi makes little laughs under her breath, like yelps. Hikaru talks us through everything he does, every action, every button press, how much tension he's putting on the stick, and his voice is calm and peaceful. And then we're getting closer to it still, and Hikaru matches its speed so that we're travelling alongside it: having it to starboard, behind its veneer. We can see the anomaly even better now, and it is less like glass here, more the surface of a puddle: perfectly clear but rippled in places, almost a murmur in the surface. Hikaru keeps doing what he's doing, pushing the boosters to their limits. We feel it inside here, on the gravity: we are pushed backwards ourselves. We match the *Ishiguro*'s trajectory, but we are moving faster than they are, and then we're at a position where, using our rear camera, we can see inside their ship almost: and they don't have their lights on. Inside the ship it is almost as dark as the anomaly itself. There is no movement, and there is nothing visible. We do not have lights that we can shine inside, even. 'Stay the course,' I say. 'They'll notice us eventually.

So we keep moving in front of them and Lennox asks, under his breath, 'What's wrong?' because it's obvious that something is.

'Why is it so dark in there?' Tobi asks. None of us can see anything, so we keep moving forward: we do not stop, and they do not stop.

111

'Perhaps the good Doctor Singer's eyes were tired,' Tomas says. The delay runs to almost a minute, I think, but I have not counted it, and it will only get worse the further from Earth we get. I don't answer him, because it would be pointless. This is not the time to wait for a conversation. The crew are looking to us – to me – so I choke orders out, to stay in control of this. To let them know that I am still in control.

'Hikaru, keep us here. Lennox, try and find something to get their attention. We must have something.'

'We can knock on their front door,' Wallace says. 'We can jettison something from the ship, to knock on the hull. They'll notice that. Might get some movement inside.'

'Good. Prepare that, then,' I say. 'We have to get out there and –'

'Look,' Tobi says. She points at the rear-camera screen, and the *Ishiguro* quickly dropping behind us. 'They've stopped.'

'They've seen us,' I say. We fall silent, and Hikaru brings us to a stop, braking – they are not brakes, they are reverse boosters, really, but we think of them as what they are, in the service of what we are used to – and then Tomas speaks. His words are so much later than my words, thanks to the lag, and it is almost as if he's correcting me, but it cannot be that.

'They've seen you,' he says. 'You should stop.' He cannot know that we already have, but we have. We are still, and so is the *Ishiguro*.

We move backwards through space, nudging ourselves towards the *Ishiguro* in tiny increments. The thrusters were here for this reason: to allow us to move close to the anomaly, to allow us to hold position and not drift. They can fire in any direction, control on every point of each axis: another

112

invention we wanted, that we bought, that we own. We are silent, all of us, watching instead of speaking: concentrating on the task at hand. We move backwards, reversing until we are alongside them. We peer into the cockpit, into the darkness inside the ship. And: to think that we nearly rejected the need for delicacy of movement in our engine system, and that this, right now, has justified the millions we spent on procuring the boosters.

'What's the plan?' Hikaru asks as he draws us to a stop. We won't drift: the boosters will anchor us, calculating exactly how to keep us steady, judging how much the ship is moving. She moves too much: they compensate. It's delicate, but they are proven. We are still, and they look at me as if I know all the answers. I don't, I want to tell them. We have to do something, but I do not know what.

'We need a plan,' I say, but then Tomas voice comes in, straight away, so quick it's almost over mine.

'Nobody must go out there,' he says. 'It might not be safe, and we don't know about the anomaly yet.' They all look at me here, as if I should argue this point. They want to know which of us is more in charge as much as I do. But as soon as he says it, I know that he is right. 'Send a probe,' he says. I nod at Lennox, and he drags himself through towards the engine rooms, where they are kept, then comes back minutes later. The thing is small and round: a research offshoot of the boosters below us, covered in tiny engines that use exhaust gases as propellant. He passes it to Wallace, who presses a button on it. Its LEDs glow blue and bright.

'I'll run it,' he says. He floats back towards the changing rooms and the airlock, and I follow him, and Lennox. He straps himself to one of the benches and brings up a screen and he types on it, synchronizes the probe with his interface, and then he throws it to Lennox. 'Put it in the airlock,' he says. 'We'll flush it out, start it out there.'

'It will definitely hold,' I say, more a question than not. These things have been tested underwater and in our labs, in the vacuums that we created. Lennox lets it rest inside the airlock and then shuts the inner door. This will hold as well: the first time we have opened up any part of the ship to space itself. The seals, the panelling, the joins: they will all hold. Lennox types the code into the panel to release the outer door and it opens. We are still alive, and still fine. We watch on the camera inside the airlock as the ball stays drifting, unaffected by the vacuum.

'We're go,' Lennox says, and Wallace types something into the computer and the blue light flashes more. It shoots gas from the back, a puff of white, and the ball leaves the *Lära* and goes out into the nothingness. Wallace calls up another screen: this one showing the tiny camera that rests in the front of the probe.

'Let's see what's out there,' Wallace says.

He sends the probe forward, moving it slowly. From here we can get as close to the anomaly as possible: seeing the sheen of it up next to the camera. Through it, the *Ishiguro*. It looks the same as it ever did. It is clean and almost new; were it not for the technological advances we have made, you wouldn't think that it was twenty-something years old. There are very few marks on it. Nothing that would suggest it had any troubles. Nothing that gives us a clue as to what happened.

'Stay here a second,' I say to Wallace. 'Tomas, do you need anything from the anomaly?' We have to wait for the reply, and it's interminable. I don't know how we ever thought that this would be acceptable.

'Not just yet,' he says. 'Worry about the *Ishiguro* now.'

'Fine,' I say, and I tell Wallace to move the probe to the cockpit and through, into the anomaly.

'We don't know how it will react,' he says.

'So we discover,' I say. He moves the probe adjacent to the cockpit, and he rolls his shoulders, gearing up for this.

'Okay,' he says. He directs the probe straight for the cockpit. It passes into the anomaly as if it was nothing; as if it had been in there the entire time. Not even like water or glass: no ripples, and nothing shatters. We see the ship come closer, but the probe doesn't slow down. Instead it heads for the cockpit glass, and it collides, and the picture on the screen that we are watching it on crackles and fades into static, and the probe spins. The picture goes; out of the airlock I can see it, the blue lights now deadened. 'I didn't make it do that,' Wallace says. He furiously types and pulls at the keyboard to get a reaction. It spurts, left and right. It moves, but only just. Something's damaged on it, and it sits there like any other piece of debris.

'What's happening?' Tomas asks. 'What the fuck happened?' The image he'll be looking at will be of such a low resolution that it won't be worth much in way of an explanation. 'Did you crash it?' he asks.

'No,' Wallace says. 'I lost control. It fucked up.' He continues typing, and I watch it there, drifting now, away from the *Ishiguro* and back towards us. It seems to stop, somehow, and just floats there. It's almost tranquil.

'It won't have just fucked up,' Tomas says. 'That's not how they work.'

'So it's the anomaly,' I say. 'It must be.'

115

'Wait,' Wallace says. He rewinds the live feed, back into the recorded footage, and then plays it back: slower than real-time we watch the probe go off, and we watch it pass the boundary, and then frames start dropping and noise comes in, and we see the cockpit for a second as it collides with the glass, and then the static takes over. 'You're right,' Wallace says. 'It happened as soon as it went over. It was dropping frames in the video as well. Must be something interfering with the signal.' He rewinds it again, to see the moment it passed through. He slows it to an absolute crawl: as many frames of static as there are of the ship. 'Fucking madness,' he says. 'We don't know enough about this thing.' He types something, and there's a hiss of static on the screen, then the footage again.

'You've got it back?' Lennox asks.

'No,' he says. 'No, it's just playing video. It's looping video.' He jabs at the keyboard. 'I can't stop it.' We see the probe go on its journey again, hit the cockpit again, spin out. The footage starts again almost immediately. Again, and again, and we watch it. Wallace stands up, unclips, and looks to see through the airlock. 'If we can get it back, I might be able to fix it. It's obviously still got some life left in it.'

'We do have another,' I say.

'Not the point.'

'Guys,' Lennox says. 'The fuck has happened?' He watches the loop, and then, when it starts again, waits until it hits the cockpit. He pauses the video, and we all stare at this still frame. There is a glimpse, barely even a split second, where we have footage of inside the cockpit: and the blue light from the probe shines in there, and we can see chaos: debris floating, detritus, parts and pieces of who knows what. On the walls run dark smears. 'That's blood, right?' He advances the footage, frame by frame, but that's all we've got. The camera spins and tumbles.

'We have to go in there,' I say. 'We have to see it for ourselves. We have to see what it is.' I try to sound convinced when I say it; I try to sound as if this is second nature to me, and not something that I am guessing at, and praying for. Lennox and Wallace are both silent. Neither knows if I am right.

Somebody needs to go into the anomaly. We don't know what it is, still; and we don't know the dangers. We have a few absolutes, certainties: we can tell that it will not kill whoever goes into it, because everything about the *Ishiguro* tells us so. Somebody is alive in there. Why they haven't seen us, we don't know. Why they haven't come to us, rolled out a welcome wagon, desperate to thank us for rescuing them – if that's what they need – we do not know. But we need people out there. They are all trained. They have all done this in simulations and real-world practice. They are all capable. Now it's just drawing straws.

We need two volunteers, and Tobi says that one should be her. She's logged the most time in zero-g simulators. She's used the boosters on the suits so many times before; there is less chance of anything going wrong with her out there. And, in case a pilot is needed for the *Ishiguro*, she will be invaluable. Wallace agrees: she's good in this sort of situation, he says. He doesn't raise his own hand, though: instead he looks down at the floor, and at his feet, and he mumbles. I catch Inna staring at him, and I wonder what's going on. Something that I do not know. She raises her hand as well, then.

'I should go,' she says. 'There could be people on the other ship who need my help.' I shouldn't worry: hers is not mine to worry about, and it makes sense, and this is perfectly safe. Those suits are built to withstand so much. But still.

'What about Lennox?' I say, thinking that he is equal parts

117

young and limber and athletic and ballsy and expendable. And I think these things, and I don't feel guilty. It is safe, but if it is not, he is the one that we can stand to lose. Not Inna.

'Sounds good,' he says.

'If somebody is injured and can't be moved, I could save them,' Inna says. 'There was blood in there, wasn't there? This shouldn't even be a discussion.' Lennox looks disappointed, but then Wallace throws him back into play.

'Lennox, you should go with them. You know how to get the ship started if you need to, right? All three of you go.' We wait for approval: from Tomas, or maybe me. But I am not the one to call this. I don't know why, but I defer to my brother.

'Fine, the three of you,' Tomas eventually says. 'Get suited.' Wallace pushes off to go and get the suits, and the other three begin to take their clothes off. Inna stands in front of me: she unzips herself, pulling her suit down. Underneath she has a vest covering herself: her underwear, thin and blue.

'Help me?' she asks. She is looking at me. We were told that we couldn't be shy on the ship. Everybody sees everything. They'll see you shower, eat, sleep, shit. All of it, at some point or other. Wallace passes me a suit for Inna, and I open it. She bends down to pull it onto her feet, and I see more of the tattoo, eking out from the edges of her white vest. There are stretched claws and wild blue feathers. This is plumage. She seems to watch me as she undresses. She doesn't make eye contact, not to hold my own gaze, but she flits between looking directly at me and not: drawing my eyes to her as she meets my stare and then looking down at her own body, to slide her legs into the full-body suit, to push her fingers, one by one, into the slight, pinched tips of the gloves. The suits aren't like they used to be. They're thin and figure-hugging, a composite designed to

118

withstand temperatures and pressures that the old ones – swollen and puffy, missing only the diving bell – couldn't have come close to holding up to. They're designed for movement, for freedom. I am sealing the suit for Inna at the back when Lennox finishes dressing himself. He pulls up a full-body screen and turns a camera onto himself, examining himself as if it's a mirror.

'Okay,' he says. 'Anything happens, you'll pull us in, right?' They're going to attach themselves with tethers to our ship: a metal-fibre wire that we can control the tension on. I don't say this, but the tethered line is a last-chance Hail Mary: if they lose consciousness, or if we lose contact (I think about the probe turning to static, dying in the middle of the nothing, just spinning out of control), it's how we get them back. He looks at the two women, both putting the final touches to their body suits.

Inna leaves the end of the zip-seal until last: leaving that part of her bird exposed again, on her collarbone. She watches me as she closes it.

'Roomy, aren't they?' Lennox says. They laugh. He's joking; he's slightly scared.

Wallace helps them with their helmets. He fastens the braces over their suits; they're tied at the waist and the chest and the back, fastened and clamped; and then the helmets are on, locked down, cranked tightly. He runs diagnostics on the helmets to check, and they're all sealed. No rips – the fabric is almost impenetrable, so it's what we expected – and they're ready to go. He calls up their helmet cameras on tiny screens: inside the glass, angled at their faces. Inna and Tobi are serious with this, but Lennox pulls a face and look at himself on the screen. This has all happened so quickly. This is what we intended: that we could make a choice to leave the ship and be outside within minutes. None of the protocols or procedures that might have held us up, causing us to miss an opportunity. This is easy. This is, Tomas and I decided, how it should be.

The three of them stand in the airlock to say goodbye. Wallace clips them to the safety cable, daisy-chained together: Lennox to Tobi to Inna. If one of them needs help, the others are always attached. They wave at me, as if this is an adventure. Inna leans out before we shut the door and beckons me towards her. I come, and she leans in, cranes her neck so that I can see into her eyes. She doesn't say anything, but there is something. She smiles at me, and pushes backwards. Wallace closes the inner door.

'Are you ready?' he asks through the intercom. We can see them through the window into the airlock: nervous, twitching, bracing themselves. This is what they're all trained for. This is it. 'Thumbs up to show you're ready.' They all hold their thumbs out. Wallace types something, and the outer door opens, and they spill out in that first sudden rush.

'They're clear!' Hikaru shouts. We hear Lennox cheer over the comms – a long, drawn-out howl of joy, the howl of a sportsman scoring a goal, of a man climbing a mountain – and Wallace and I watch their cables become taut through the seals in the glass. They're so free. It's like swimming: driving through the darkness, the tiny boosters on their packs propelling them forward.

'When do they reach the anomaly?' I ask.

'Ten seconds,' Hikaru says from the cockpit.

'Slow down,' I say to them, but that's easier said than done. I intend for them to stop at it, to examine it briefly; to see if it is tangible. There is something that we refer to as a wall: this must be something. But then they pass through it, and it is as if they do not even notice. One by one they break it, and they carry on as if nothing even happened.

They do not realize. Hikaru turns on the intercom so that we can speak to them. 'You guys okay? You're inside it.'

'Holy shit!' Lennox says. He somersaults; he spins, around and around, tucked up. When he stops, he is facing the darkness that stretches off in front of him, and he reaches out towards it. 'So weird,' he says, 'like it's not there.' He turns to us, and his face. We can see his face on the monitors. 'What the fuck!' he says.

'What is it?' I ask.

'There's . . . It's like fog. It's hard to see through this.' Inna and Tobi turn and look as well, and their faces match. 'Turn up your lights,' he says, 'it's easier to see with the lights on.' We do.

'It's like looking through ink,' Inna says. 'It is so strange.'

'The mission,' Tomas says. 'You all should get on with this.' They do. No questions. Lennox swims forward, deeper into the anomaly, towards the *Ishiguro*, his arm outstretched.

'I can see my arm, but nothing past it. Can you see this? It's so weird.' He turns and pushes back towards us, his arm still outstretched. Wallace switches one of the screens to his camera view, so we can see what he sees. 'Are you watching this?' Lennox asks. It's patchy, and static-filled, and loose. His ouststretched arm: there is nothing there. Wallace flicks to show Tobi's camera. She has nothing in her view except the expanse of the anomaly. It's the darkest blackness I've ever seen. It's not like black paper or black metal, because it's nothing. The signal is frazzled and crackling with static, so the picture is fractured, but the gist is there.

'Tobi, what can you see?' Wallace asks.

'Nothing.' She sounds terrified. 'If I couldn't see my own hands, this would be like I was blind or something.'

'Put your flashlight on,' Wallace says. Tobi reaches up and

flicks the switch, and the light comes on, but it deadens in front of her. There's nothing to illuminate.

'My God,' she says. 'Can you see this?' Her voice crackles through the speakers.

'We can see it,' I say, as if that is the right phrase. There is nothing to see.

'Listen,' Tomas says, over the intercom, 'you need to go to the ship. We have to get on with this.' I wonder how much exactly he can see down there. How bad the picture is: the static from their feeds mingling with the static that he'll be picking up from the bounce. They don't argue: all three of them turn to the ship. We keep watching their cameras as they move towards it: and it looks so mundane suddenly, so dull, just another billion-dollar piece of technology floating further from home than anybody's ever been before.

Wallace talks to Lennox. 'There's a panel on the side of the ship, near the airlock. You can open that, start to cycle the airlock from that.'

'Isn't that dangerous? For them inside?'

'It seals the inner door when you open the outer one. It's an automated process.' I wonder why he didn't go out there himself. He would have been much more suited to this. I look at him, so dishevelled and tired.

'Should we knock on the door first?' Inna asks.

'You can try,' he says. 'They won't hear you, though. The metal's too thick for that.' Through Lennox's camera we watch him swim towards the panel. He reaches it.

'This one?'

'There are grips on the side. Pull them away and it'll swing loose.' He does – it's a strain, and we see Lennox struggle with it – and the panel opens. It's a mess in there, even I can see that. Some of the wires cut. Some of them tangled.

'It's not meant to look like that,' Wallace says.

'Can you still open the airlock?' I ask him.

'Yes,' he says. 'That part looks fine. It's the comms that are ruined in there. They'll have no satellite use, I reckon. Probably why we haven't heard from them.' He talks Lennox through what he should be doing, and then tells the other two to get to the entrance hatch. 'It'll open as soon as the internal one is shut,' he tells them. They pull themselves around to it, all clinging to the hull. Their cables snap and slap across the ship, and we can hear them reverberate inside *our* ship, where they go taut at their attach points. 'Ready?' he asks. They wait. 'Not long now.'

We wait and watch. 'Did he do it right?' Tomas asks, because of the lag, and then the door starts to hiss open, only a crack, a smidgeon. They are going inside. We see glimpses on their cameras of the inside, past the airlock window: how dark it is.

But there is movement in there. There is something moving.

'What was that?' Lennox asks, and then he hears something and snaps his head to face the rear of the ship, and the engines on the *Ishiguro* kick into action. They flare up and the light – which is blue, like the burn of a blowtorch, rather than the flame-yellow of a fire or an explosion – fills the monitors, each of them. They all look at it, and the *Ishiguro* lurches – bursts – forward, away from them. I see it happen, and it is as if it's too slow: as if we are not watching this for real, but we are on Earth in that second, watching a video. This is why you don't go into space, we are being told. Chaos and death will only follow.

'No!' we hear, Lennox's voice this absolute mess of panic; and Wallace howls and launches himself towards the safety wires and hits the button to pull them back to the ship, and

123

they start winding up but it's too slow, much too slow. On each screen we can see them turned towards the blue flames, coming through the static like exhaust trails, and then their monitors blink off one by one, no signal at all. It's not the static or the interference; it's the engines. The suits were meant to withstand temperatures, but the cameras weren't.

'Oh shit oh shit,' Tobi screams over the feed, through the static masking her voice, 'oh shit,' and then she drops away, and Hikaru goes to start our own engines but I tell him to wait, because we don't know exactly what's happened yet, although we do.

'Help me get them in,' Wallace screams. I am drifting: I am, I realize, not doing anything. This all happens in seconds. I stand next to Wallace as the cables retract, and we watch for what we're going to see: charred, unconscious bodies on the ends of them, and no idea if they're alive or not, because their life monitors have disappeared from the screens along with the camera feeds. We didn't predict anything this violent happening. Nothing this terrible. From here I can see their bodies: limp and drifting, all three of them. And inside the ship, in front of us, their cables rewind.

What has happened? This was to be my triumph.

'Nearly got them,' Wallace says, of the cables, but then they stop dead: stuck on something, jarring. 'What the fuck?' he asks, and there's an absolute desperation in his voice. It cracks, and he's suddenly crying. 'Fuck, please,' he says. His voice breaks through the tears, and I don't know what to do.

'What's going on?' Tomas asks, over the intercom. 'Is everything all right?' That almost makes me laugh. In another time, it would have made me laugh.

'No,' I say. 'Everything is not all right.' I wait for the reply as Wallace rushes to try and manually pull the cables, but there is no hand crank, and he will never get purchase. That's not how they are designed.

'Look on the cameras,' Wallace yells at me. 'They're not moving. They're stuck on something. Try and get a camera angle we can see them better.' I press buttons, cycling the exterior cameras on the ship. It turns my stomach: the possibilities of what I could see out there if I catch this at the right angle, the right magnification. What if I see cracks in their helmets or tears in their suits? They're meant to be fireproof, untearable, but nothing is actually those things. It's all scales of what can be tested in a lab. Heat anything up enough and it will burn, or melt, or both. Put enough pressure on something – the pressure of the *Ishiguro*'s engines, say, which I'm betting hasn't been tested – and anything will crumble and bend. What if I see them dead: burst, burned, ruined inside their helmets? Hikaru calls to us as I'm trying to get a decent picture – yet, honestly, I'm looking but not seeing, because this is all too much – and I panic and shake and leave what I am doing and pull myself through the corridor and to the cockpit trying to forget for a second our teammates who are somehow seemingly snagged on nothing at all, and on his screens I see the *Ishiguro* off in the distance, screaming forward, engines fit to burst, shuddering with how fast it is going; and then it starts to peel itself apart, like one of those videos of cars hitting walls, the dummies that were proxy flying through windscreens or hurling themselves around the interior. This was the self-destruct sequence. It was designed to break apart if it needed to, on re-entry: separating cleverly so that the seating area, fitted with a parachute, could complete the rest of the descent by itself. But why destroy themselves? Why here, and now? Shards seem to splinter off first, and then whole chunks, spinning off from the bulk of the ship with force, all of them propelled away

125

from it. What's left of the ship scatters them in its wake. I can, from here, see inside the ship: it's not illuminated, but there they are, the insides of the ship. I have studied it: watched videos of it before the launch, seeing all the crew in their positions, narrated by their very own journalist; seen pictures of it; seen scale models; used it as research for our own craft, both in terms of what to do, and what not. And here it is now, in the flesh. It is so close that I could almost touch it.

Then I see them: two of the *Ishiguro*'s crew members floating away from their craft into the darkness. One in a chair; the other clutched to the first, spinning away from the remains of their ship. That's all they have, and there's no way that we can save them. We're too far away, and they are moving too quickly. Not towards us, but towards nothingness, deeper and deeper into space, or the anomaly, whatever it is.

But now, we have our own problems. Maybe there are things more important than answers.

In the airlock, Wallace types furiously to try and get the safety lines to work harder. I look outside, and I see them pressed up against something: their suits flattened. 'It's the anomaly,' I say. 'They are trapped inside the anomaly.' Wallace looks as I pull up overlays, and they are: it's where they crossed, that's where they are trapped. They have been able to pass through it, but cannot pass back. Perhaps this explains why the *Ishiguro* never came home. 'Stop,' I tell Wallace, so he does. He is drenched with his own tears, and it's so curious to see them: out of his eyes, onto his cheeks, peeling away and drifting into the air between us. 'How much air have they got?'

'If they're still alive?' He looks at me as if this is my fault, and his. We are mutually responsible. 'A couple of hours, minus however long they've been out there,' he says. I suck in air through my teeth. I have to keep this together.

'What are we going to do?' Hikaru asks.

'I'm thinking,' I say. When they're not looking I take a stim, and I cling to the safety rails, and I tell Tomas to contribute anything, if he has any ideas. The delay feels even longer than usual. Maybe he's choosing to not answer.

'Okay,' he finally says.

I have never felt as useless as I do right now. As I look at them out there, and I wonder what we can do. And I talk to Tomas, who says that he cannot do anything. He says, 'Mira, this is on you. You are the one up there,' and it feels as if he is removing himself from the blame. I wonder what he is doing down there. I wonder what they are all doing: scrutinizing their low-quality versions of our camera feeds, wondering which of the crew are dead. Maybe they all are.

We get confirmation of one before they do, because of the lag. I am watching the screens on my own. I don't know where Wallace is, because he left me here by myself, and Hikaru is in the cockpit, scanning to see what caused the *Ishiguro* to blow up. I am by myself when one of the cables slackens, slightly; and the one of them closest to us on it, Lennox, begins to drift back towards us, pulled by the tension. It is only him, the other two are still against the anomaly wall; I shout for Wallace and Hikaru to come and help get him in, amazed that Lennox somehow made it out of the anomaly, but the others do not come. I am alone when Lennox reaches the airlock: and he drifts towards the camera, and I see his face, and I just know.

8

Lennox's body is inside the hatch, and I can drift down to floor level and see it: his eyes shut, as if this was peaceful for him. This was nothing. A dream of death: going to sleep and never waking up.

'We can't bring him in until the others are through,' Wallace says, when he finally arrives. He doesn't seem surprised that Lennox is dead; he is cold to it. The tether wire blocks the outer door, so it can't happen. I wonder if it matters. Lennox is okay here: his body crumbled, pressed up, but peaceful, and at least he's here. We can do something with him after all of this. He can have a funeral, when we get home. 'I said that he should go,' Wallace tells me, but he says it with no pain in his voice: a blunt statement. No more tears; this is, I think, his way of focusing on the task at hand; at what needs to be done. 'I said that he would be good out there.' We are not to blame. I wonder if I should say that, or if this is okay: leaving it as a guilt that we may always feel. I do not know the best way to grieve when you are implicit. He pushes himself to the doorway. 'Why are they still there?'

he asks, but he knows the answer, as much as makes sense. He wants me to say it.

'I do not know,' I say.

'Do you think they're alive?' He makes eye contact. He's taken a stim, I can see: his eyes are focused, not twitching. Totally still as they stare at mine.

'Yes,' I say. 'I think that they might still be alive.' We both know what that means, even as we cannot explain it.

'Okay.' He nods his head, processing this. 'I want gravity,' he says.

'No,' I say, a snap reaction.

'I need it.' He doesn't look at me, and he doesn't actually sound angry in his voice; but I know that there will be no arguing with him about this. He brings up a console. 'Hang on to something,' he says. I reach out for the rail on the wall, but I am too slow.

We fall, collectively.

My feet touch the ground, and they try to take the weight, as they are used to doing; as they have been trained, over years and years, to do. They are shaky, desperately so. We haven't been here long enough to do permanent damage, but there will always be an initial weakness. If you spend a week lying down, you can barely walk for a few hours. Now I shake and lurch for the rail, and my whole self feels implausibly heavy. Another time and place this might be funny: I need the safety bars when there is no gravity; we put the gravity on and I still need them. I am useless, I think. I am in need of assistance in everything. Wallace massages his calves, and he moves forward slowly and clumsily, but better than I. We were meant to be doing exercises, but I have ignored them the entire time. I wonder if he's been doing them: when he goes back to his engine rooms, grabbing the bars and forcing himself to squat against the wall, pulling himself towards it to work the legs and arms as best he can.

'Okay,' he says. 'We work out how to get Tobi and Inna back now.' Force, defiance in his voice. He is driven.

'If we could have done this differently,' I say. I don't know how I'm intending on finishing the thought. We wouldn't. This would have always gone this way. I stagger to the cockpit in his wake, and he sits next to Hikaru. I am left behind them, clinging to the rail. My legs cramp. I cannot moan. I cannot cry about this. I tell myself: this could be so much worse. The three of us discuss the options as if this is the most natural thing in the world. We are cold about it, no emotion here. We do not allow ourselves to panic. There is a timer on one of the screens, I see: a countdown of the air that they have left. Hikaru must have set it, and while it's only approximate, it's terrifying. I cannot stop looking at it as we talk, and for brief moments I lose attention and I picture Inna. I picture her coughing for air, struggling. I wonder if she will know what is happening; if it will hurt.

We have options.

We go in there, to rescue the two of them.

We force them through the anomaly, using the winch. Wallace does something that might make it more powerful, and we exert that force on their bodies, whatever the cost. We get them back one way or another.

We accept that they are a loss. We say goodbye. We watch them die, because we are scared, and we want to save ourselves. This is not a real option.

As we discuss, we all try to not shout. Wallace doesn't speak as Hikaru, myself and Tomas offer our suggestions. The conversation is stilted, stopping and starting with abandoned ideas.

We argue inside ourselves, none of us sure what the anomaly is still. I wonder whether we shouldn't have concentrated on it, rather than the *Ishiguro*. We could have spent our time examining what would happen if we passed through. But we – Tomas, myself, all of us, really – are scientists. We are here to discover. If you do not discover, you are nothing. You solve questions, and the question that was most immediate was about the *Ishiguro*: its crew, how it was here, what it was doing.

Tobi's line goes slack as we are talking, and the slight recoil pulls her towards us. We pray that she is somehow free; but she doesn't answer her radio, and her body is limp in the darkness, bent in the middle as if she is being carried by something, as if she draped across some unknown person's arms. Wallace runs and retracts the cable, and brings her in. Her helmet is melted; her face the same. I turn off the camera as soon as I see her. We do not need to see this.

It is more evidence. Somehow, Inna is on the other side of the anomaly because she is alive. Somehow, because they have died, Tobi and Lennox's bodies are back with us.

'What's happening?' Tomas asks. None of us answer. Wallace presses his hands against the internal airlock door, and he cries. I swear I can hear the beep you hear in a hospital when somebody dies, even though there is no beep at all.

According to Hikaru's clock, Inna has maybe an hour of air left. She is left floating there, still presumably unconscious. There is no reason for her to wake up. The suit will regulate her temperature: she will be neither hot nor cold, and then she will just die. Maybe she will wake up when she runs out of oxygen. Maybe she'll look at us, desperate, and then work out what has happened. We have abandoned her, she'll think. We've let her die in there.

I think about her as we stand around and wait for her time to run out, and I imagine what might have been. I don't know, and I don't know if I am right, but I imagine that maybe we could have had something. I have never had a relationship. I am my age, and I have never had this, or anything.

'Look,' Hikaru says, and I expect Inna's body to be creeping towards us, her limbs slackened and dead; but instead she is shaking, and she is awake, and her eyes are open.

'What's happening?' she asks, in a tiny, terrified voice. 'Please god, what's happening?'

She's alive.

I think that I have been in love, but know that it has never been reciprocated. I have loved women, and I have idolized them. I have met them and learned their names, and I have thought, I could be with you. We have had common interests and beliefs, and they have wanted to know about my work. They have asked me if I can see a future with them, and I have wondered. I have wanted them; but now, with Inna, this is something different.

I cannot explain it better than that.

'Can you hear me?' I ask, and she screams, so I tell her to calm down. 'Please, Inna,' I say. 'We want to help you, but you have to listen to me. You have to answer me.' She stops.

'It hurts,' she says.

'Can you move?' I ask her.

'I don't know,' she says.

'Do you know what's happened?'

132

'I can't move. No,' she says.

'Tell her to not try, then,' Wallace says. He is watching, sitting on the floor behind me, back against the wall. 'Tell her to save her energy.' He knows what I know, or what I have posited: that she is here until she runs out of air, and then she will die. I wonder if I should just be making her comfortable, trying to make this easier on her. That is what you do when it is inevitable.

'Listen,' I tell her, 'try to stay still. We are doing everything that we can to get you back here.'

'Why can't you come and get me?' she asks. She is asking me, I think: not the rest of the ship. Why can't I. 'Please, Mira.'

'It's complicated,' I say. 'There is a problem, with the anomaly. I need you to see if you can move, and to check that you're okay. Check that you're fine.' I watch her move her hands, flexing them, and her arms. She flexes and looks around.

'Where are they?' she asks. 'Lennox and Tobi, where are they?'

'Don't worry about that,' I say. 'Do you remember what happened?'

'The ship started,' she says. 'The ship started, didn't it?'

'Yes,' I say.

'I can barely see you through this,' she says. 'Please, turn the lights brighter.'

'Okay,' I say. Wallace does it, and the relief on her face is immediately visible. I look through her camera myself: it's better, but she's right. This is like looking through the murk of dark ink.

'Tell her to push the anomaly. To see what she can do. Maybe she can find a way through it or something.' Wallace speaks

133

quietly. I tell Inna to do it, and I watch as she presses the wall in front of her. From here, it is as if she is trapped behind glass: a prisoner, desperately pawing to get out. Her hands move against it, as if she is a mime; as if this is all an act.

'What is happening?' she asks, and she sounds desperate. She breathes quickly, gasping air in, and Wallace pushes himself to standing. He doesn't look up; he stays hunched at the side.

'She needs to calm down. She doesn't have enough air to start panicking.' He rubs his side, with his hands; and then moves one hand to his neck, and rubs that. He is breaking, I know, but I need him to hold it together. I don't know if this is something I should say to him or not; if that might risk pushing him over an edge of whatever he is facing. 'You need to get her to calm down.'

'Can we get her more air?' I ask.

'We can't open the airlock until she is back or we cut her safety cord. We can cut the cord, if you want.'

'But she can't come back until she's dead.' We stand and watch her panic: from here, even, I can see her breath fogging up her helmet.

'Can't she use Tobi's?' Tomas asks, and we realize that he's right.

'She would need to get the body back,' Wallace says, 'and she'd need to unclip hers, plug the spare in. That's assuming it's intact.' He bends down to look at their bodies in the airlock, and he tries to examine the packs. 'Lennox's is gone. Burned out, looks too melted. Tobi's . . . It might be okay.' Her helmet is cracked: her face behind it pale and dead. She was so worried about her eye, but did it matter? In the end, the time she spent concerned about it? Was it worth it? 'I can talk her through it,' Wallace says.

'How long will she have to do the changeover?'

'Seconds. If she doesn't panic, stays calm, it should be fine. Tough part is the seal, because that's behind her head. You can't see that. The suits weren't designed for this.'

'Let's do it,' I say. I make the decision. One way or another, I seal her fate. Wallace leaves, to get one of the spare suits and to practise himself, so that he can talk her through it. I stay, and I talk to Inna. I explain to her what happened to Tobi, and to Lennox. I tell her that they are dead, and that she needs to pull Tobi's body towards her to take her air supply or she will die as well. She cries, because it's too much to take, but she does it: I watch Tobi's body slink through space towards her, and I watch Inna pull the body closer, facing away from her; and then she holds it there, so that it cannot turn. She doesn't want to see her face. She must have seen the faces of so many bodies; now, she is choosing not to.

'What do I do now?' she asks.

'Just wait,' I say. 'Not for long.' I watch Wallace doing the manoeuvre; he can barely get it right first time. He tries again, and again. At least he doesn't look upset, now. He looks like he has something to preoccupy him. Keeping busy: it feels like a way past this tragedy.

Wallace stands at the glass and talks her through it. He holds the suit in front of him to make this easier. She has twenty minutes, and then she's dead, and this has all been for nothing. The anomaly; the *Ishiguro*; Inna, Tobi, Lennox. Hikaru and I watch as Wallace talks to her.

'The air in the other suit, that's going to help you breathe for longer,' he says. 'So you have to move this one to your suit.'

'How long do I have?' she asks.

'Long enough. We'll do this, okay? I'll talk you through it.'

'What happens then? When I can breathe again?'

He looks at me, and he lies. 'Then we come and get you,' he says. 'We have to sort this first. We're close to working out how to get you out of there.' I want to ask her what the anomaly feels like, really feels like: to take off her glove and touch it. I want to ask her to get a sample of it, to carve or dig at it, to see what she can do. I want her to help us, because we might not get another chance if she dies. Who will willingly send another person behind that wall? To test it, to see what they can find? I wonder if I am a bad person for thinking of science now, rather than Inna. Tomas would have an answer to that question, I'm sure.

'You only have one shot at this,' Wallace says. 'We want to get your camera working first. Can you reach up? I want to see if it's broken, or just fazed. There's a button on the front of the helmet, like a depression. Press it.' She does: on one of the little screens, her face appears, crackling through static. 'Excellent,' Wallace says. 'We've got you.' She smiles a little. Like she feels that this is putting her back towards normality. 'Now, on Tobi's body.' He pauses; then continues. 'You need to get the oxygen tank, find the cable that runs through to the back of the helmet. You know which cable it is?' he asks, and we watch her pawing at the suit ineffectually. She stumbles on the cable by luck rather than judgment. 'That's the one. You need to find the catch on the end of it. Unscrew it. It'll be tight.'

'Won't this let the oxygen out?'

'It's a membrane,' he says. 'Can't come out unless connected to the suit. Stops leakages.' She unscrews it. We can see Tobi's dead face for a few moments, with its eyes rolled back and its cheeks blue. We try to concentrate on what Inna is doing. 'Excellent. You'll need to pull the oxygen tank off now, and then hold onto it. Okay?'

'Okay,' Inna says. She sounds more with it, now. More like herself. Survival instinct has kicked in. Everything else fades into the unimportant. Inna manages to do it, to free the tank, and she brings it close, coddles it. She steadies herself with one hand against the anomaly, and I want to ask her what it feels like: to do my research, even here and now.

Is it like treacle? Is it like tar?

Wallace continues. 'Now this is the tough part, Inna. You with me?'

'Yes,' she says.

'You need to unscrew your oxygen and screw this one in. You'll still be sealed into the suit, but you won't have oxygen for a while. And you have to screw this new one completely on, or it won't give you oxygen. You understand what I'm saying?'

'I understand,' she says. She is shaking. Her eyes are so wide. I watch as she reaches behind her. It's an awkward angle.

'Don't do this rashly,' Wallace says, 'take your time. Feel the connection first, and work out how you're going to do this.' She's only got ten minutes left. Not more than that, certainly. She can't take too long, but I don't say that. Nothing worse than extra pressure in a situation like this. 'So you unscrew it, then lift the other canister into place, then screw that nozzle on. The same place you unscrew the old one, that's the place you put the new one. Remember that.'

'Okay,' Inna says. She fingers the connection a few times and then takes a breath, a deep one, and she unscrews it.

'Good luck,' I say, but I don't know if it's loud enough for her to hear me. She unscrews the old capsule fully and then lets it hang loose, and – her face the perfect picture of composure – lifts the other hose to her back, to the same spot. We all watch as she tries to find the hole but misses, so Andy tells her to take her time, find the hole with her finger and then attach it, but she misses again, and that's all it takes. She's flustered. Her eyes panic. Her mouth opens, and she breathes again and again, gasping in the last air from the helmet, and then there's nothing left. She jabs the hose down over and over, trying to find purchase, and then by pure luck she gets it onto the hole – she can tell something's right, because the panic turns to relief for a second – but then she tries to turn it the wrong way, and then the right way, but it won't catch. It won't hold. It doesn't work. Her fingers twitch as she turns it weakly, and then they twitch again, and she stops turning the attachment altogether. 'You're nearly there,' I say, but I don't have the enthusiasm, because I know that she is gone, even before I see her face go still, and before I see her eyes turn dead.

None of us say anything because there's nothing to say. We took a chance and it didn't work. I leave the airlock and I sit in the lab and I start writing something for me to read to ground control, maybe something more public. Some sort of apology. We dabbled in that which we did not understand. We took risks. They did not pay off. Wallace slumps and sobs on the floor. He is lost. I tell him to wheel the bodies in, but he ignores me, and I stand there, ineffectual. It is as if no part of me works any more. Hikaru has started plotting a course home, I can see: but we must wait for official confirmation. What else is there to be done? I bring up Inna's

138

face on a screen, the monitor inside her helmet. It's curious: how quickly one can look dead. How quickly the blood drains, and how grey the skin can become. I wonder if that has really happened, or it is simply how I perceive it to be.

This mission has been a failure. I say this to Tomas, and I tell him that he needs to talk to the UNSA. I wonder what they already know: how much he has shared. I don't worry about the lag. This isn't intended to be a back-and-forth conversation.

'Okay,' is all that he says.

'That's it?'

'What else is there to be said? What if we tell you not to come home? Can you stay there, now?'

'I don't think so.'

'When are you leaving?' Tomas asks.

'Soon,' I say.

'Will you take more samples at least, before you leave? More readings? It seems a shame for you to be there and us to still have no idea what the anomaly is.' He is right. I do not say it, but he is right. I question what is inside me, because I want to mourn, but there is more to this. 'And the *Ishiguro*. That you should see it, here and now! The chances of that, Mira. They're incredible.'

'I know.'

'Infinitesimal, almost.'

'I know.' He knows that they are not, because it has happened. He's trying to get a rise. 'We'll try and take some readings,' I say, 'before we go. I think it makes sense.' I don't know what they would be, but he's right. We've come this far. Time, and money, and space. We are only as good as the work we do; as the results we uncover.

I go back to the airlock, to pull Inna back in. Wallace is

nowhere to be seen, and the room is dark and cold. I am about to press the button and wind her towards us, away from where she has been drifting, loose inside the anomaly, when I hear a noise: a rush, an inhalation, a shock, a scream.

On the screen, Inna opens her eyes.

'What's happening?' she asks. 'Please god, what's happening?' I don't say anything: she has been dead too long to suddenly come back with no intervention. I do not say anything. She panics, and says some words in Russian that I don't understand: her rolling tongue. And then she asks for me. 'Mira? Why aren't you answering me? What's happened?' She begins crying. I know that this is impossible: and yet, here she is. She gasps. 'Where are you?' she asks again. I look at her face on the screen: the colour back in her cheeks, and how alive she is, all of a sudden. She puts a hand out to the anomaly. 'Hello?' she asks.

'Hello,' I say.

PART TWO

Death is not an event in life: we do not live to experience death.

– Ludwig Wittgenstein

9

I spend the entire first time – or maybe this is the second time, I don't know how to think of it – desperate to save her. When she replies to me, I ask her what she remembers. She remembers the *Ishiguro* powering up its engines, and she remembers things going wrong. She asks where Tobi and Lennox are, because she cannot see them. They are both on this side of the anomaly. She asks where we are, because she is scared. I try to make it better. I tell her that I am here. I tell her that we are going to save her, and I call Wallace and Hikaru into the airlock room and we fight about this, screaming at each other about what we do. They do not understand this; I do not understand this. Tomas stays quiet, conspicuous by his absence. Eventually I am forced to ask him.

'What do you think, Brother?' I ask, but he doesn't reply. Inna begs for reassurance, and we tell her that it's okay, that we're working on something; and then she tells us that she is having trouble breathing. She says that she feels light-headed, and she starts to cough. We're too shocked to make this work; too ruined. We dread to think of her out there, and what she is going through. When she dies, it's like a replay. It is always the same way, too similar for comfort, or coincidence. She asks for air, sputtering. She is begging for air, as if it's something we are depriving her of. Then she dies, just like the first time. We stand, and we shake, and we hang our heads. None of us say anything; and then she opens her eyes again, and takes her first gasp for the third time. The first time she was awake, maybe it was something else. Something that we couldn't explain, something like that. This time, the next time, I know that it is destined to happen again, and again. It is cyclical.

'What's happening?' Inna asks as she gasps herself to life again, the same way that she has the past two times.

'What do you remember?' I ask her. I change it by interfering, but the general routine remains the same. She wants answers, and I cannot provide her with them.

'The ship, we were at the ship,' she says. The parts in between: they are gone to her. But I remember, and Hikaru remembers them, and Wallace remembers them. At the end of this cycle, two hours later, she paws at the anomaly wall like every other time. Then she dies, screaming and howling, tearing her throat ragged in that sealed bubble of a helmet; and then she wakes up again, and asks the same question.

'This is curious,' Tomas says. I don't know what I want to say to him, but it is so much more than that.

It is awful to watch her, because she always dies the same way. Something about that makes it worse: as if you want the chaos of death to make it seem real, somehow. You want to believe that it cannot be happening, whereas her deaths only reinforce the terrible nature of her situation. Each time she coughs and chokes on her words in the exact same way that she did before. Wallace doesn't leave the airlock. He sits there on the floor and watches her, in the distance. Not her face on the screens: the nothing, and her in the middle of it. He says, 'This is so fucking cruel. How can this be happening?' but I don't know what to say to him in reply. It feels rhetorical. When Hikaru tells us that we have to remove the artificial gravity, because the batteries are suffering, Wallace clips himself to a rail and floats there, right where he was. The four of us – I'm including Tomas in this, even though he is a minute late to every decision, every conversational note – talk about how to get Inna out of the anomaly. If we even can.

There are rules here, even though we are not wholly aware of them. We are piecing them together as we go. The anomaly is as a semi-permeable membrane. Anything can pass into it; but then they cannot come out. Detritus, scrap, corpses: only non-living matter can return to this side of the anomaly wall. (This is a logic that we have reached by observation rather than the regular scruples and tests we would apply to such a theory. We would test it, had we a rat or a dog or anything else living that we could send over there. Instead, we have Inna, our only test subject, and we can pull the rope that connects us to her, but she doesn't move. Lennox and Tobi were like her, trapped; but they died. Now they are on our side. We spend time during Inna's next cycle – this is almost like a video game, I think, when we used to call the ability to replay moments Lives, as if that was normal, to have multiple attempts at something with no penalties involved – trying to pull her through, to force the matter, and I ask her to press against it at the point where the tether enters and exits, which she does as she cries for us to save her, but she cannot get her hands through – there are no points of entry or exit – and then she beats the cable and the anomaly both with her hands in melodrama, or what would be melodrama if she wasn't so slowly and gradually dying.) I wonder about the *Ishiguro* – why it was where it was, and what we saw, those two bodies floating off. How deep they might get, propelled by the explosion. Hikaru wonders if we can't just drive the ship into the anomaly, get Inna and then leave. The ship is not living. Metal passes through it fine. I think about the *Ishiguro* and I wonder. It's nothing. I can't explain it to Hikaru and Wallace, but I tell them that I don't think it'll work.

'It's too much of a risk,' I say. 'What if we all end up stuck on the inside of that thing?' They nod. I know more about this than them, in theory. They're not so desperate to get her back that they would mutiny. Or, at least, Hikaru isn't. Wallace seems lost in this. He doesn't stop staring into the middle distance. They have a word for people with his look in their eyes. I forget it. A psychological term to describe them.

'He's thinking of something,' Hikaru says, when we talk about it. Wallace is asleep: passed out, drifting in the airlock room. 'He's been through a lot. We all have.' Later, Hikaru says that he thinks that I should sleep as well, and he should. We should all sleep. 'We can't do this if we're falling apart,' he says. We agree – I take another stim, but I agree to the theory, that the two of them need to rest or we won't be functioning at 100 per cent efficiency – but one of us needs to stay awake, to watch Inna. To be here with her, as she goes through this. She is suffering, and this is the least that we can do. And what if something changes? We wake Wallace from his drifting slumber and put him into his actual bed, and I tell Hikaru that I have the ship. That I am absolutely in control. While he sleeps, I talk to her. We go through the motions. I find it hard to believe that they are already rote: but what else can they be? She doesn't change her script, so I am the only one able to adapt; or, to pretend to adapt.

On her fifth cycle I wonder, with her dying, if I should be mourning her. Is she truly dead if she keeps coming back? Is she dead already? Is this simply a prolonging, a dragging out of her life beyond her natural time? Is this, whatever the anomaly has done to her, simply life support? She is out there, and she dies. Maybe she only comes back because we are watching her. Maybe it's because we want her to. I cannot explain this. There is still science here, there must still be answers, but they feel so far away from us. I wonder if she would know if we backed away, slowly, silently. She cannot see us. Eventually, she would just be shouting into the darkness; crying out, and then she would die anyway. Maybe that way is peace.

I watch the camera inside Inna's helmet. I watch as she struggles and dies; and I wait for the moment that she comes back to life, a hyper-exaggerated Lazarus. That moment, where she wakes up and breathes her first of this new burst of life: it's the same as her smile. Maybe this is how she wakes up every morning, to greet the new day.

Over and over she falls from the ledge. She wakes up and she cries, I don't know how to help her, she chokes, she dies, there's a time of placidity where nothing happens and then she gasps her first new breath of air. She repeats. She doesn't remember the times before, which is a mercy. We know this because all I can do is ask her questions. But all of this feels like a lost cause: because how do we stop this? How do we stop her?

'We pull her out when she's dead,' Wallace says. 'That seems like the right thing to do.' He doesn't look at her on the screen – he won't make eye contact, even though she cannot see him – but he seems to feel some empathy with her.

'That's interesting,' Tomas says.

'She's not dead,' Hikaru argues.

'She is.'

'No. Because she has a life sign more than she doesn't, right? Which means that the suit is malfunctioning. And we can hear her. That's a better argument for her being alive than . . . something else.' Sleep has made Hikaru unblinking. His internal logic – where we ignore the thing that's happening that we have no way of explaining, because what we cannot explain cannot be true – is flawless. But it's also broken: we can't pull her out of the anomaly, and we cannot explain that. I don't push him. But I ask Tomas' advice, and he tells me what he thinks is happening.

'The anomaly is keeping her alive. The other two are dead. Somehow, whatever it is, it's bringing her back to life. As long as she's inside it, she's alive again, until she runs out of air. If you bring her out when you get the chance, she'll die for good.' He stops talking. I don't fill in the gaps. After a while, he starts again. 'Are you there? I think you would be killing her.' He wants us to stay here for longer. He wants us to run tests on the anomaly again while we think of a way to save her.

'What tests would you have me do?' I ask him.

'I don't know,' he says. 'I'm sure we'll think of something.'

I sit with Wallace, clamped to one of the rails. He is terrible. There is a carton in his hand, a cardboard construct: our sole concession to a food or liquid in the crew's private possessions, a private supply of something or other. He initially asked for scotch, that he might celebrate with a glass of it. Instead, he is drinking it now.

'Are you okay?' I ask. It is rhetorical. He doesn't offer me the drink, or look at me. He carries on regardless, drinking. We are silent for too long before he speaks.

'What do you think this means?' he asks.

'Inna?'

'After we die. Do you think it means anything?'

'For her or us?'

'Us.' He drinks.

'I think it means what it always meant,' I say. 'I think it means that there is nothing.'

'So Tobi and Lennox: they're just dead?'

'That's right,' I say.

'You never believed in a heaven?' he asks.

'I have always had too much logic for that,' I say. He finishes the carton and crushes it.

'What do you think she sees, when she's dead?'

'I have no idea,' I say.

'We can never ask her, because she doesn't remember it.'

'No.'

'So it might as well be nothing.' He lets the carton fall from his hands and it drifts off. He dips his head and shuts his eyes. I do not stay sitting with him, because I do not know how to talk to him when he is like this; and I do not know how long he will stay like this for.

In the lab, I listen to Inna die again. The final stretch of desperate cries and shudders, always the same. Utterly truthful: a pained realization, that this is it, for her. I have her camera feed in front of me, but sometimes I shut my eyes and let it wash over me. That feeling of loss. I need another stim. I can feel myself wavering. It's such a good job that these things aren't addictive, I tell myself. I would be a wreck if there was some real dependency on them, rather than my desire to remain awake for far more practical reasons. Then Inna comes back to life again.

'What's happening?' she asks. I don't say anything at first, because I find this too hard. I wait for her to start crying and pleading. I don't want to interact with this: I don't want her to know that I'm watching her die again. Maybe it's cruel, I tell myself. I am selfish, letting her go through this alone. Maybe I should be out there every time, holding her hand, telling her that this will be all right. Maybe we should just kill her, drag her through, put her to an ending. Tell Tomas that it just happened, damn the results, the tests, the answers. This is her umpteenth performance, and she is screaming her lines to the cheap seats. 'Is anybody there? What's happened?'

'Inna,' I say. 'I'm here.'

'Why am I out here?' She panics. Almost hyperventilates. She always almost panics at this point, and then she drags it back. If I don't talk to her, she *does* hyperventilate. That feels like enough of an experiment by itself. 'We were by the other ship and the engines started. What happened? What happened?' I am trying to treat this as something worth watching: research into whatever the anomaly is. This was Tomas' idea. Watch her: the moment that she comes back to life, maybe there is something. A spark, a flash. The last time, we told her to undo her oxygen tank. We lied to her, because we wanted to replicate the first time around: to see how it was somehow reattached to her helmet, somehow full of oxygen again. We have videotaped this so that we can watch it back at our own leisure. As if the constant recurrence of it isn't enough. 'Mira, please talk to me! You're scaring me!'

'I'm sorry,' I say. 'Just wait a little while. We are working out how to come and get you. Bring you back onto the ship.' I call for Wallace and Hikaru to come here, and I find the spot on the footage where it must have happened, but I can't see anything. So I slow it down, play it back again. I focus on her oxygen tank: the one thing we cannot explain in any real way. It becomes reattached. That's not science: it's magic. On the video, in one second the hose is there, floating slightly free of her body; the next it's attached again, and firmly. One swift movement with nothing between points A and B. I slow the video down even more. Even more. Wallace arrives first, and he sees the screens – I have forgotten to pull them down, so my obsession with her face is exposed, but that's the least of my problems – and he screams at me.

'What the fuck are we doing?' he asks. He turns and leaves. I hear him hit the wall: no howl of pain, just dull thud. It's hard to get the power up without gravity. Hikaru waits in the doorway and watches him leave, and then he shakes his head at me, as if I would go after Wallace and try to calm him down. That isn't me. We watch the screen together.

'When are you going to save me?' Inna asks.

'Soon,' I tell her. 'We're coming.' I slow the footage to a crawl, to see single frames; and I find the exact frames in the footage where the changeover happens. There's nothing in it. No Inna, no oxygen tank. The frame before, she's dead, and the frame after, she's alive, almost exactly as she was hours and hours before. In the space between, it is blank. 'Do you see this?' I ask Hikaru. He nods. I wheel it back to the exact frame, and we concentrate on it. There's nothing there: not even the stars, because the anomaly has had those too.

Wallace comes to me when I am alone. I thought he was asleep but he isn't. I am not, because I am watching her. I have turned the sound off: now she screams silently. He speaks quietly from the doorway, as if he doesn't want to disturb me. He doesn't make eye contact.

'I asked you this before,' he says, 'but this time I'm really serious. Please: I want to call my family now.'

'We might be going home soon,' I say to him. I don't know why I am trying to put him off, but I am. I want him to save it; in case he really needs it. 'You can tell them we are coming home when we know it for sure.'

'I don't care.' He looks at me. His eyes are red and dark. 'Let me call them now. Please.'

'Okay,' I say. He doesn't leave.

'Can I have the lab?' he asks. 'There's privacy. I just want to be alone with them a while.' I unclip myself and pull myself past him. In the corridor I turn, to offer my help to him: to tell him how I hope he feels better after this. He has already shut the door, and I message Tomas, before he makes his own connection.

'Wallace is calling home,' I say. 'Let him. It's fine. I think he needs it.' Tomas doesn't reply, which is good. He would question it, maybe. Let him. I have made a choice.

In the main living area I bring up Inna on the screens. I talk to her and make it better, because this is what I feel like I should do sometimes. I lie to her that we'll be saving her soon. She asks me what we are going to do, how we are going to get her back. She asks what the plan is.

'We have to work out what the anomaly is first,' I say. 'We are closing in on that.'

'How did you get Tobi and Lennox back?' She doesn't know that they're dead, this cycle. I haven't told her.

'In the blast,' I say. 'When the engines started, they were thrown out. I'm sorry that you are there, still. We are doing everything we can.' I haven't told her the strangest part of her story, in any of her lives: that she's died before, over and over and over. I talk and I talk, and she asks questions, and we relax into this. She trusts me. Why would she not? I am in charge of this. I understand it all. I have been here since the beginning: planning this, working it out. We talk, and then she says that she is tired, that it's getting hard to breathe. I have lost track of time. Wallace is missing, still; still talking. I imagine the cost of that. The bandwidth being used. How angry people will be. I flick through the screens, opening the outward signal. I can see into his conversation. He is terrible and sad, so sad. His face is red with tears.

'I love you,' he says. He touches the screen, because they must be doing it as well. I cannot see them, but I imagine them crying at his words, his gentle manner. He is finishing this. 'Look after your mother. I love you all so much. I'm sorry.' He severs the connection. That is wrong. Something is wrong. Why would he apologize?

'Wait there,' I say to Inna, even though she has so little time left, and she will be gone, dying alone; and I unclip myself and push towards the office, but the door is locked. I cannot remember the code, so I call for Hikaru, but he cannot remember it either – why would we lock the doors?

– so Tomas steps in, and he unlocks the doors from their end, and we wait and wait.

By the time I get to him he is dead.

Tomas tells me that it isn't my fault. 'He would have done it whatever. He was that personality type.' I was the one to cut the cable that Wallace had tied to the floor; that had tightened itself naturally as he pushed away from it; that had choked him, and that he could not get back from, even if he wanted to. 'Some people see things and they cannot cope,' Tomas says. Hikaru sits with Wallace's body. He put it to bed, and he says something. A prayer, even though Wallace didn't believe whatever it is that Hikaru does. I don't stop him. Hikaru has stayed calm, somehow. Maybe it works. Maybe whatever it is that he believes is somehow a leveller. I would worry that he would take the same route as Wallace, were he not so scared of death. His religion – some obscure thing borne out of the riots in the American Mid-west at the start of the last decade – says that death is the end; it is something to be feared. There is nothing afterwards, so seize the day. The white foods are to prolong life. White is the colour of light; of health; of life itself. I think about the irony of the anomaly out there: absolute blackness, and yet, how it is prolonging Inna's life, and preventing her death.

We are now a skeleton crew. Tomas says that it will be all right. He reminds me that they can offer assistance from their end; like when he unlocked the doors. That was the point of what we designed: if he needs to, he can get us home. Inna goes through cycles by herself: she died while we tried to save Wallace, and she lived again, and then died once more. She isn't even a sacrifice any more. She's a curio we can return to when we have dealt with our current crisis. When Hikaru has prayed as much as he is going to, we seal Wallace's bed. He can do whatever decaying he likes in there and we won't be able to tell. Let the people back on Earth deal with it. The trip is a tragedy. We've already ruined this. The *Ishiguro* had the mystery to sustain it in history: we will have only the massacre.

Tomas tells me that he's getting the press in the next day. That he's prepared a breakdown of everything for the various heads of the UNSA, along with the assorted conglomerates and governments who have put money into this mission. This is the point at which they deserve to know everything. It's a dangerous game he's playing, I know, because he's assuming that they will tell him to deliver results. He wants them to say, Stay. Work it out. After this much tragedy, we cannot return with this being in vain. And what does it say of the anomaly? I ask him how much he's going to tell them about it.

'Nothing yet,' he says. 'I'll say that we're doing tests into it. That it's during those tests we've had accidents. That we are getting results. That this is worth it.' He's playing the game. He knows what he's doing better than even I. He's had the media experience I missed out on as I watched him from backstage. 'You do think it's worth it, don't you, Brother?'

I deal with Inna by myself, sitting with her – or, rather, sitting in the airlock. I watch the screen of her face. She is desperate, and I do not want to lie to her. Not this time.

'Are you coming to get me?' she asks. She has fifteen minutes of this cycle left. Less, if she starts breathing too heavily. I should tell her to be light with her breathing, to calm down. That would be the sensible thing to do.

'I don't think we can,' I say instead.

'What?'

'The anomaly you're in. We can't pass into it to get you out.' She's silent. I can see her eyes: they're darting. I cannot be the one that has betrayed her. She trusted me. I would be her captain. 'There are ways we could try to keep you alive for longer.'

'Until you have a plan,' she says. She sounds so Russian in that moment.

'I don't have a plan,' I say. 'I don't. I think that you are going to die.' Her face doesn't change. But she looks so disappointed in me.

Tomas sends me the press release that he's put out. It is not for me to check; he's already broadcast it to the wider world. This is just for my information. It's frank and nearly officious in its use of language. It says that we have reached the anomaly, and that we are conducting tests. It has not been without its tragedies as a trip, however: and he lists the names of Lennox and Tobi as our dead. No mention of Wallace; no mention of Inna. Our suicide and our mystery will be left for another day, or until we get home, even. He's playing this. He knows that too much death and we'll be recalled. The equipment – the true cost of this expedition – must be returned. It's vital. The press release ends by saying that we are making great strides. That we are realizing our research into the anomaly, research that has lasted over three decades in total. The crew of the *Lära* are still achieving all that they set out to achieve, he promises, and that there will be answers to some of humanity's deepest questions upon their return.

I open a line to him. 'Seems optimistic,' I tell him. I wait for the lag to reach him, and then minutes after it, but I think he must not be there. He is somewhere else.

156

10

I look at the outputs of the software that we wrote to track the outline of the anomaly. I have almost forgotten this, the part that we thought was the most important. Fly to the middle of the wherever, find this thing, explain it. This is what science is.

The orange shape is whole; or, at least, what we can see is. It is drawn in solidly, a line around. It is enormous. I cannot tell the sides, especially now that we are so close, but it stretches off so far in every direction. Up and down and left and right, we are surrounded.

'Have you seen this?' I ask Tomas.

'What do you think we've been doing down here?' he eventually replies.

I ask Hikaru to edge the ship closer, as close to the line of the anomaly as we can get. I use Inna to help us plot the thing. During one of her cycles I tell her, in a desperate, panicked voice, that she has to find an exit or else she will die, and I instruct her to move her hands across the surface of this thing. She confirms what the pings say. I let her use every part of her oxygen, reiterating to her how urgent it was, knowing that she would die; and then I witness her snapping back to her starting point as I blink my eyes shut. Then I start again, only this time I tell her to head in the other direction. When I am satisfied that the results are correct, we start work on gathering samples from the anomaly. I ask her to try and break a chunk from the wall, using the leash she is attached to, wrapping it around her fist to attack it, just to see if it makes a difference. It does not, and she manages to hurt herself; she wonders, as she lurches towards death, if she has fractured it. The next time around, when she wakes up, she feels no pain in her hand, and there is not even a bruise. Death means very little to her, now. Or, maybe, her death means little to me. This is like a game. It is something to be pushed and explored. It's almost crippling as a distraction: to see how far I can push these limits. I could tell her to take off her helmet, and she would: simply because she believed me. She looks at me with implicit trust every cycle, every time I tell her that I can help her. She stares at the camera sometimes, even though she doesn't know she is making eye contact with me.

I am not sleeping any more, because of the stims. They are like replacement batteries, and they are ideal for my situation, as I have no desire to miss any of this. And I do not want the worry, the stress of what would happen if I tried to sleep. The stims are astonishing, really. I have never used them before. Tomas routinely used them – or an early version of them, when they were still loaded with addictive properties – during his finals. He started revision later than I did, and missed a few more classes on some of the lesser modules. He claimed that he was more naturally adept, which might have been true if he had also coupled that with the work that I did. I remember him taking the stims every evening for a two-week period. Perfect clarity, they promised, and that's what he had. Talking to him as he was riding off the immediate rush of one was almost inspiring. Seeing how his mind connected with itself, and how it maintained those connections. He slept for two or three hours every few days, as if he were simply recharging himself. He called those periods of sleep 'nights' – as in, I haven't used a stim tonight – but they fell where they fell, whatever time of day, and there was no routine to them or his life. After a while, they began to lose potency. He would wake, get a good four or five hours before his body began to shut down, and then turn back to the pills. But they pushed him through the exams. They weren't illegal, because they weren't performance-enhancing. The knowledge had to be remembered regardless; the thoughts and concepts entirely your own, no matter how awake you were, how clear your thoughts. He would take one half an hour before the start of an exam and I would be the one who bore the brunt; alphabetical order dictating that I ended up sitting in front of him in the exam halls, able to hear his furious typing right behind my shoulders. He typed faster than anybody else at the best of times. He'd taken a course in touch-typing where the rest of us all used three or four fingers, and he hammered the pad so hard I wondered how it didn't crack. When the exams were done, he struggled to stay off the pills. He slept for days. He called it a hangover, but I knew the truth: the shivers, the headaches, the fever, like the old symptoms of influenza. Almost indistinguishable.

Hikaru doesn't know that I'm still not sleeping; or he doesn't care. Either way. He is still and static, and humourless. He has become a shell. If I didn't know better, I would think that this hadn't affected him, that's how calm he has remained. In many ways, he is acting as if this hasn't happened: we are still here, and still on a ship in the middle of nowhere, and still on a mission. We've moved much, much closer to Inna now, and to the anomaly. Hikaru has been put in charge of making sure that we don't drift – I have no intention of crossing that line – and nothing else. I am dealing with Inna.

And Tomas: he claims that he is helping. It's something that they cannot rehearse on Earth, but they have ideas. That second where she dies, they're wondering if we can play with it. Use it, somehow. Maybe snatch her through as she comes back to life, or at least a part of her, and that might give us purchase. I worry that the anomaly wall is just that: that, like the slice of a guillotine, it might somehow chop off any limb that we dared pull over to the near side of the anomaly. And I worry that she is alive because she is in there, and that as soon as she leaves it will be over for her. Tomas is intent to the point of preoccupation on getting a sample of the anomaly. I tell him that it's impossible from where we are. He tells me that we'll find a way. He sounds convinced.

I sit in the lab and work, going over the results that we have. The knowledge that we have. We were naïve to think that we could simply come out here and find out the answers. How long has it been since humanity had to reach for something? To truly push themselves and make a discovery that changes the face of who we are and what we understand? This is one of those discoveries. Out there, in the anomaly, time means something different. Life itself means something different. If this is something we can harness, it could change everything. Every single aspect of life on Earth could be altered. And if it cannot be used by us, then it is something to explore and to divert time and energy into understanding. It is a marvel; it is the likes of which we have never seen before.

I have ideas. We have tools that Wallace brought up here: designed for taking samples from rocks. Diamond-tipped drills. If I cannot work it on my side, I can ask Inna to do it on hers. I do math, as well, working out how far the anomaly is from us right now, so that I can limit my tether when I actually go out there, to prevent me accidentally crossing the border. I am uncomfortable with this. When they were training in low-gravity situations, I was doing work. Actual work, hard grind, to ensure that we would not die on this mission. They forgot, I think, how important this was. I feel like I could say it again and again and they would never understand the enormity or importance of this. That is something that only Tomas and myself understand.

I go into the airlock room and take my clothes off, before pulling my spacesuit from the locker with my name on it. You would think that, with the layers of the suits being so thin, they would be cold to wear; and with the fabric being such a bizarre composite – metals, plastics and wools all working together, all coated in treatments that are the result of decades of work and millions of dollars of purchased patents – you would think that they would be heavy, or scratch your skin. Inside the suit you're all but naked, but you can barely feel the suit even touching your skin. I prefer loose clothes in general. I find shirts and belts to be claustrophobic in the way that they stitch the halves of your body together. I undo the buttons on cuffs. But the suits here are smooth and warm – the perfect temperature, in fact, regulated by the readings taken from your own body – and they feel like nothing. You are free. Even between your fingers, where they could be so tight and constricting, they simply seem to fit. They're made from a single piece of the new fabric, that's part of the reason: no seams. They stretch for every body-type, despite being custom fitted. They're a marvel.

I look at myself in the mirror, because they're also – for a man like me, of my age and lack of build – mildly unflattering. Tomas is probably in better shape than I am. He is more tucked-in. In another time, another place, I would worry about how I looked. But Hikaru will not judge me, and Inna . . . I will not rescue her this cycle, so she will die again and forget that I was ever out here, and forget how I look in this.

I switch on the monitors, to see where she is in this cycle – because I want to be out there when she wakes up, to really make the most of the time we can have together – but she is not panicked and terrified as I thought she would be. Instead she's almost smiling, calm and peaceful. She is talking. I hear her, saying that it will be all right. That she knows we are doing everything we can. She asks what happens if we don't have a solution. She asks how much air she has. He answers, somehow; zero lag, Tomas, playing as me. He must have done something; I cannot work out what. He tells her that he doesn't know how much air she has – a lie – and then he says that he won't lie to her. He says that they are doing everything they can. He says that he can't wait to get her back on the ship. He is speaking these words to her, acting as me. I think about interjecting, but she will forget. She will forget him, and this version of me. She is happy, even though her death is inevitable. She trusts me.

I sever Tomas' connection to her. 'What are you doing?' I ask. I wait for a reply.

'I'm trying to make this peaceful for her. She was alone. What did you expect?'

'I can't talk to her all the time,' I say.

'Of course you can't. So I was doing it for you. I worked out a way around the lag: I know what questions she will ask, so I can predict it. We were speaking out of sync, Mira. It was really quite the thing.'

'Don't do that,' I say. 'Don't pretend to be me.'

'What are you doing now?' he asks.

'I am going out there.'

'Oh,' he says. 'Good.'

In order to open the airlock door, we have to close the outer door. We cannot do that until we sever and retract the cable stitching the three of them together. As soon as Inna begins, I play melodramatic, and I tell her that it's urgent that she unclip herself. I don't give her a chance to ask why. She does, and I retract her tether. It snaps through the nothing, back towards the ship, and it coils itself inside the airlock. I shut the outer door, and the inner door opens in turn. Lennox and Tobi's bodies are in front of me; I have to deal with them. I call for Hikaru to help me, but he doesn't. He says that he has to keep the ship anchored. He's lying, but I can't force him. He is all I have left, really; so I move them myself. They are easy to move when there's no gravity. You can drag them and they don't snag on anything, and there's no mess. Their suits are sealed, and I try to pretend that they are not even people. They are suits, nothing more. They are an experiment. It's not like I haven't seen a dead body before, but still. Regardless.

I seal them into their beds next to Wallace. Three of them now, lined up and ready for a crew who are not me to take them and worry about them. As if they're sleeping. This is what they did with the captain of the *Ishiguro* when he died: they put him to bed for the rest of the trip. No burial in space. Instead, you journey with the corpse of the man who died. It's practical, if not horrific. They are with us, as much as they can be. My mother used to say that ghosts stayed in the places that they died. That a quiet house was made louder by the presence of the spirits over the years: this is why old houses feel the way that they do. She really believed in that stuff. We sneered when she said it. And then she died, and we said, Maybe she's here, in this hospital room. Maybe this is where she will stay forever. But we didn't actually think it was true, because we didn't believe in God or in ghosts or in anything like that. What's it that they say? You can either be logical or fallible. There's no halfway point.

Afterwards, I sit and wait in the airlock room. Inna tries to talk to me, to get me to tell her the rest of my brilliant plan that involved her cutting herself off from the rest of us, but I am silent. Even as she begins crying, and cursing my name. An experiment: to see if the tether cable resets as her oxygen supply does. My hypothesis is that it will not. As Tobi and Lennox are outside the anomaly, and remain dead, so too will this cable no longer be a part of Inna's cycle. She will awake and assume it was lost when the *Ishiguro* interrupted their jaunt. This entire process will take time, now. It will take time and sacrifice, but that has to be acceptable.

She dies; she wakes; the cable is inside the airlock. Over her next life I prepare the tools I will need, and I attach myself to the tether inside the airlock itself, and I tell Tomas that he will have to open the airlock doors for me from Earth; that Hikaru is distracted.

'You're comfortable with this?' he asks.

'No,' I say. I have an unbalanced inner ear, and I am clumsy on my feet, let alone drifting in the ether. I am graceless, and I haven't adjusted to the lack of gravity on the ship, because I ignored the training. Because I am not this sort of man. 'But I have little choice,' I say. 'Needs must.'

'That they do,' he says. I put the helmet on, and I press to fasten it to the suit. I wore one once before, when we received the trial versions, to check that the visibility was acceptable. It feels tighter here, now, even though I know it's exactly the same model. Exactly the same size. The helmet hisses as it attaches to the fabric and creates the seal, and I'm no longer breathing the *Lära*'s air: I am breathing my own portable, personal oxygen.

'Open the door,' I say, and wait.

'Okay,' he says. No farewell, godspeed, no stay safe. The door opens, and I am outside.

I cannot describe this; there is no need. It is singular, and fantastical. It is nature, even though it is not what we would immediately think of as such. It is, despite everything that brought us here and that protects me and that enables us to be here, and the death and the unexplainable nature of the anomaly: through that all this is nature. This is the purest I have ever been with the universe, and that is really something.

The boosters on the suits are tetchy and sharp, and they spit out in a way that I do not expect. I have not practised enough with these, which is a disadvantage. I didn't foresee having to do this. Truthfully, I didn't expect to ever wear my suit. Maybe to drift; to revel in the nothingness if I could. But I didn't expect to be out here, and I didn't expect to have to work in these conditions. I push myself forward, but I have to be tentative. There is too much chance of me getting this wrong and overshooting. I do not want to end up in there. What would happen? I would die with Inna. Over and over, perhaps, if that's how it works. But I nudge towards her, shuffling almost, and then I am right in front of her. I can see her perfectly as she dies: close enough to touch, if I wanted to lose myself. She sees me, her final few breaths. I am close enough to comfort her, but I do not.

She dies, and she wakes, and she sees me, and her routine adapts.

'You're here,' she says. 'What happened? Why are you here?' She reaches for me, and she touches the wall.

'You can't,' I say. 'I am outside the anomaly, and you are inside. But I have come to try and help you, to help you get out. Can you see me okay?' I ask. She nods, but she's unsure. 'Make the torch on your helmet brighter. That will help.' She does, and she sees me more. She smiles, a little. Just a little. She raises her hands and feels the anomaly wall between us. She feels it every time, but now I am here, close enough to touch. 'I'm stuck,' she says.

'Yes.'

'I'm a prisoner here?'

'I don't think it's like that,' I say.

'But you came for me,' she says. I should have kept a tally of how many times she has died now, for the results of whatever this is. So that, when I come to write this up, when I am delivering my paper to whoever wants to read it, there are exact numbers. Details: science is all about the details. I'm sure that Tomas will have been doing it, or that he'll have somebody else doing it. She presses her hand, and she cranes her neck. 'You say it isn't a prison, but look at me.'

166

'It's the anomaly,' I say. 'We don't know how it works, still.'

'Where are Tobi and Lennox?' she asks. 'Are they safe?'

'Yes,' I say. Lying is easier. Lying moves this on. I am learning from each time, just as she is not. I grow; I evolve. A harmless lie is easier than the truth, when time is pressed and Inna is dying. 'Tomas and Hikaru are working on how to get you back onto the ship. They'll have an answer soon. I have to do work until then. Will you help me?' I have to give her a use: she has responded well to tasks during previous lives. It serves to keep her mind away from her situation. It lets her know that we're all working together towards a common goal; that we haven't forgotten about her. She will not simply be left to die.

I pass tools through the anomaly, and she takes them at the far side. She and I move them back and forth, passing them through the wall. She rests a hand against it all the while, making sure that I keep my distance. I have to watch my drift. It's easy to reach out and forget and suddenly your hand is through. I don't know what would happen if I were to have a limb, or a part of me through the anomaly. Would I be able to retract it? Or would it render me stuck forever, unless I accepted the inevitable and followed it into the darkness? For a second, distracted and daydreaming, I see myself and Inna: together, in an embrace. Holding each other, dying over and over. We share oxygen. We wake. We die. We wake. Seconds together, snatched and desperate. Is that what would fill our dying moments? Is that what we would see?

I pass her a scalpel, holding the blade myself, as you are taught to pass knives, and she takes it and tries to cut into the anomaly wall – putting her hand to it, pressing hard, splaying her fingers and cutting between them – but the blade finds no purchase. There's nothing there for her to work on, and the scalpel passes through. If I held my hand out, it would cut me. We try with the drill, to take a sample, but again there is nothing. This might as well be air. Were it not for Inna's hands on it, and for what we have seen, and for what we cannot see inside it, I would say that there was nothing there.

'I'm sorry,' she says.

'It's not your fault,' I tell her.

'Are they ready to get me back onto the ship yet? It's getting harder to breathe.' She looks tired. I don't tell her that.

'I'll head back and find out,' I say. I wave as I go, so that she feels safe. Maybe she will just drift off to sleep this time, rather than panicking and choking. If I talk her towards her death, that might be better. I seal the doors and cut the communications, because I can't stand to look at her as she dies in this cycle. It's too much: seeing her up that close, and with my lie to her still hanging. I like to imagine how she dies this time; imagine the peace that I wished for her.

Something of this reminds me of these books that Tomas and I used to have as children. My mother said that they were her brother's, from when they were young – and he had died when he was a teenager, so she kept them, as something worth keeping – and she gave them to us when we were old enough and told us to take good care of them. You read the first page and then it gave you a choice, and you picked one of two options. Each led you to another page, where you might fall down a pit or meet a monster, and you would have to keep making decisions to try and reach the end. Some ends came quickly, with death or early accidental glory; some went on for pages and pages, circling around, leading you on a chase. Tomas and I would play the same book one after each other, trying to see who could get further. We turned it into a game: which one of us had the better instincts? The better gut reaction to a situation, the better wiles to lead them through the *Maze of Death* or the *Journey to the Ocean Sand*: the brother who navigated the choices with the most skill, he would be the winner. There was no prize other than gloating, but regardless. And the winning itself was tricky to determine, as what one of us thought to be a win – so, abandoning their submersible and swimming to a desert island, but still having escaped the Kraken – was determined by the other to be a false option. The debate carried on past the book.

'You would die of starvation,' the non-playing brother would say. 'On that island, with no food source, no weapons, no means of escape, you would die. That isn't a win; it's delaying the inevitable.' So the argument would go, and the winner would add the book to their own personal pile. It would be theirs then. We both treated them the same way: with some level of reverence in their physical object. As soon as the game was over, however, the text was destroyed. We broke the rules and read them beginning to end, finding secrets and routes and pathways and endings that we would never have stumbled on before. We reverse engineered them, to work out how to reach the different areas. The main character escapes the submersible, the same as countless other times, but this time he meets a beautiful Atlantean, and she kisses him, giving him the gift of water-breath, and he can survive and then the mermen rally and help him kill the Kraken. The Kraken's head is a trophy: how do you reverse engineer such a situation? We would read these sections and be totally in awe. It made us take risks, in the next book. Because maybe those risks would pay off? They rarely did. Most times, we ended up with the same endings: death, or the island, or some tepid, muted victory of circumstance and luck rather than judgment.

Now, here, talking to Inna, it's like that. Choices at the foot of a page, nothing more than selecting different dialogues. If I start the conversation differently, she will respond differently. There are seemingly infinite ways I could start it, or things I could tell her, and yet they all end in the same approximate way: with her crying, and begging me to save her, as if that's a power that I somehow have but am keeping from her.

I send Tomas a message, direct to his console. I do not bother trying to speak to him, because I want to be certain that he will receive this. 'I think we have to come home now,' I say. I will try to forget about Inna. I will try.

According to Hikaru, we're on about 50 per cent of our life support – a number that would be much lower if we were supporting a fully live crew, rather than one that is all but deceased – so we can't stay here much longer. Stolen from the *Ishiguro*, we need the rumble of our engines to recharge us: a sense of moving forward to sustain us. There are limits, and protections, and cut-off points that we do not want to reach. I am contemplating, always contemplating telling Hikaru to start the engines; I cannot predict how he would react now, if I suggested abandoning Inna. Tomas will turn us around if everything falls apart. We agreed, when designing the systems, that the overrides from ground control would be final. You never know what can happen up here, but there they would always be in control.

Hikaru is speaking to Inna this time. He said that he
wanted to talk to her, to try and ease her through this. I told
him to be my guest. I do not watch them, because nothing
about this can surprise me any more. Instead, I go to a
cupboard and count the stims we have left. I take another.
We are fine. We have so many on board it is as if I knew
that I would need them, when I was checking the inventories.
I try to reach Tomas on the comm as I am still in that tablet's
rush. By the time I get his reply it has passed, and I feel
normal again.

'Brother,' he says.

'Where have you been?'

'I've been in conferences. We have been trying to decide
what to do.'

'Oh,' I say.

'I got your message. We all took it into consideration,
that's for sure.' He gulps something. I picture him, his stubby
glass, his single malt. We both know what it means before
he says the rest. 'You have to get some results, Mirakel. Then
you can come back.'

'For fuck's sake, Tomas.'

'The board reminded me of the cost of this. The spend.
And it's the best we can hope. We know that this thing isn't
normal, as well.' The pauses are unnatural and elongated. I
cannot parse them in the patter of normal speech. 'Didn't
you want to leave your mark?'

'We have left it. We have three bodies on our hands.'

'But their blood isn't. They signed the waivers, just as you
and I did.'

'And you're in such a risky position, there, with your
fucking drink and your fucking baker.' I laugh at how ridiculous this argument is. That I won't even call her by her name.

He goes silent. There is always silence between us, and it is always me that it falls upon to break it. 'What do you want us to do?'

'That's harder,' he says. I hear the click of him lighting a cigarette. 'They want readings taken from inside the anomaly.'

'We are not taking the ship in there.'

'It doesn't have to be the ship. Send a tablet over: get pings from that. See how deep it is. Use Inna: give her the equipment on her side. She needs to send signals inside it, see if we can read them from Earth. Just to see.'

'She'll want to know why I'm not coming in to take the readings myself.'

'So you tell her a lie,' he says. I can hear it in his voice; in the drag of the smoke, the exhale with the impatience. 'You've done it before.'

'There are two of us left, that's all. You think that this is going to end well?'

'What do you mean?'

'Do you really think that we're coming home?' I realize that I am shouting. I wonder if Hikaru can hear me. I hope he can, because maybe then he will react, and I will not have to. 'The longer we stay here, the more likely it is that we will die here.'

'They want readings. We all want readings. And we want for you to rescue Inna, as well. Or maybe you're just happy to leave her there to die, again and again and again, for the rest of all time?'

'Don't,' I say. 'Fuck you.'

'I don't care what you say to me,' he replies. 'Take the ship closer, and take the readings.' Then he's quiet. The argument, driven by the lag, makes me wonder if there's more coming. It's too tense: the silence between the words. 'I'll talk to Inna for her next cycle. Give you some time to relax.' Then he's gone.

I stay in the lab. Bring up the map of the anomaly that we have been making: the spinning orange, still being made from the dots, still having gaps filled in. I calculate: estimating the size of the thing if this is essentially an orb, as deep and tall as it is wide, using the trajectory of the curve to estimate where it is heading. I move my finger into it, breaking the line of the anomaly, and I move it back and forth. I put a pin into the image where Inna is, another where we – the ship, myself and Hikaru and all our bodies – are, and I move the ship closer to see how close we can be before this all becomes truly dangerous, and I chicken out and turn the ship around myself.

I wonder what would happen if we managed to get the ship back to Earth. If I found a way to supersede the instructions that Tomas would desperately send to prevent us. The mission wasn't military, so I couldn't be court-martialled. It wasn't governmental, so there's no way I would be committing some law-break that might earn me jail time. It's private: business and investors and some degree of public faith. They would lambast me, and they would attempt to sue, I would think. They would claim that we – and I suspect that Tomas would be thrown under the bus as well, unless he sacrificed me – had squandered their money. That, in our weak-willed frippery, we had travelled this far, spending billions of dollars, and that we had returned empty-handed, with four deaths under our belts. (In the scenario where I flee, I tell them that Inna has died. It is true, at least a part of the time.) The anomaly, they would say, is still out there. It is still a potential threat. Do we understand it any more than we did before these two ran their hands over our space program? We do not, they would say.

We are, in fact, more in the dark. Because how do you lose so many crew members? How does a crew of six go up, and only two come back down?

I wouldn't have an answer for them. I call Hikaru into the lab and tell him what it is that we're going to have to do in order to appease them. I show him, on the map, how close we need to get. He nods, and he chews a bar made of re-formed bleached chicken, and I can tell that he has no faith at all in our ability to survive this, but he will never say that. He will not let me know.

11

Persuading the crew to come out here was easy. This was always to be a trip that would be remembered, and the probability – we told them – of a tragedy such as that which occurred with the *Ishiguro* happening twice were next to inconsequential. Tomas used to say: The chances of one ship going missing in space are pretty slim. The chances of two going missing in the same place? So close to nil as to be almost impossible. We will, Tomas and I wrote to each of them in our letter of persuasion, guarantee your safe return. They needed that persuasion, because they were happy before we found them; or at least comfortable. They had families and jobs and lives. We wrote personalized letters to those candidates we most desired for the roles that we had to fill. Paper letters, hand-written, mostly by me, as Tomas' handwriting left a lot to be desired. He preferred the speed of a quick draft where I favoured the dedication of precision and care. But they were our words: a joint effort. A month after the letters went out we fielded visits from a few of them: that was when we found Hikaru and Tobi. Both in our first round of choices. Both so strong and capable. They were interested, because how could they not be? What a chance this was, for all of us. We told them about the training that they would need to undertake and the work we would be doing. We told them about the risks involved. We told them that they would have to take out their own insurance policies, knowing that they would not be able to. Everything about this is a risk, we told them; but without risk there can be no true reward.

'What is the reward, exactly?' Hikaru had asked.

'Answers,' Tomas had told him. 'Science is a pursuit. Answers are there, and we seek them. We need answers to a question, because humans are made to question. Now we have a question that nobody can answer, but we might somehow be able to. Think about that. Wouldn't you like to play a part in getting an answer to what might be the biggest question of all?' They didn't ask what the question was. That's the thing: they never even wanted to know, not really.

It's amazing: standing in the airlock and leaving the external door open, and being able to see right across to Inna. This is how adjacent we are: she opens her eyes when we have stopped moving, when the thrusters are only there to maintain our position. We're like lovers, greeting each other on a dock: she cannot see me through the fog, but I am there. She only has half an hour left, and she will die. So it goes.

Hikaru and I prepare the tablet to give to Inna. We designed the computers to be detachable in part, so that we could work outside if we needed to. They were tested for pressure, designed to have special haptic interfaces that would work with the suits: we were prepared for this. This is forethought. They have attachments, and we configure one to be able to send a ping out: only to judge distances, but it's something.

We haven't been able to see deep into the anomaly before. We don't even know how deep it is. Maybe, I think, it could go on forever. It is a tunnel. It is a hole. This thing looks like any other tablet computer, so we agree to ask Inna to take it, hold it while we remotely control it, and then pass it back for the results to be uploaded. Should be simple: easy to use, nothing she won't be used to in her life of medical instruments and tricorders. We need her in control, so Tomas suggests that we wait until this cycle has ended. I couldn't agree with him more, but I'm glad that I don't have to say it. I wonder if Hikaru is starting to hate me for the ease with which I let her die. He can maybe see how I would be with him. I would be the same, I know. Maybe more callous. I feel something for Inna, I think. I have a desire for her that I do not share for him. I wouldn't blame him if he hated me. I don't know what that says about me. I think that, when we get home, I should maybe speak to somebody. I wonder about myself. I see something inside me, or maybe I do not see it. Maybe there is simply something that is not there.

I see the toll that it is taking on Hikaru as well. With him, it seems deeper (but then, I suppose that the afflicted would always say that). I thought that he was tuned into his religion, his powerful self-beliefs driving his action. The more time I spend with him, however, it simply seems as if he is broken. I have offered him the chance to speak to his family, but he has turned it down. Perhaps he knows that it was the last thing that Wallace did before he ended it, and perhaps that carries a significance for him. It's his own business. In my reports, I will write that I believe he is suffering from post-traumatic stress disorder. I will recommend treatments, but I am sure that he will refuse them.

I pull on my suit and am ready to go. I am a heavy breather, and I tell myself that I must be light to preserve my air. I have to pace myself. I stand in the airlock and we listen to her die, because we have to know as soon as she is alive again. She gasps and screams and asks what is happening, and I speak to her. I tell her exactly what we need.

'Quickly,' I say, 'we don't have much time.' I explain to her that there's been an accident, and Hikaru starts the airlock cycle. She asks me why she can't see me properly, and I explain that I am there. I am with her, I say, but the anomaly blocks her from looking out. I say, 'You have to help me. You're stuck there until we can find out how to get you free, and you are running out of air. We have to be quick, and then we can get home. The device I want you to use, it'll help us.'

'Why can't I come back now?' She requires a delicate balance when being dealt with. It must be scary, to be out there, alone and on a countdown. I know that it is scary. It has scared her countless times before this.

'You're trapped', I say, 'in the anomaly. Do you not remember?' Treat her as if this is her mistake. As if she should know more than this. Assert myself.

'Of course I remember,' she says. She's so hurried and frantic that she lies to me, because she knows that it's easier.

'We need to find out how to get you free.'

'And this will do it?'

'Yes,' I say. 'This is how we begin to get you out.' I pass her the tablet. 'It turns on at the top,' I say. She presses the button; there're a few hours or so of battery on it. More than enough for what we need to do, and for her to pass it back before she dies and it gets lost, or drifts off, or whatever. 'It's all controlled on the screen. Do you see the apps you need to run?'

'Yes,' she says. 'Do you want me to open them?'

'Work left to right,' I say. 'Open them one by one, and set them going.' She concentrates on the buttons. She presses them as if she has never worked one before, but I know that's just nerves.

'It's okay,' I say. 'Take your time.' She seems her age, here and now. As if this has revealed it all to her: everything that she has done and been, all of it, suddenly rushing back into her face. Undoing whatever care she's taken of herself, or work that she's had done. She looks scared and old and tired.

'They're running,' she says. 'What do I do now?'

'This is the easy part,' I say. Now you just hold the device out. You point it all around you, turning it every minute or so. Turn it just a fraction of a degree. We need readings of this whole anomaly, to help us understand it. It will find a hole in the anomaly that we can use.'

'You couldn't come over here and do this yourself?' she asks then, out of the blue. She holds the tablet out, though, and then she moves it slightly. More than I would like for the desired results – I want exact angles, ideally – but I cannot labour the point now. I am picturing the signal blaring out in every direction, waiting for a response. I am picturing her handing me the device when she is done, giving me the results, and then us leaving. I do not answer her question, and I take too long, and she realizes that there's no way out of there. I wouldn't risk it; she is being used.

'Look,' I say, but she doesn't care. She knows.

'What was the plan? Were you ever going to tell me the truth?' Her mouth is pinched. Her cheeks are red. 'Or were you going to string me along until the very end? Would we just play that I was going to be saved at the end of this?'

'It isn't like that,' I say. 'This is important.' I do not think

179

she will understand that. 'It could help us rescue you,' I say, 'but we do not know until we try.'

'Oh, good. If there's a chance,' she spits. 'What is this? How does this help me?' She holds the tablet down, losing one of the results. She knows that there's far more wrong here than she first thought. I want to reach for the device, in case she breaks it or throws it. I think of Tomas, and how those results are a ticket home.

Am I this selfish? Am I really this man?

'Please hand the device back,' I say. And she does. She cannot see me, but she looks forward and into my eyes. She is crying. Not hysterical, not begging. Just so desperately sad.

'What has happened to me?' she asks.

'It's the anomaly,' I say. 'It won't let you die. You were out here days and days ago, and you ran out of air, and you died, but then you came back. You keep coming back, and we don't know how to stop it yet.' She nods – I see her helmet bob with an almost tidal smoothness – and then reaches behind her, and I see her hand find the nozzle for the air and unscrew it. 'Don't!' I shout, but even then I wonder why I'm begging her not to, because it's inevitable. I could reach over there and stop it – my hand on hers, to stay it before she does this to herself – but I have no idea if I could bring it back or not, or if I would be stuck, destined to die slightly after her, destined to come back again back to life just like her, in this perpetual loop.

So instead I am forced to sit here and watch her dying from behind, and it isn't until I turn and start back towards the ship that she wakes up, desperate, having learned nothing. I get back onto the ship and shut the door behind me.

I plug the device back into the computer and start

180

uploading the information. I need to analyse it. There's nothing there, though. Nothing of any use to us and our research. I take another stim, dry swallowing it. I am a master of it now.

'Successful trip?' Tomas asks.

'No,' I say. I leave it at that, for the time being. I don't tell him the rest, but he might have been listening, for all I know.

Hikaru asks me if I mind him going to sleep. He looks ill. His cheeks sallow; his hair greasy. His eyes are so tired. I tell him that he should rest.

'We're heading home soon,' I say to him. 'And you're our only pilot. You'll need your sleep.' He nods. He doesn't believe me. This is what he's doing: he's accepting his fate. Has he made peace with it? Is it possible to make peace with something that might not happen? 'Goodnight,' I say to him, and he lies down in his bed and fastens the magnets. He is lying in between Tobi and Wallace, but he doesn't seem to notice that, or care. He shuts the door behind him, and the glass goes dark.

Then the ship is quiet. Inna is out there alone, but I try to pretend that she isn't. I wonder if I shouldn't sleep as well. I can feel my eyelids shake and tremble in the way that they do when the pills wear off, but I do not know how to sleep. I think that I have probably forgotten. That was the problem all along. I inject the sedatives. I feel it on the third, the fourth. There is nothing to miss, now. I lie down at the end of the horseshoe of beds; and next to me is Inna's empty bed. I shut the lid as well, because maybe then I can pretend.

Even though I am sure that I am asleep, I can hear a noise that I did not make, that reverberates around the ship, coming through it all. It wakes me, but it's so dark and I do not open my eyes, and then I cannot hear it again. It's as if it was never there. Then, when I am sure that I am nearly asleep again, I hear it in the distance. It is, I think, similar to the noise of somebody banging on a door.

'Tomas?' I hear myself ask, mostly asleep.

There is no answer from him, and I drift. I dream of darkness, and of home.

'Wake up,' Tomas says, 'and be careful. Seriously, Brother. You need to be careful now.' He opens my bed for me, and I unclip myself. I'm startled and worried, and in that moment between awake and asleep, when everything feels half-lost. I am here but not. I clutch on.

'What's happened?' I ask.

'You need to bring up a screen of the exterior,' he says. 'Do it from there. Stay where you are.' So I do. I raise the screen, and I flick through the cameras, and look at where we were focused before, but Inna isn't there. I wonder if this has closed: if she is done. Then I flick to the next camera and she is outside the ship: pressed to the side, clinging to the metal. She looks weak; her hand feebly tapping the exterior airlock door.

'How?' I ask. 'She's free?'

'No,' he says. 'She's moved.' On the screen she splays her fingers and starts slapping the metal. 'Or the anomaly has moved. But she is still dying. She has died once, out there.'

'You didn't wake me?'

'I tried,' he says, but he's lying. As if I do not know the tells in his voice.

'Am I inside it?' I ask. He leaves the pause too long. He is fucking with me.

'No,' he finally says. 'We're guessing, based on the pings. Still sending them out to the sides, assuming that the aperture of the anomaly hasn't changed.' Everything is speculation, and I feel my guts rise. I am scared, because that is not what I want. I want to be alive. I want to do what I can. There is no guarantee that, inside there, I will not be able to get out, but we have to work within the confines of what we know. What I know is that Inna is stuck. What I know is that, for some reason, the *Ishiguro* never left, not until the day it exploded. The anomaly is hell. It is death.

'Does Inna remember anything more?' I ask.

'No. She's more confused, certainly.'

'You haven't let her in yet.'

'Would you have?' He's right. I would have made the same decision. I wouldn't have wanted to risk the ship. She is now a variable: she might be the thing that stops us pulling the ship out of the anomaly, were she inside. 'You'll have to talk to her,' he says, 'or not. It's your decision, Brother.' I flick the camera to show the inside of her helmet. She is desperate. We're here, next to her, and she has woken up alone and in the dark and we could just open the door but we have not. She will be wondering why; if we are all dead, maybe. Nearly, I want to tell her. We're getting there. 'She's at the end of a cycle,' Tomas says. The variable is nearly dead. Soon she will begin again, and this will be fresh to her. I click her face away. I do not want to see her die here. I think it might be different: even more confused, even more desperate.

'Where can't I go?' I ask, and he tells me to bring up the screen he's sending, so I do. I look at the line of the anomaly: carved through our ship. It slices through the engines and pretty much splits the ship into two: down the central corridor, with the airlock and bathroom on one side, the lab on the other; and the beds and lounge and cockpit also divided. The line is nearly straight – the curve of the anomaly so long we barely notice it in here – but we aren't. We were on a slight angle, so the line matches that. I have more of the lounge and cockpit than the anomaly does. Inna is not the only variable; Hikaru's bed is firmly inside the anomaly, now.

'Hikaru is still asleep?'

'Until we know what to do,' Tomas says. 'We don't want him to panic about this.' How much has he been watching us? When did this happen, sneaking up on us? 'Unless you think we should wake him.'

'No,' I say. 'Not yet.' I look at the picture. 'We need to reverse,' I say.

'So we have to wake him.'

'You can do it from there, can't you?'

He takes longer than usual to answer. The lag hides a multitude of sins. 'It's safer if he does it. From here, what if, I don't know, what if it crushes him while he's in his bed? What if that's how it works? He should do it. You'll have to wake him up.' I think he is gone, and then he speaks again. 'It will sound better, coming from you. Less alarming.' I try not to think about Inna, still out there. I ask myself, deep inside, if I am a bad person. And if I am, does it matter?

The ship looks as it should from the inside. The anomaly has no colour, no smell. The air is the same: no change in temperature as you approach it, no front that suggests anything different than what we are used to. I contemplate chalk or pen: something to draw a physical line down the ship. I do not want to be caught in this. Accidents can happen. They can be so unbearably fatal, or eternal. The same. On my side of the anomaly: my bed, Inna's bed, Wallace's bed, even though it's full. I have the kitchenette, and the food. In the lounge, they have most of the table, the medical cupboard, a chunk of the floor space, one of the three computers. In the cockpit, they only have half a seat. With Hikaru's bed still sealed I can't even hear him sleeping. I cannot reach over and open it, so I tell Tomas to do it.

'I can't get a signal,' he says. 'I'm pressing it, but it's not responding.' I think about the slight static on the connections from inside the anomaly; and I think about the remote probe suddenly becoming unresponsive as it got deeper into it. Three items of electronic interference: almost enough evidence to be definitive. I bring up a screen and try, but again, the bed doesn't open. 'You don't want to reach over there and open it manually?' he asks. He is joking, but he doesn't laugh. I clip myself by my belt to the rail and watch the bed.

'We'll have to wait for him to wake up of his own accord,' I say.

'I suppose so,' he says. I wait there in silence, staring at the room, trying to work out if the anomaly is going to move – or grow – any more, and if it might swallow me whole. I'm thinking about that when I hear the banging start again, which means that Inna died, and she's back again, full of air and energy and desperation, banging on the door, begging to be let in. What was that story from when I was a kid, something about a Monkey's Paw? I haven't wished that she was still alive yet, but that banging is so insistent. Desperate, as it should be. 'Tell me about what's going on down there,' I say to Tomas. I stare at the beds and wait to see if he will answer.

I think about anything else, after a while. I stare at the beds and wait, and Inna's banging is a drum inside my head. A constant, unending rhythmic reminder. In my pocket I have a pack of stims, and I take one as soon as I catch myself yawning, because I am still somehow tired. The body needs to recover. You can put it through the ringer, torture and punish it, and then you have to let it recover.

I think about how I can come back from this. How I can ever hope to recover who I was; and I wonder, briefly, who that person even was to begin with.

Hikaru's bed hisses open. I have been listening to Inna's hand become weaker, and the sound drop off inside here. The hiss comes as she falls silent, which means that this life is ending for her. Another will start. This is the new cycle. Hikaru lets himself up. He stretches. He cracks his shoulders, rolling them, rubbing them with one palm. He turns his head to look around.

'What the hell?' he asks. 'What's happened? Why are you so dark?' He sees me: through the ink of the anomaly. I bring up a screen of one of the cameras, to see what he sees: myself, through a black fog, almost, the internal lights dimmed. I make them bright, but still it is hard to see every detail through this. He brings up a window, and looks out, and he sees the darkness; how there's no fringe of stars on his side: just the blackness of the anomaly.

'I'm inside it,' he says. He rubs his face. He has most of a beard on it now, and his skin is greyer than it was. 'And I suppose you are not, somehow.' I don't know how to deal with this. Likely that this has to be a plaster, rapidly torn off: a wound exposed to the air, for the benefit of healing.

'The anomaly moved.'

He nods. He's either not taking this in or he implicitly understands. Maybe I don't need to go through this all. He

186

unclips himself and swings his legs out, as if there's gravity and he's just going to put them on the floor, but then he starts drifting. He pushes towards me with his hands out, and I watch them fold up against the dividing line in mid air: like the world's best mime. His eyes sag even more as he feels the wall. How it's inside the ship, how it has cut a swathe through everything: questions that I cannot answer. I wonder if we'll ever have answers, or if I will return home to accusations. How all that mattered would be the deaths and the enigmas, spoken of as fraud and lies as we attempt to bluffingly explain the unexplainable thing that we have encountered out here.

'It moved, not us.'

'That's what Tomas tells me.'

'And he's sure?'

'He's sure.' I watch Hikaru. He looks around every part of his side of the ship. He doesn't look at the anomaly wall, at where I should be. It's nothingness; I don't think that I would want to look into it either, not if I was in his shoes. This feels like hostage negotiations, I think: he is suddenly a man on the edge. I don't want to say the wrong thing, but I have no idea what the wrong thing is. 'We were both asleep. Maybe it's related to that.'

'Was Tomas awake?'

'Yes,' I say.

'And you trust him? There's no way he would have done this. No way he would have moved the ship.' Tomas is listening, because he must be. He is always listening. 'Or, you know, not moved us backwards, when he saw what was happening. He's not so fucking driven, so desperate to get answers, that would never have made him do this.'

'He didn't,' I say. 'And we'll get you out of there.'

187

'Like we have with Inna,' he says.

'That's different,' I reply. 'You aren't dead.'

'Yet.' He doesn't look up. He looks so grey.

'Listen, now that we have you on the inside, working out what this thing is will be much easier.' He rubs his face with his hands, his whole head. Running his fingers through his hair. I've lost him, I think; and then the banging starts. She's back.

'What's that?' Hikaru asks.

'It's Inna,' I say. I won't lie to him.

'She's still outside.' He turns and pushes towards the doorway, down the hall. I chase him, slower than he is. Still less able. I drag myself along the rail and I watch him, and I shout. 'We thought it was safer, because we didn't know what we were going to do. We didn't know how affected you were!' He ignores me. I get to be in the hallway and watch him bring up a terminal, so I do the same. I tap to lock the door, to enter the override code that only Tomas and I know, but the system rejects it. It's on the other side of the anomaly; I cannot do anything. The equivalent of the static, I suspect. 'Hikaru,' I say, 'I want her back just as much as you, but this could ruin the entire mission.'

'You can't leave her out there to die,' he says. She isn't really even dead. I don't know if she is even really alive. I see him hammer the buttons to start the airlock cycle, almost in rhythm with Inna's hammering on the side of the ship. He speaks to her through the comms as the door opens. 'Inna,' he says, 'you should come in now.' He's her white knight; the one who saved her. I am the one who stood on the other side of the fence.

'Hikaru,' I say, 'be careful what we tell her. About what's happened. It could be distressing to her.'

'I won't lie to her,' he says. The banging stops, and there's a different sound. Pawing. Scraping, the noise of Inna dragging herself along the hull.

'I will,' I say. And then there she is: gasping in her helmet, even though she has enough air. Inside, then, and frantically looking around. Hikaru shuts the door behind her, and the air floods into the room, and she pulls off her helmet and presses the walls of the decompression room as the helmet floats about behind her.

'You saved me,' she says. She is weak and tired, gasping in as her lungs get used to this. He reaches for her and props her up and pulls her to the rail and helps her take hold of it. I am pathetic. She is crying so hard. 'What's happened?' she asks. She pulls at the straps of her suit, tugging the zip down, and the suit peels away from her chest and shoulders. Her bird tattoo: I had forgotten. Where does it go? What does it mean? 'Mira,' she says. 'Come and help me, please.' She looks at me, but I stay where I am.

'I can't,' I say. 'I just can't.'

I explain everything to her, apart from how many times she has died. That can come later. Hikaru watches me while I talk to her, and I wonder if he will be the one to say it. He has brought her in from the cold; maybe he will tell her the truth. If he does, he can be the one to deal with that. When she was outside and I told her, I saw how it ruined her. To know, suddenly, that death means nothing inside the anomaly: it must change you. (I have thought about it myself, but I am so distant from it: I have tried to consider the implications, what it might do to the mind, but until faced with the very real possibility of what the anomaly offers, I cannot firmly contemplate how I might feel.) She will find out eventually, I know, but that doesn't have to be now. Hikaru doesn't say anything to her: instead, he says that he needs some quiet. He says that he needs to think. I don't think he believes that we are ever getting home, at this point. I tell myself that I will tell her eventually, when we're free of this and headed home. If that is possible, then so too will the truth be.

Instead now I tell her that she passed out. I truncate time, and say that Tobi and Lennox have not long been dead. That Wallace killed himself just after that, and that Hikaru and I have been trying to get her back ever since. She doesn't question the timescale, because she's just happy to be back on the ship. She is wrapped in a towel, having showered, and she coughs and sips from a water bottle she keeps tethered to her wrist, nibbles at a food bar. She is ravenous, she says. As she eats, slowly, so slowly, I explain about the anomaly wall, and how she and Hikaru are stuck that side of it.

'It seems safer that I stay outside it for as long as possible,' I say. She presses a hand to the wall. She's sitting on a chair opposite me, strapped down.

'So what is this anomaly, then?' she asks. She looks so tired. She and Hikaru both, but it shows even more on Inna. Where you can see the surgery scars, suddenly, as the skin slightly sags over their thin laser-lines; and where she tries to smile but the skin won't allow it, because it's been too smoothed over. She is in her tank-top, and the bird reaches for her neck, its beak only slightly parted. I'm sure that there's a hint of a tongue in there. 'You must know something now.'

'Nothing,' I say. 'You know how often we can't explain something?' She doesn't reply; it's rhetorical. 'Never,' I say. 'Because we make up explanations. We take whatever we've got and apply logic and get somewhere.'

'I want to go home,' she says.

'So do I,' I say, but I do not know if that is true. Not without answers. Because what are we without answers?

Hikaru agrees to run the tests I ask of him, even though he questions their point. Now, I can tell that he is lost in himself. He is not the man that he once was, but he understands enough of how this has to work. He has no control, and he is like all of us: expendable. While he sends pings out from the front of the ship that is inside the anomaly, Inna examines the bodies of our dead comrades. She says that she is only making sure that they're preserved, but I suspect that she wants to ensure that there hasn't been any foul play. She says that she trusts me, but there will always be a doubt. I catch only a glimpse of Lennox's charred arm before I stop watching her examination. She asks me about Wallace, about what drove him to do it. I tell her that some people can't cope with the unknown. She doesn't buy it. I have asked myself the same question, over and over. What piece of knowledge pushed him over the edge in the end?

The day is quiet and strangely muted. It's almost as if nothing happened, and we're a crew getting on with this. I don't know, really, how I expected this trip to go. Maybe that we would have come to the anomaly and found nothing, that would have been ideal. Not for science, but for the safety and state of the crew. Maybe it could have turned out to be the equivalent of the aurora borealis: a trick of the light, a convergence of science that gave us something strange but harmless. (Does that mean that I see the anomaly as harmful? Intrinsically, in itself? I don't know. Every pain it has caused has been our own. It is simply the iceberg that collided with the *Titanic*.) The anomaly would have been something that we could shrug off, and we would learn from, and there it would lie: charted in the stars, plotted for eternity, as something that we would name – Hyvönen, maybe, the Hyvönen Anomaly – and that would always be there. People would search for it in the skies with their high-powered garden telescopes, to look for that ripple, like the haze of heat rising from tarmac, only stretched across the stars, and they would wait for the optimal conditions to see it, as they do with meteors and planets. It would be a thing that existed past us, longer than us. Our name would be unfaltering. That would have been a result: past the excitement of the trip, and the thrill of this whole endeavour, a thing that we could name and be remembered by. Science in its essence.

I remain desperate to stay awake. I cannot keep this up forever, I know. I don't know why I am so scared of sleeping now. I am worried, perhaps, that if I wake up I will have missed something: another death, or myself becoming swallowed by the anomaly. And I cannot take a shower, even though I desperately need one, because it is on their side. I am itching from the dirt and sweat, my scalp and pubic region needing a wash. Instead I take bottles of recyc-water, and I go to the engine rooms. I strip and spray the water at myself, all over, rub myself with a bar of soap and then try as best I can to wash it off; as the water tries to follow the lack of gravity and flee I catch what I can to smooth it across myself. I am also growing a beard. I can see it in the mirrors of the screens, but I am not able to judge what it looks like for myself. Inna says that I look distinguished, but I do not necessarily believe her. The beard itches as it comes through. Inna has offered to find and give me the shaver, but I don't need it. I think I like this. I like the idea of, when we land, me looking completely different to Tomas. He will have the birthmark; I will have the beard. I spray the water all over me, onto my head, my face, my groin and armpits, my arse. This can't be hygienic, having the waste float around me like this, drifting into the engines and the walls. I dress and avoid it, and then step outside the room before decompressing it. I listen as the air and water and whatever's spewed off my body are sucked out into the vacuum. I leave it sucking everything out for far longer than I need to. There is something curiously comforting about the thought of a vacuum.

I take another stim. I remember when you used to have to wait for headache pills to kick in. Now, they're working as soon as you even touch the tablet, surging through from fingertips to nerves in the most fluid and driven of motions. The stims bolster me. Everything is perfectly clear for a while. I squander that clarity by myself in the lab.

I watch Inna on the monitors when I am not with her. There is something about her that I want to clarify. I want to run tests on her, and I want to hold her and reassure her. The two can be attached and interchangeable, I suspect. Sometimes I catch myself thinking that she has died too many times to even be real, now.

I am forced to piss into bottles. I do this by myself, in the engine rooms. This is my private indignity. When I return, I find Inna sitting at the table, a screen pulled out in front of her. She's watching the footage that we recorded of her dying. Playing back that moment of pure nothing over and over.

'Why didn't you tell me?' she asks. Hikaru is crammed into the cockpit, asleep in his chair, leaning up against the anomaly wall. 'How many times did it happen?'

'So many,' I reply. 'Too many.'

'And you didn't rescue me.'

'We couldn't.' I know how weak this is going to sound

before I even say it; how she will resent this, because I would. Anybody would, knowing as she did that they were left to die. 'You were on that side, and we were here,' I say. 'And we had to stay where we were because it seemed like the only chance we would have of getting you back.' I don't say: and ourselves. If we went in there to get you, we would all have been stranded.

'You've got me back now,' she says. 'You could have come and done this straight away, couldn't you?' She rewinds it and zooms in: her face as she dies. That moment where it stops, where the terror and screaming give way to something like peace, but it's an accident. And then the scratch and blank frame and she reappears, her eyes opening like it's morning and she's been asleep, and then she realizes the enormity of the situation.

'We haven't got you back,' I say. 'You are still in there. I am out here. We can't go home.'

'We haven't tried,' she says. 'We haven't even tried yet.'

'I'm sorry,' I say. 'We need results from inside the anomaly. We have to get them, and then we can try. I am so sorry.'

'You aren't sorry, Mirakel,' Inna says. Every r, so softly rolled. She stays looking down.

'Ask Tomas when we can leave,' Hikaru says. He has been awake the whole time. 'I've asked him, but he won't give us an answer. Do that for us.' He doesn't sit up. He stays in the chair, his eyes still shut, and that's the end of the conversation.

I float in the lab and begin talking to Tomas. 'I want to see you,' I tell him, and I wait.

'What?'

'Initiate video,' I say, and the call goes through. I wait: the bandwidth isn't built for this, and the resolution is terrible, and the lag almost makes this unworkable. I sit back and wait, and there he is, recognizable even when he is so pixelated: my brother. He is in that suit, just as I thought, but he's not comfortable in it. He straightens his hair and stubs out a cigarette in the glass ashtray behind him. He smoked long before they made them harmless, and it's a habit he's thrilled to revel in. It's funny: his birthmark is how I see myself, I think. That here is my point of reference for how we look, even though my face is clear. Never even a spot of acne, nothing on it but the skin – and, now, the beard, of course – but I can still tell that this is having an effect on him. That, maybe, the calm in his voice is an act. His tie is loosened; his top button undone. The image is broken and only three twenty by three twenty, maybe, but still: I can see him.

'This is a surprise,' he says. 'What do you want, Mira?' Behind him, a crowd: they peer and try to see the screen. It will be just as low-res on his screens, I know. He could have stretched it out; filled the wall, even. He puts his earpiece in, so that only he can hear me. 'We're just as busy as you are, you know.'

'What do we want out of this, Tomas?'

'What do you mean? You know what we want.'

'We wanted to find out more about the anomaly. That was our mission. Find out if it was a danger or not. Find out how big it was; what it was. We were to get answers, right?' I do not wait for him to reply. 'Well, we have them. We have answers. We do not know what it is. We do not know exactly how big it is. We know nothing, and that is the best answer we can hope to have right now.'

'I see,' he says. He looks at my eyes: the camera being embedded in the screens means we have eye contact. It's a look I've seen before: disappointment, mainly that I am not the man he is. I am not willing to go as far as he is.

'They want to go home.'

'Well, they can't.'

'You don't know that,' I say.

'Then let them try.' There is a pause, longer than the lag alone, and then he speaks again: 'Although it looks as if they already are.' He disconnects and I push out of the lab and into the hall. I have to be careful in being frantic, but the ship is rumbling: the engines spinning, warming up.

'Don't!' I shout, but it's too late. We move, lurching forward. Hikaru is controlling us, pushing us away. He has misjudged this. The *Lära* barely moves, but Hikaru and Inna do. Their bodies are slammed to the wall, crushed between the insides of the ship and the anomaly. Inna is against the table, her back broken, her spine snapped; Hikaru in the cockpit, squashed down, pressed as if in a vice. There is blood, and death, and Tomas says something over the speakers. I scream, because I did not want this, and I think about going over there, to save them, but I cannot move. I shut my eyes, only for a second, because this is too much – Inna's shocked face, Hikaru so mangled I cannot see where he ends and the ship begins – and then they are just as they were. Inna is at the table, watching herself die; Hikaru is asleep in the cockpit.

Inna looks at the darkness as I gasp, as I know what it is that I am looking at. 'Why didn't you tell me?' she asks, still searching for me. I tell myself that I should try to remember what it was that I said before, to make this play out again as if this was just the first time. But I don't. I act like I am not there, and I stay silent, and I push away.

*   *   *

Tomas speaks to me when I am alone. 'There is no uniformity,' he says. 'The way it works, the time it takes. Hours with Inna when she was outside. Minutes here. Twenty minutes? Maybe less. I wonder how it is chosen. I wonder if it is arbitrary.'

'I don't know,' I say. I feel sick, and I try to eat, and I try to stay calm. My mother taught me breathing exercises. She taught me self-control, and so many ways to keep your head. If you let it slip away, you are likely to ruin yourself.

'I wish I could be there to see it,' he says. 'To be that close. We have never seen anything like this, have we?'

'What do you mean?' I ask. I want to stop and think on this; to take it all in, and let it have a chance to become real. I cannot compute it, and I cannot understand it. I am not even sure, in this second, that I am meant to. But Tomas drives forward, wanting answers.

'I mean,' he says, 'as humans. We have never seen time be this fluid. We have never seen it act this way. It's fascinating.'

'It's not time,' I say.

'Oh?'

'It can't be. We are as we were. It's not changing for us. Time cannot be different in two places at once.'

'You'd think that. But the rules are different, maybe. We do not understand it, Brother, and maybe we should not try to. Not yet.' This is not something we can test, I think. Not as he would have us do. 'Anyway: I am locking them out of the engines. I'm bringing full control here, so that Hikaru can't do that again. You understand?'

'Yes,' I say, but I want to ask for a chance to talk Hikaru down. To tell him to change his mind; to say that I know what he's planning. I do not. Tomas is in charge here now, because I have seen too much. I need to stay here. I need to be by myself.

When he is gone I make sure that the door is shut, and I lock it even though there's no chance of them getting to this side of the ship and opening it and getting me, but then they start shouting, or Hikaru does. He has tried to turn the engines on and found that he can't. He can't do anything: his controls are completely locked out, passworded and under blankets of security that he cannot hope to bypass.

'What the fuck have you done?' he screams. 'Mira! Come out here!' He shouts, but he can't do anything. I am safe in here. I flick through the internal cameras, and I see how disappointed they both are. Inna looks at the screen, of herself dying. She watches it over and over. I have been there myself, I think.

12

They both sleep, but I stay awake. I don't want to risk them waking up and finding a loophole, or doing something that ruins us all. I wonder: Can they cause an explosion? Could they, if they wanted to, make the whole ship useless, cause us to explode? Wreck life support, meaning that they would come back but I, presumably, would not? They could hold me hostage. They could do anything that they wanted, then. There is a flare gun in the emergency landing pack. They could shoot me, if they wanted to. If they told Tomas to start the ship or they would kill me, he would have to listen to them.

Inna doesn't have a bed to sleep in on that side of the ship, so she's attached herself to a bench in the changing area. I can see her, just about: the side of her head, and her shoulder, and the tattoo. It rises and falls as she breathes. I don't know how she can sleep; I would worry that I wouldn't wake up again afterwards. And hasn't she slept enough?

While they sleep, I look at numbers, and I try to imagine that I am worthwhile. That something I can do here can make some sort of difference. I do not believe that I can. I do not know what any of this is proving: these numbers, these pings, these results. Our mission was for answers, but increasingly I wonder what the questions even were. Or if we were asking the right ones. Tomas tells me that I should be using Hikaru and – now – Inna more.

'They're inside it,' he says. 'Get them to go out outside and bring in debris from the *Ishiguro*.' It's still out there, chunks of the ship, bobbing around. It's in the distance, but nothing that we couldn't cover with the scant amount of air the suits allow us. That's not the point, I think.

'What would you have them look for?'

'That ship survived for decades. I want to know what happened to it. There was a black box, wasn't there?'

'There would have been hard drives.'

'They might have survived.'

'I'm not asking them to go and get them.'

'Why the hell not?'

'They will say no. They hate me, because of what you did.'

'We had to do it, or they would have killed themselves. Do you prefer that idea?'

'I'm not asking them,' I say. He goes silent. 'Do you have any more ideas how we get out of this thing?' I ask.

'We're working on it,' he says, but I know that that means nothing.

'Worst case, you'll have to send somebody to get us.' He doesn't reply. There's another ship: a second ship still in Florida, which remained unnamed but was still constructed and tested, as everything else. It was our backup, in case the first had a problem. We made everything in duplicate during the manufacturing process. It cost a fraction of the price of the first craft: creating two of every custom part made perfect sense. Each part, in fact, has another copy, sitting waiting, unassembled, in some warehouse somewhere. It made sense to have these things: a backup ship, a backup crew, a backup of everything. 'It could launch,' I say, 'and we – you – use some of the other crew who went through training. Most of them know enough to get out here fast as anything.'

'Perhaps,' Tomas says. 'It's certainly something worth discussing.' He doesn't say goodnight, obviously. No need. I understand the finality of that. I take another couple of stims. I need more, or I will. Only a few left. Worst case, I tell myself, I have to sleep. I shut my eyes and relax, and let the cards fall as they may.

Hikaru is locked out of the computers, so this falls to me, now. The maintenance of the ship; the care and caution of our lives. I check the numbers: how much battery we've got left in the charge, which means life support. It means, how long we have before we fall into darkness and start to drift as the boosters shut off, and we die, for the last time or not. We were never meant to stay still this long. Hikaru can't have looked or he would have said something, and Inna wouldn't know how to look, I don't think. I send a link to a screen grab of it to Tomas, so that he can see, and then I float to my bed. I am lying down when I remember that I am not allowed to sleep; and I only took stims a while ago, but they are working less and less. I take another. I stay awake.

We can't risk being swallowed, I tell myself.

Tomas and I did this once before, when we were children. We built our first spaceship as soon as we moved to a house with a big enough garden, after our mother married her second husband. We used cardboard boxes from when he had a brand-new sofa delivered, and we taped items to it and glued them, and spent the morning painting the whole thing with whatever he had in his shed. A thin grey for the outside; reds and yellows for the panels. He was desperate to be fatherly, so he spent the morning doing anything we asked of him, as did my mother, and they tried to be romantic about it: this is a spaceship of new familial love and pastel colours. We didn't care about that. We were strict and told her what we wanted: we wanted science. We already owned books about spacecraft, and there had been a documentary on the television about shuttles, real things – this wouldn't have been long after the Indian disaster – and we wanted to do what they used to do, back before. Her new husband understood: he went to the shed again and came back with a handful of wires and cables that he had torn out of the back of some ancient and ruined computer monitor, and then he gave us the circuit board from the computer itself. We glued it in; a handful of old hard drives for the systems themselves, underneath the glass window given us from the monitor also. And then controllers from a video game console, to guide us to where we were going. It was perfect.

I have photographs of the two of us sitting in it. Our problem was a lack of imagination. That you could give us the ship and we would sit in it and wonder why we could not actually take off and see the things that the adults around us were telling us we were seeing. My mother got inside the ship with us and tried. She looked to the moon, and then her new husband pretended to be an alien, but that only destroyed the illusion more. We were steadfast. The point of the game for us was to see if we could do it. We had built the ship: now the fun was in the ship itself, not the journey that we were supposed to imagine it taking.

So more of the fun: the disassembling of the ship. The

laying out of the different sections flat on the lawn. Telling her new husband that this part was due to be used again in another craft, but that *this* part was scrap, destined for use in microwaves or refrigerators. Useless for space travel, we told him. Better off being used in the home, I think. We laid them all out and then collected them in, putting the bits we wanted to keep into a box. All we kept for the next trip were the hard drives and the joystick, nothing but memory and control. Everything else was able to go. We burned the cardboard that night and sat around the campfire it made in the garden, and they smoked and we cooked hotdogs. I remember not being able to see our mother by the end of the night – she had gone off inside – and we both asked where she was, and her new husband said, She's gone to the stars! like he was carrying on the game, but he was joking, and he laughed at his own joke. We thought he was laughing at us, and we didn't get it when he said that he wasn't. Not at our age, not as excited and anxious as we actually were.

Even on a ship this small, even with the anomaly wall physically between us, Hikaru and Inna begin to ignore me. I do not say their names, and I do not try to get them to talk to me, but they are in their own worlds, so distinct and separate from mine that I feel alienated. I feel pushed to one side. They are angry with Tomas and me, both of us. If they knew why he did what he did, maybe they would understand. You cannot feel as we do about answers unless you are the ones asking the questions. As they are awed by this, they lose their heads. Tomas cut the ship off from being able to control itself because it would save their lives, and because it would save the mission. There are three of us left, in a way, and we can be saved; and we can return with what we came out here for.

Eventually I strap myself to a chair and sit opposite them, watching them. They are both still and silent, both staring at nothing; Hikaru stares at the screens in the cockpit, Inna at screens of the anomaly itself. I wonder what she sees in it. If there is something that she wonders, based on when she was out there, floating so free and loose inside it.

'Tomas was only worried about the anomaly,' I say, and they ignore me at first. 'You know how long we have worried about it for. You know that. It's not like it's a shock to you, that he would do this.' But it is. 'We need answers, you know that.'

'Why did you cut us off?' Hikaru asks.

'Tomas did it,' I say, which sounds defensive. I do not want them to hate me. They can hate him: he is safe and sound, warm and cosy.

'Okay,' Hikaru says. It's so dismissive.

'We need to find out what the anomaly is,' I say. 'How it does what it does.'

'And what exactly is it that it does?' He slams his hand, flat-palmed, on the anomaly wall. 'It's nothing.'

'You know,' I say. 'You saw what happened to Inna.' My voice is apologetic. Inna cocks her head to her name, my invocation.

'Why did we get cut off, Mira?' Hikaru asks. He knows, I'm sure, or he suspects. 'How did you know I was going to start the engines? How did you know that was going to happen?'

'We need to get you out of there,' I say. 'That's all I know.' Tomas would have told them, I think. He would have been cold and delivered it as a fact. You died. You came back. Once is enough. But he is not on the comm right now, which means he misses this. The decisions made now are my own.

'We aren't getting out, though,' Inna says. She doesn't change where she's looking. She doesn't even try to find me. 'We aren't leaving here, and we aren't going home. We are going to die, and we have to make our peace with it. Hikaru and I are starting to. Now it's just you, Mira. This is finished.' She looks so calm. I would like to look that calm, I think.

'It's not finished,' I say.

'Of course it is,' she tells me.

'We can get out of this and make it home, Inna. We just have to work together, and we will find a hole. We can get you home, I am sure of it.' My lies. I do not know what I believe: if I think it's possible, or if I am telling her this to keep them going until Tomas says we are done, and that they are sacrifices. And when that happens, will I be satisfied? Will I be able to go through with it?

'We can't go home, Mira. Don't you see that?' She walks closer; puts her hands out until her skin presses onto the wall. I can see her veins, in her wrists; the blood pumping around her body. 'Why are you the only one who doesn't see that?'

'I'll find a way,' I say. 'I will.' I don't let them reply. I go to the lab and I call Earth, and Simpson tells me that Tomas is asleep, and I rage at him. 'Get him,' I say. 'Wake him up and tell him I want to speak to him.' I wait. I bring up the orange ping-map and I try to think about work, but I don't even know what that work is any more.

He comes onto the line. 'What?' he asks. He doesn't sound as if he was asleep; he sounds stressed, yes, but I know our voices when we are just woken.

'They have no faith in us, Tomas. They have none. They don't believe we are getting home, and I have nothing to tell them.'

'Okay,' he says.

'It's not okay! What do you suggest? What the hell should I say? Do you have any ideas down there? Any plans? Anything for us to try?'

He sighs, and I know what it means. It is my sigh. It is even my mother's sigh: when she told us that she was sick, and that she would not be getting better. 'We have nothing,' he says. 'There are no plans.'

'There must be something,' I say. 'We need to do something.'

'Make your peace, Brother,' he says. He has no faith in me, in himself, in us. No faith that we can survive this. Death is the only answer, and inevitable. 'I'm sorry. Goodbye.'

'What have you done?' I ask him. 'Tomas, did you know?' There's no answer. The line is silent. I message a few more times, try to instigate a video call, try to send data packets, but there's no response. I shut my eyes. I think of the anomaly, and I wonder what will make it move; and how long I have.

In the lounge I tell the other two that I have accepted it. They tell me to cross over, towards them, and to keep walking. I say that I cannot, because I don't know what it will mean. And they say, this will last forever. After you cross to us, you will never die, because you cannot. I wonder how I look, to them; grey and vague, through the anomaly. If they can ever truly see me from where they are.

And then I find myself sitting in the cockpit, in one of the pilot's seats, propped up. I think that I've been asleep. I can't remember if that was a conversation that actually happened or not. Inna and Hikaru sit at the table. They are eating together: as Inna once said, it is important to do things in a social way, to enhance the feeling of solidarity, to stress that

206

you are not out here all alone. They cannot see me, but I watch them, and on this side I eat as well, as if I am with them. Hikaru isn't eating white food. He's eating one of the normal bars – I think it's meatballs, from the colour, meatballs and vegetables and gravy, Swedish style, one of my requests – but he doesn't look as if he's enjoying it.

There's something on the scanners. I notice it when I'm staying awake, my last couple of stims, as Hikaru and Inna both sleep again. Sleeping until death; until the batteries go, and life support ends, and this is over. The something is in the distance. Indefinable because it is so small, but coming towards us.

'Tomas,' I say, 'are you watching this?' I don't get a reply. I don't really expect one. Even though I know full well that he's watching, and listening.

In the lab I bring up a screen and put a marker on the object and then I realize what it is, but it takes me a second because I'm slow with tiredness, even through the stims, and I put the marker in and it makes sense. I bring up video footage from the bounce, the long-range footage of whatever this thing is, and I plot it against the map of where we are. I go into the hard drives, to the time stamps of what we saw before, when we first met the *Ishiguro*, and I bring that up, extend it and enlarge it, and try to match the two. The blur looks the same from here, as tiny as it is; and I spend all day watching them, trying to see if they're exactly the same; and they are, soaring along inside the anomaly. It makes sense, and I finally have answers to one of my questions. How did the *Ishiguro* survive out here for so long? Answer: it didn't. It has been cycling, like everything else that dies inside the anomaly.

I don't say anything to Inna and Hikaru, not yet: I sit and watch them. 'I have déjà vu,' I say, hoping that Tomas will correct me; tell me that this is not déjà vu, this is sitting through something again, an experience that reminds me of the first. Déjà vu is a chemical response to coincidence that causes a rush of endorphins. This – watching the two versions of the *Ishiguro*, one from before, one now, and yet both somehow old – makes me realize how much the anomaly is like the video players. It is not changing time; it is simply replaying that which has already happened once before.

I spend my life here watching it as it gets bigger, losing track of time. It's following the exact same line. I tell Hikaru and Inna that I might be onto something, that there might be something happening soon. I don't say that it's a way out, because it isn't. I don't say that it's the *Ishiguro*. I match the trajectories exactly, using the recorded pins as an overlay, so that I can see if anything changes. It's safe to assume that they are like Inna was: relatively mutable, able to alter what they do each go-around, depending on circumstances. Still, they won't have changed a thing, I shouldn't think, because there's nothing external to influence them. There is no me, telling them lies through a headset. Assuming that they don't know that they're in the cycle – because why would they? – they will do exactly what they did before. Why would you change a decision that made perfect sense the first time around?

As it gets closer and closer I can see the ship. Their path is an exact copy. Where they stop, it's at the same time in the same place. When they start moving again, ditto. It's almost too incredible.

'Are you seeing this, Tomas?' I ask, but he doesn't answer, and of course he is.

Hikaru tells us that he wants to go for a walk. I cannot stop him, I know that. He says that he wants to see what it's like.

'I never had the chance when we were still on the mission,' he says, even though the mission is not done, and we are not finished, 'so I think I should probably do it now. Before this ends.' He is convinced that we are over. This is Hikaru on a death clock. If Inna was doing her job properly, she should be worried about him. He's a prime candidate, more even than Wallace was, and look how that ended. He preps an O_2 tank for the helmet and gets changed outside the airlock. Inna helps him: even as she fastens his suit for him and aids him in attaching the helmet I can tell that she hates it. What it reminds her of, to look into that slightly mirrored glass of the front. I watch them through the corridor, but I can barely see the airlock from here. I change the view on the screens to track him when he's outside – I imagine him doing something stupid, and know that I have to watch it if he does – and I strap myself to a chair and reach for my stims. The blister pack is empty. I tell myself that it's okay. Fastened here, barely sitting, almost floating, I am gone.

I wake up to the noise and bluster of Hikaru coming back: the flurry of him working the airlocks compared to the silence of Inna sitting by herself. I don't know what she was doing.

'How was it?' she asks him. She knows what her time was like; what it must be, she's thinking, to have had a trip into that darkness that passed without incident.

'Yeah,' he says. He thinks, and then, 'Pretty amazing.' I pull myself to the corridor and peer in at them. 'You should try it,

Mira: going out into the anomaly.' There's no joy in his suggestion. He is the villain in the darkness beckoning me closer to
his side of the ship. 'It's not like real space, you know? You
feel so alone, and there's nothing. Even a foot in front of your
face, there's nothing. It's an answer in itself, I think.'

'I'm fine,' I say. I flick back to the *Ishiguro* on the cameras.
It's only a day away, maybe. I am trying to think of ways to
get its attention, to let it know that we're friendly. If we
combine forces, maybe we can break this thing? Maybe then
we can all get home?

I wake my crew and tell them that we need to talk. They
are sluggish and wary, but I tell them that this is important.
I tell them what I have discovered: that the *Ishiguro* is out
there again, and heading back towards where we are. Hikaru
nods along as if this is the most normal thing in the world.
Suddenly nothing is incredible.

'So they're in a cycle, just as I was,' Inna says. As you
may be still, I think, but I don't say that out loud. Wherever
they are, whatever they are doing, if they die now they will
begin again. Everything replays itself; all that has happened
becomes new again. Inna has been in the anomaly since she
died the first time. Would all her cycles before count as a
single cycle now? If she and Hikaru died, would they all be
a part of their joint experience? She stares at the screen I
bring up, showing them it. I put it against the wall, make it
large. She treats this as a window.

I am the only one out of this. Really, if I break this down,
I am all that is left of my own free will; my own ability to
do what it is that I want. If I were to die now, I would stay
dead. I would join my other crewmates, sent out of the
anomaly before they had a chance to restart their lives. I

210

would drift; they might be able to drag me to their side but I, I assume, would remain dead. They would put me into a bed, probably Hikaru's, to preserve my body.

I would be in that state for eternity: done.

I have never before had thoughts this dark. Once, Tomas told me that he had considered suicide. As a teenager he had wondered about it as a way of expressing himself. An experiment. He asked me what there was left to conquer – this was before we had set ourselves on our paths – and said, This is a way to explore that which can only be explored now. To really discover something about humanity. It was a child talking, the idea of a fool who talks before thinking. Maybe it was under the influence of something – he got quite into drugs as a teenager, mushrooms that our stepfather grew and approved of us trying, an experiment to open our minds (and which directly led towards him leaving our mother) – but it made sense to him for a minute. Death: a final frontier. He had those thoughts. I wish that I could speak to him, now. Ask him what he would do in my situation, even though I know the answer. He would say, Be strong. I am not as strong as him though. Not in that way.

'Are you all right?' Inna asks me, but I can only gulp her question – and my answer – away, and I slope off down the corridor and into the lab. She follows, down her own section of the corridor. I stay around the corner, out of sight, but I don't close the door, and I can hear her voice calling to me: 'Mira? Mira?' She sounds concerned for me: as if, all of a sudden, she wants to ensure my safety again, and that I am okay. Her job, and maybe something else.

'Go away,' I say, but I don't know that she can hear me, and I'm not really sure that I mean it.

* * *

211

I think about it all day. Here, on the one hand, the *Ishiguro* is getting closer and closer: and with it comes a chance to witness something truly incredible, to step outside the bounds of science as I understand it, to define a scientific theory. The reappearance of it, the seemingly immortal cycle of life inside the anomaly: it could change the world. This is what we wanted to find, even though we did not know it.

And the other hand: the reality of what is left, and how my days will end. Because Inna doesn't remember her cycles, and I would hazard that the crew of the *Ishiguro* don't either. If they could, it is likely that they would be doing something different with them. They wouldn't be back here, revisiting old glories. They would be trying to find a way out of this. Twenty-three years of this, and they surely would have found something better than echoing themselves.

So there is a way out. I think about how I would do it. Wallace's route worked for him, but I could not do it. We have blades, scalpels in the medical kits. And we have pills: we have enough tranquillizers in the medicine cupboard that it would be easy. They say it's like sleeping, drifting off in a fug of something or other. A haze.

If I could find the courage, this would be my last chance.

I watch the *Ishiguro* get closer and closer. It is so unnatural: like a ghost, almost, coming through the nothing. It is solid, but it has exploded and been lost (I assume) so many times before. I wonder what they're doing in there. I wonder if they know what we know, on this cycle. Maybe this time they have worked it out. It stops. It did this before, the first time. (I laugh at that thought: the first time for me, but how many times for them I wouldn't even like to hazard a guess. Maybe I will run the numbers one day: it should be easy enough to work out.) It is close enough now that they should be able to see us. We are not chasing to catch up with them: we are ahead of them, not debris or a meteor or anything else you might see in space. We are like them. I wonder, if they see us, how we will look: the half a ship inside the anomaly, divided up. What that will look like to them? I tell Hikaru and Inna what has happened, and where it is.

'How do we get in contact with them?' Hikaru asks. I can hear hope in his voice. I'm not sure that he even knows it's there, but it is. I wonder if he suddenly regrets eating his non-white food. 'There must be some way,' he says.

'We tried everything before,' I say.

'You could try hailing them,' Inna says.

'We've already tried that as well,' I tell her. 'We tried different radio frequencies, and they didn't answer. They're too automated.'

'So we're in front of them. They'll see us through the cockpit now, won't they? They'll want to know who the hell we are.'

'Yes,' I say. 'Of course.' But we float and wait, and nothing comes from there. Hikaru gets nervous, and paces as much as somebody can up here; pushing himself in a small space, from wall to floor to ceiling. He bites his nails: so different from the man we brought up here. That man was calm, still. This one is a nearly a wreck.

'I should go out there,' Hikaru says. 'I could get them out.'

'No,' Inna says. He isn't thinking. Or he can't remember. It seems like so long ago.

'It would make sense,' he says. 'They're close enough, right?'

'Don't be fucking stupid!' she shouts. I picture them – Inna, Lennox, Tobi – out there, trying to do what we thought was best. Then the *Ishiguro* firing its engines and roaring forward in that way we never expected. How it didn't flinch: all their engines, pushing it onwards along the inside line of the anomaly.

And then, realization. We are not where we were; or the anomaly is not.

I push myself to the lab. I get the maps up, where we and the *Ishiguro* are now, the video of where the *Ishiguro* was before. Something's changed: the *Ishiguro* was never on this exact trajectory. It was further away, further from the Earth. It's moved, clinging to the front-line of the anomaly, as if it was a tide, maybe, and we are on the edge of the wash; and I watch the video of what it will do now and we're in its path, trapped halfway between the anomaly and not. On the video projection, as an overlay, the *Ishiguro* roars past us and explodes. It moves through where we are. It moves into us, and if we are still here, we will die, as it will break every part of us.

I do not want to die. Sometimes, the promise of that is enough to give you the answer; seeing it happen, almost, is enough to put you off the idea.

Hikaru tells me that there's no choice but to move the ship forward. He pleads with me, that it's something we have to do. He says, 'We don't want this to be our everlasting,' which seems to me an odd way to phrase this. I wonder where the cycle would start from with this death; if there is any logic or reason there, any science. (I wonder, for a second, for a fraction of that time, if this could be down to God. This is the first time since I could breathe that I have contemplated with any seriousness the concept of a deity. I almost feel a fool.) I tell Hikaru that there must be another way. This all seems to play too slowly: as if we're struggling for what to say and think. I wish we had Tomas' input. He might have an opinion.

'Don't be an idiot,' Hikaru says, as he seems to always say or think now. 'There's no other way out of this. You will die, Mira. Is that what you want?' Preservation of the self, I think. This is what he's displaying, even though he's turned it onto me. Inna pushes herself towards the wall of the anomaly. She rests against it. The flats of her palms are white with the pressure she's putting onto it.

'Please think about this,' she says.

'I am,' I say.

'You told us that there was a way home.' I was placating them. 'You said, we can all get home. You cannot get us all home if you die, Mira.' She's terribly scared: she knows that it's my death and mine alone. What will happen to them? Would they relive this moment for eternity? What happens to the me in their cycle, when they come back? Would that dictate their own loop: leaving them with that solitary moment of death, over and over, unending and ceaseless? When do they die? When does this begin again?

'Put in the override code and give us control back,' Hikaru says.

I watch the *Ishiguro* start its engines on the screen. It rumbles on the video, the hull shaking, and it seems to lurch – drawing backwards, like a toy car that you pull then release – and here it comes. These are the moments that define us.

'Brother,' I say, wanting him to do it. I want him to release the controls, to save me. This is a test. How much am I a sacrifice? But there is no time to have faith in him, so I bring up a console and type the override code and release the controls. I am surprised: there is a part of me that expected Tomas to have changed the code, but it is as it always was.

Hikaru is ready, and he taps buttons with a purpose I haven't seen from him since before this happened. Our own ship rumbles, and lurches; not out of the anomaly, as when they died, but the other direction. I am not strapped in, and neither is Inna, and we suddenly have gravity. We fall, and I hit myself on the wall, surprised. This is speed like I haven't felt, speed like the launch protocols demanded we were to be protected against. A burst, and I know we're clear before we stop, because we have gone so far. Hikaru slows us down with the boosters, and he leans into the yoke and he grins. He looks so happy; and he looks at me, now one of them: our fate shared. I am inside it, and it feels like nothing.

There is no time to dwell.

I hit the screens, panning the cameras to show us the *Ishiguro*, to track it, and we watch as it carries on just past where we were – it would have killed us, no question, or me, at the very least – and it explodes. It happens just as before, only we're closer now, and I can see it from this angle: as the ship begins to tear itself apart, spitting out the detritus and the furniture and the consoles and the beds. Most of it flies out of the anomaly, dead and gone and lost and free. But then there are those two bodies as before, one clutching the other. I can see them from here: the one in front is the journalist, instantly recognizable from his pictures. They were everywhere, for a while. Cormac something was his name. Easton. Cormac Easton. The other is harder to see, but he is bald, and thin. Dr Singer. He clings to the journalist and they move forward, towards us, deeper into the darkness, away from the rest of the ship.

There isn't time to think. I pull a suit on, slapdash, almost, and a helmet, not even stopping to check the seal properly, because this could be something: it could be a way of saving ourselves. Having Dr Singer here with us could change everything. Together, he and I could find a way out. That's what he and I both have been missing: a brain to play off. Another scientist.

'What are you doing?' Inna asks. There will be a minute, two at most before the pressure out there kills them, or they choke to death and their cycle begins anew. I can interject; I can save them. I tell Inna to be ready, that they will likely need medical aid, and I start the airlock cycle before my suit is even fully sealed, and I wait by the door and I squeeze my hands into fists and then out again to palms. Fists and then out to palms, over and over, as the door opens.

And then I am out in space. I hit the boosters, and I am clumsy still, but better than I was. Perhaps I am learning. They come towards me, and I them. For some reason Dr Singer pushes the journalist away from him, his back to me, and I go faster. I can feel the heat of the boosters through the suit, at my back; not burning me, but the suits can withstand so much I know how far I am pushing them. I ignore the journalist. He is not my target. He is nothing. He was nothing then, and he is nothing now. I aim for Dr Singer, tackling him almost, and he crumbles into me. He feels so frail and thin. I can save him. I let the journalist die out there in the darkness. He wrote, once, that he felt like an explorer. He can carry on exploring.

I turn, the boosters in the suit pushing as tight an arc as they can manage, and I head back to the airlock. I don't know if Dr Singer's already dead. I don't know anything. I hope that Inna can save him. I cling to him as we go.

Inna shouts at Hikaru to get the gravity on as soon as the airlock door opens, and I drop to my knees. I am unprepared, but this is no longer about me. Dr Singer is coiled up, curled inwards, fetal. Inna rushes in and flips him to his back. I see her face first, and then I look at the body on the floor: it is barely a man. I cannot explain it. He is wrinkled and shattered and old, so much older than he should be. His skin is translucent, almost, hanging and sliding from his face, his features visible through it. His eyes are black and white and red in seemingly equal measure, and they lie open and lifeless. He isn't breathing: we would be able to tell, as the rise and fall of his chest would still happen, even as emaciated as he is. It would be, on this frame, all we could see.

'He's dead,' Inna says. She is uneasy even touching him, handling him as one does a dead cat: fingertips and hesitation. For a second, he reminds me of those old drawings of aliens, the kind we would find in our books, deciding whether to make peace with them or not: grey skin, oversized head, dark eyes. I think, for a second, almost a joke to myself, that here is the discovery we were looking for. Life, and yet it is dead. She is unsure whether to save him or not; if she should see whether this is something she can turn around.

'Try,' I say. I think about what I risked, and where we are now. This cannot be for naught. She slides a syringe into his suit at his neck, and holds a mask to his face to force oxygen into his body. I worry that the settings are made for a normal man, and that he will reject this: or that maybe it will split his insides. His shrivelled lungs torn at all the air. Perhaps I am wrong? Perhaps the ship has not been in the cycle? I thought. But we saw it crash twice, and Easton was so perfectly young. Nothing about this makes sense. The corpse's chest swells with the oxygen; it almost creaks. The adrenalin should make his heart pump, a kick-start to an engine. What is this that we're saving? She starts to manually work his chest, and I hear cracks: the sound of ribs breaking. She is in danger of making this irreparable, and then I remember that he will come back. He will die and, somewhere down the line, come back to life. We can try again. All we have to do is survive until the *Ishiguro* comes back, maybe, and we can be quicker, prepared. We could save them both, maybe. I move my arm to stay hers, but then it coughs. No, *he* coughs, and it sounds vile: a thick rigid mucus inside him, a lurch of his whole body, making his bones clatter against the floor. His spine bends and everything seems exaggerated owing to his frame, and the flesh that remains seems draped over him. His eyes don't lose their peculiar colour; now, they dart. They're quick, no lag, snap from face to face to face, from me to Inna to me again.

'It's okay,' Inna says, but he doesn't listen to her. He pushes backwards. He's terrified, and he reaches the door of the airlock and forces himself against it. He looks at us still, doesn't take his eyes off us. Everything about him is fallen. Everything about him feels wrong. I have no idea who this man is, but he is not Dr Singer.

We leave him in the airlock. We shut the door on him, because we do not know who or what he is, and we watch him as he tries to stand; as he leans his hands against the glass and seems to try to walk himself to upright. His thin legs buckle like a foal's, and he falls to his knees, which look as if they should shatter at the impact of the metal floor. His frailty in every part reminds me of my mother, at her end: atrophied on her bed, her body giving up. He hasn't tried to speak to us yet, nor we to him. Or, we haven't tried to entice him. Inna tells me that we should ask him his name.

'Maybe he remembers something,' she says, but I am hesitant to assume that. We open the airlock slightly and throw a meal bar in. He turns away from us and devours it, forcing it into his mouth. He tries to keep it down and fails; it doesn't matter to him, though. He paws it back into his mouth, a monkey in a cage eating his own vomit, and then he looks back at us over his shoulder as if we owe him another. He's not pleading with us. She gets one of Hikaru's white bars, stripped of everything, bleached food that tastes of nothing and gives you only the proteins and vitamins you need. The man in the airlock sniffs it and then eats it. He's feral, and it goes down in bites. He has no teeth that I can see but he gums it to pieces and swallows them. I am sure that I can see the lumps travel down his throat, passing his exaggerated Adam's apple. Inna says, 'For a man of his frame, he should be dead.' She leans close to the airlock. 'What's your name?' she asks. He shoots her a look of something, I don't know what.

'He is too gone for that,' I say.

'What's your name?' she asks again, over the intercom. She says it calmly and quietly, and she puts her hand on the glass of the airlock. She wants him to trust her.

'I am Cormac Easton,' he says, 'and I am a journalist,' although it's slurred and drab through his mouth, and harsh on his throat. He's the same one he was seemingly carrying as a young man, being thrown from the explosion of their ship.

He is hesitant, but we get words out of him. Inna examines him as much as he will let her. She rattles off what is wrong with him: early-onset dementia; massive bone loss and muscle deterioration; a mind-boggling list of psychological ailments; scurvy. She tells me that it's a miracle he's alive. I tell her that it's not a miracle. When I have time, as she examines him, I talk to Hikaru. He seems better since I ended up on

220

this side. He tells me that he doesn't feel as alone any more. I think about how it's as if we're rebuilding our crew.

'It is unsettling, though,' he says. He rubs his hand with his thumb: pushing it into his palm.

'He's still human,' I say. I fear how unconvincing I am, even to myself.

'Him and Inna. They're the same. Neither of them should be alive.' He says it so coldly; I do not tell him that he has died once before himself. 'Do you think he's been looping as well?' He doesn't want an answer, and he doesn't wait for one. 'It's not natural, is it?'

'It is what it is,' I say, 'and Inna is herself. Exactly as she was before it happened to her.' He asks what we do now, and I tell him that we have to work on calming our visitor down.

'He's a phantom,' he says. 'You see that, don't you?' And I do, but I don't tell Hikaru that. I tell Hikaru that he could be necessary to our getting home. 'We're not getting home,' Hikaru says. 'We go deeper into this thing, maybe we'll come out the other side.' We never found out its depth. The pings meant nothing, finding nothing, returning no results. Now we have that to think about: that we could head deeper into it and never reach an end.

When I'm done with Hikaru and Inna and Easton I find myself alone. I think about where we are, and how I could have escaped this. But I am a coward, or sensible. Too sensible, maybe. I'm alive, I think. I *assume*. At least I have that. I'm destined to stay alive until I am no longer alive, and then I'll come back. I contemplate Easton, and how he is here. How he was there twice, and what that must have meant. Something was wrong with his time, but maybe something different to ours. Inna died and then came back, but what if we had left her? What part did we play in her cycle? The cycles, the loops, the lives, they are seemingly random in length. There are no answers: it is as if we are being played with. I wonder when the loop began for him. They went far deeper into space than we did, because that was where the anomaly was then. When did their cycle start? Or was it only Easton's cycle? Were the rest of them just passengers, de facto parts of it, destined to be as they were until he reached his end?

'Tomas?' I ask. I wonder if it even matters that there is no answer. We nurse Easton back to health and maybe we will have one. Maybe then we can get closure. Or we make a closed experiment of this: a test that can provide a definitive answer. I think about writing myself a note, scrawling it onto one of the boards in the lab about what I am going to do, and then lifting a razor to my neck and sliding it through the skin, through the arteries and veins. Feeling them pop under the weight of the blade, and watching the blood arc out. I wonder how long it would take me to start a new cycle; and when I came back, if I would still feel the pain. If the blood would remain. When I would start the cycle: in this room, with razor in hand? Partway into the slice? Or before I even contemplated it? Before I had even written the note to myself?

Before this mission even began?

The others are antsy, staying where we are, leaving gravity switched on. Hikaru looks at the battery and worries, because the charge loses every second that we sit still. He questions whether the ship's batteries will still work the same inside the anomaly; so we might end up with this being our last. We should save it for life-support systems: on their own, what we have left could sustain the four of us for nearly a month, that's how efficiently they run. I tell him that I want to talk to Easton before we switch it off.

He is lying on the floor, head down. He is perfectly still, and his hands are splayed, flat on the floor. His fingers are like nothing I've ever seen: pink silk draped over broken twigs. He can't bend them properly, they're too gnarled. He lies here because of the gravity. Because it's so hard for him to lift his head. His muscles can't cope with it, and they're relaxing. I ask him questions and he doesn't answer them. It feels pointless.

'I'm letting go,' he says as I stand up to leave, to tell Hikaru to remove gravity. He's barely audible, so I lean in, and he repeats it.

'Of what?' I ask, because I feel like I should. He doesn't answer. He shuts his eyes. 'Are you even glad that we saved you?' I ask, but of course there is no answer. 'We are about to lose gravity,' I say, and then we do. I watch him float upwards, and he hangs there in the middle of the airlock, weightless and gone, entirely limp, like a rag doll with no spine to give it structure.

I pick a blister pack of stims from the medical cupboard and pop one out. I can stop now, I tell myself. We're swallowed, deep in the belly of the whale. Inna comes to me as I hold the pill in my hands.

'He's sick,' she says.

'I know.'

'What do you want to do about him?'

'Can we make him better?' I ask.

'I don't think so,' she replies. 'If we had a hospital, maybe. Nutrient drips. Years of therapy.' She means both kinds. 'Here, I don't think we can.'

'Okay,' I say. 'Then we make it as easy for him as possible. He probably deserves that.' I try and sound convincing. We don't know anything about him. He might have mutinied and killed his crew for all we know. Somehow he survived and they did not: and somehow he has aged, and they are all just a part of his cycle. We can't explain it: I dread to think what will happen to us out here now. If one of us will become him, outliving the others, somehow going around and around at a completely different pace, in a completely different loop.

'I'm scared,' she says. 'Of what might happen now.'

'I know,' I say. She floats up to me and puts a hand on my leg, and I see her fingernails, the chipped nail-polish on them. That she made a token effort before and I didn't notice it. I wonder if it was done for me, before. I hope that it was. She squeezes my arm.

'You didn't stand up for us,' she says. 'And you didn't come to me.'

'I thought that it was the best thing to do,' I tell her. It is not a lie, one way or another. 'I wanted to make sure that we got home.'

'We still could now. We could find a way.'

'Yes,' I say. I think, Lies are no foundation for the start of a relationship. That is what this feels like.

'This doesn't stop. We were here to find out more about the anomaly, weren't we?' She looks hopeful. That my answer will be the truth she's believed.

'Always,' I say.

'So that will not change now. Now we simply have a better point of view.' She bends in towards me, and I think that this could be when it changes. For a second I am not here: I am anywhere else. I have forgotten our location, our crisis, our pains. I have forgotten the deaths we have suffered and the calamity. I have forgotten the *Ishiguro* and Tomas back at home and everything else. She kisses me on the cheek, on the hairs that have grown there, so close to my mouth. And she whispers, into that skin there, that she forgives me. 'All we have left is the reality of the now,' she says. 'We shouldn't sacrifice that. We shouldn't lose it.'

I think, I have nothing to be forgiven for. But I cannot say that to her, because this, to her, is all, and she has given it to me. I let the pill drop from my hand, and I put the blister pack back. I do not need them now.

My mother, before she died, was in a hospital. I visited her with Tomas one Saturday when we were close to the final stages of our pitch for the UNSA contract. We were busy and tired and lost, and, to us, this was another blip. She had been in and out of the hospital for years, a seemingly perpetual cycle of treatment and recovery, and each time was given what amounted to an all-clear. Then, two months later, something would be found. It was always a step ahead of her, and of us. (Her then partner told us that if we had put half the effort into curing her that we put into our adventures – his word – we could have saved her. He said, Think of the good you could have done. He spat on Tomas' shoes, and we said, Well, you left her, just as she was sick. We were all guilty, even though Tomas said that he was not.) This time, she was taken in as an emergency. We flew across from the US, where we were preparing for a meeting with important men who could add funding to the proposal. Part of the process was showing the UNSA that you could play the game, and it was crucial. Going in without some base funding would have been fatal to us.

So we flew over on the Saturday morning, working on the flight, and we sat with her all day. She did look sick, we told her. Not that we thought what she had was hyperchondriacal, but that she often put a brave face on for us. We asked her what the doctors had said. She said that they didn't know what they were talking about, and we said, Okay, but what did they say? They had said that it was in her spleen, now, and her stomach, and her bowel. They would have to tear most of her out, and what would they be leaving? (I distinctly remember picturing her as one of those dissected mannequins that they used in biology class, with the pregnant baby in: you take the baby out and there are all the organs, removable one by one, carefully stacked so that they don't just tumble out and leave the woman hollow.) So we sat with her, and we queued up movies on the television that we knew she loved, and we just sat and watched them.

She asked us how it was going with the project (which is what she called the mission, as if we were still in school). It's going well, we said. We're doing our best. That's all you can ask, she told us. She said, I'm in a lot of pain. So we upped her morphine, just that second, because we wanted to help. She said, You could name something after me, couldn't you? Of course we could, I told her. Tomas said, We could name a star, but I didn't want that. You can buy that from the internet, I said. Anybody can be named after a star. We'll pick something else, I told her, and for a second I was best child, again.

She said, Give me more morphine. So we did, because she was in pain, and who could bear to see that? We worried about if she would die when we left, when we were in another country entirely, and couldn't make it back to see her. But it was immaterial. She asked us to up her morphine and we did, and again. She died in the night, that night, and I said to Tomas, Well, we name the ship after her. That's the thing that will be remembered in the history books. Remembered, preserved in a museum: the story of us and our mother, alive for eternity, having been to the stars and back.

I tell Hikaru and Inna and Easton that I am going to sleep. I climb into my bed, resisting the urge to stay awake; to find the stims and take them. They are not addictive, but maybe that feeling is, I reason: the feeling of being awake, of having yourself fully there. I undress as much as I feel comfortable, knowing that Inna and Hikaru are there. Especially Inna. I wonder if I have let myself go more: if the thinness in my body makes me even less physically appealing. They say that they're staying awake to watch over Easton, so I don't need to worry about it. I shut my eyes, in the darkness of that bed, and I talk to myself. I tell myself all that has happened to me, and I think of Tomas, and I think of Inna. I think that I sleep, but I can feel myself as if I am awake. I wonder if the stims have damaged me. I wonder if it's possible to ruin the part of you that sleeps, and rests, and recovers.

When I wake up, they are all asleep. I am alone. I look at Easton, curled up, floating in the middle of the airlock; and then the other beds, their screens all dimmed. I clip myself to a rail and watch them, and I ask for my brother, over the intercom, but there's no answer. I do not know if this is because he can't hear me at all, now. There's nothing when I click through to Earth. I send a message for him, telling him what happened, in case he doesn't know. Maybe he will want to save me. I beg him to: I say, I cannot be alone up here without you. Have I ever needed him like this before?

I notice that Inna's bed is open, and she is watching me. She has seen I don't know how much of me talking to Tomas, snivelling and crying. She doesn't judge; instead, she pushes out of her bed and towards me, and she opens her arms wide and envelops me. She is comforting: her skin is warm against mine.

'It's okay,' she says. 'This is okay, you know.'

'I do not know who I am,' I say. 'Without him, I don't even know what I can be.' Her hands rub my back, and they find their way to my hair, and I cry onto her vest, soaking her shoulder. The tears peel away, and I notice them, and I think, I have seen that before. Everything has a part to play in my memory of this.

'We only have ourselves,' Inna says. She moves back, and she raises her shirt, only above her belly, to show me more of the tattoo. She exposes the bottom half of the bird that starts at her shoulder. In its claws it carries a word, as if it were a dead mouse. Pak, it says. It is so dark, but now I can see surgery scars with my thumbs, and the tattoo following them: the lines of the bird, loose and fluid, along the flat, crease-free skin that shows where her body once failed her. I can see all of her written out in the tattoo. She has had the darkness inside her, destroying her organs, just as my mother did. I wonder how much of her has been taken. Life has a way of making this happen. Some would call it fate. 'We are all we are left with,' she says. She covers herself again, and she holds me once again. For a brief moment I do not know which of us needs this more; but that moment passes.

We hear the scream as we're asleep: standing with each other, magnetized to the rail, in some comforting embrace. When I wake up, it's to look into her face, and there's a second before I hear the scream again. We detach and push towards it. She is faster than me, through the doorway first and into the corridor. It is Hikaru's voice, the scream: wet and pained and like a full-stop. He is on the floor, only a few inches above the ground, his body in the pose of a kneel, of praying, a genuflection; and there is a jagged shard of plastic in his neck, blood thudding out in baubles of thick red, dabbing the walls in dragged-out smears. He pulls the shard out and immediately lets go of it, and it looks as though he is doing it in slow motion. It floats in front of his eyes, taunting him. Inside the airlock, the journalist Cormac Easton: his hands red with Hikaru's blood. The computer panel outside the door has been activated: somebody was trying to do something with it. I wait at the back, shocked and scared and so ineffectual. Inna rushes to Hikaru's drifting body and screams at the phantom inside the airlock.

'You monster,' she says. 'Why would you do this? What did he ever do to you?' She's angry, and it's a gut reaction: she reaches for the button to lock the airlock, to trap Easton in. I am in the doorway, and I am slow to react. He is faster. Easton is used to this: he is somehow at one with the lack of gravity, a fish thrown back into the water. He shoots forward, his arm out, and he takes the shard, and he kicks off the floor. He lashes out with it again. Not a stab, this time, but a swipe. The tip scratches across her neck. It is a scratch at first, and I am glad that he missed, that he was ineffective; and then her neck opens up, a second mouth lower down, lipless and slowly gaping as she gags. Her blood joins Hikaru's as her hand hits the panel, the right button by some fluke of chance, to close the airlock and seal it. It hisses shut, driven into Cormac's frail body, and I hear the cracks of his bones as he is knocked backwards. He is trapped inside, no longer a threat, and I can move now: my faculties back, freed from self-imposed rigidity. I rush to Inna to see what I can do to help. Hikaru is already too far gone. It's pointless, thinking that I might save him. But Inna: her injury is fresher.

I pick her up in my arms, draping her arms over my shoulders, and I try to walk-swim back towards the living area with her. Her blood soaks into my clothes, which is good, because this way it isn't flooding out, soaking the rest of the ship; and I finally reach the table that we ate from, or sat at while we ate, and I lie her on it. I open the medical supplies cupboard, no real idea what I am doing, and I take gauze and sealant. I know to make injections with the sealant, to stem the flow of blood, and when I have done them I try to stop the blood by pressing the gauze down. He neck feels loose under my hands: as if it is slipping as I press on it. I apply pressure regardless. I remember that being something that I should do.

She keeps breathing. I can hear it. I can see her chest. I am afraid to leave her, but I need more than this. Inna passes out, but she is still alive. The sealant appears to have worked, and she is still breathing, but I cannot feel a pulse. When she is settled, still weakly breathing, I think that I should check in the other room: to see that Hikaru is dead, and what has happened to Easton. As soon as I leave her and get into the corridor I shake until I have to stay perfectly still, and I feel – I see – myself vomit. It's a reaction that I can't control.

I see Easton inside the airlock. He's having trouble breathing: his chest is bloody. Ribs puncturing lungs, I'd imagine. He is suffocating, dying, pawing at the floor. He looks at me, and his eyes are so big in his drawn face that they're almost comical.

I'm dying, he seems to be saying, though his maw of a mouth. He mouths it: open and close, open and close.

I'm dying, he says.

'Good,' I reply.

PART THREE

O dark dark dark. They all go into the dark.
                                          – T. S. Eliot

13

Inna lasted nearly a day. I never found her pulse again, but she kept breathing for a while. It was too shallow. She didn't wake up. She had no last words, not to me at least. Only what she said to Easton, and I couldn't even remember that as I held her body.

I didn't think about the cycles. About how often I would have to watch that scene play out.

The loop begins with Hikaru in there as Easton sleeps, attempting to do as I ended up doing: seal the airlock doors and trap him. Maybe he intended to flush him out; I cannot tell. Hikaru moves slowly and quietly. He begins to tap on the keys to close the door, but he's not the stealthy one here. Easton has been awake the entire time. He launches himself around the corner of the airlock, faster than Hikaru can react – and since then, with the time that I have had to myself, I have contemplated his deterioration and the effect that it has had on his body, and how adept he became in that time at adapting to the weightlessness, turning it to his own

233

advantage – and then he stabs him. I have been able to examine the blade over time: presumably torn from some part of the *Ishiguro*. What I thought was a single piece is not. It is the construct of hundreds of thin wires, torn and stripped from the interior systems of the ship, I would assume, wound around and around, then carved and smoothed, heated and melted together to form a new single blade. It is the product of some work, of time and effort. It is quite elegant, I suppose.

He slides the blade into Hikaru's neck and then scutters backwards through the air, and there's a look in his eyes: almost as if he's shocked at himself. Self-preservation, that's all it was. He knew what Hikaru was planning. I don't know what happened on the *Ishiguro*, and I don't suppose that I ever will, but something made him this way. He is broken and gone, a product of time and circumstance. I feel sorry for him, sometimes. When I try to think of him as a man other than this: away from this situation, from the deaths that he caused; or causes; or will cause. When Inna arrives he seems to panic further. She is another potential threat. She is only trying to help Hikaru but she's so aggressive in how she speaks to him. He lashes out. He's trying to keep her back. He's just unlucky with Inna, I think. There is no malice in his murdering her. I wonder how this has worked for him: if he's been looping but somehow ageing at the same time. How long has he been alive for? How long has he been out here? And when he dies, if he wakes up and doesn't understand what has happened, how can he excuse what he has become?

I can see myself in him, or him in me. Especially now that I'm all alone. The last one left, really; the only one actually alive. I am, however, as much a part of this as they.

It begins when I am not in the room: when I am back at my starting place, looking away from the bodies, head bowed; an actor designated a part, a starting position behind a curtain.

For a few cycles I took Inna from the room and saved her briefly, convinced that I could do something differently. I had everything prepared, so that when I looked away and the play began, I could get her and save her. I have tried every option that I can think of. After a while, when I got tired, I began leaving her there. I would watch it happen on video, because I didn't want to be there in person. Would she think that I was betraying her? Of course she would. It would be the third time. The cock would crow, and she would never be mine again. So I leave her there. When she's not aided by me, she dies a lot faster. She bleeds out in minutes, and she tries to save herself, flapping uselessly, coating the room in her blood. It's hard to tell who dies first: her or Easton.

Sometimes I find myself staying with them because I can't stand the thought of it starting again: so I stand in the doorway and watch their bodies after they've passed away, and I try to stay there for as long as possible. It's a battle of wills. How long can I stare at them; how long can I wait while they die.

It's been three weeks since they died, and I don't know how many times I have watched it, but I am not used to it, and I don't hate their deaths any less than I used to.

The ship has been quiet. There are no echoes in space. I should know. I talk to myself, because why would I not? I do it simply so that I can hear another voice in the void. Despite his betrayal – and I see it as that, surely and definitively – I miss Tomas fiercely. I try to talk to him, and I send him more messages, telling him what has happened, explaining how alone I now am, and yet I only hear my own voice coming back. Still: at least this voice is something we share.

Now, I have no trouble sleeping. I shut the door on the bed and in there it is silent, and it is still. When I wake up, I wonder if anything will be different, but I know the answer. Even though there was no audience, the play continued. Every day I use more of my air and get closer to having to move the ship or die. And if I die – if I choke to death, unable to breathe – all that will be guaranteed is that I will have to live that death over again.

I wonder where I would begin from.

I have done things to try and help me understand this. I have seen if I can play with the scenario. I cannot stop it: the cycle never begins until I am away from it, and I cannot reach it in time. Chaos theory was wrong: it plays itself out, always exactly the same. We are doomed to repetition. There are never variations. I have tried to tamper with the room before a cycle begins, to see if I can affect it. If I suck all the air out, for example, can I knock them all out before it begins? Drag the key players to other areas? Lock Cormac in before he can do his damage? Open the airlock as soon as the cycle begins, maybe? Nothing sticks. All my work is undone. I cannot explain any of this, and thus I have become neutered: a scientist who understands nothing of his surrounding or situation, who can prove or disprove nothing, who can never attain answers.

One time, I dragged Inna's body from there as I did that first occasion, only faster – I am becoming more adept at the path to the table, knowing when to turn my body and hit the walls at their best, even if the collisions leave me with bruises, all to get Inna back within the shortest time possible.

236

I cannot save her, so I try to make it easier on her. I make her comfortable. I find myself wondering what's wrong with her; pushing aside her top, and then seeing where the scar lines the tattoo, how much of her side is the fake flesh that they used to seal her up. She never had a chance to let me see it in the light. Here, looking at it with as close to scientific eyes as I can muster, I can see that there is art in both. I wonder which came first: the desire for the bird tattoo or the scar? If she saw the line of the scar when she was healed, saw the different tone of the synthetic skin, and through some almost-pareidolic reaction she saw the bird on her chest, deciding there and then to make it somehow more real? I look up the word that the bird carries on the computer, and of course it is Cancer. She was shedding the past, looking to a future. Would that I could.

We – that is, the ship and her crew, in whatever form we might take – have drifted. I don't know exactly where we are, or how much the anomaly might have grown – or moved – from our original position. On the maps, we are a way from it, but there's no real way of tracking what the anomaly is doing. I repeatedly sit at the console in the cockpit and think about pressing buttons and seeing if I can fly this thing: program a new destination. I have never tried to fly this. But I would assume that it couldn't be that difficult: we designed how it should work, and we watched them build it, watched the trials. We had simulations constructed in the early days to give us an idea of how the yoke would work, the joystick, and how the remote controls would work given the lag and so forth. I took the controls then, once. The heft and power of the real thing can't be that much different.

Sometimes I think that there might be an exit on the other

side of this thing. That I could travel through it and maybe there I would find a way out.

I go through cycles myself: where I have to leave them alone to play out as they will; or where I cannot take watching Inna die again, so I attempt to save her, despite knowing the outcome. I think of it as a duty: every few times, I want those final few moments with her. I wait until it's started, with my back to them and my eyes closed, and then when I hear the action start I put myself in position. As I try to save Inna she seems to know what I am doing. She appreciates it. I am there with her in her final moments, and I try to give her peace.

I think about the great discoveries in our lifetime, in the lifetimes of those who came before us, and I wonder what they must have first thought: how inexplicable it was to contemplate a round Earth, to see and understand comets and meteors, to uncover evolution, electricity, the atom bomb. As we took those first tentative steps into space, inventing a means to explore that which had previously been something close to hearsay. I used to wonder how it must have felt, as somebody who had seen two wars at the start of that century, to watch that launch on the television at the time: to see where we had reached. To have watched *Le Voyage dans la lune* as a child, and then to see it realized. No face in the moon; no mermaids or aliens. Instead, only footsteps and flags and dust. Just as incredible, when you think of it. And now, if I return, they will know of this: that I discovered something truly inexplicable. Here is a space that makes no sense; space in the truest sense of the word. Not the void that we describe with that word in our regular lives, but something else. When the *Ishiguro* didn't come home, hypothesis was everything. Now, I could tell them so much more.

Tomas still can. Even without me he has enough. I wonder if he's told the world that I am lost yet? I wonder if he's told them that I am dead? I tell Inna, on those times that I save her, that we will make it home. I know that, for her, it is a lie. But in those moments either she believes it, or it makes her feel better, and then she dies with more of a smile on her face. She still trusts me, even after everything.

I have lost track of how long this has taken; how long I have been here, doing this for.

It is one of the times in which I save her. I pick her body up and let the blood soak me again, into my suit which has been soaked so many times. The blood stays on me: I am out of this cycle, and my suit is darkened with Inna's life. Each time it happens there is something so warm about it. It's almost comforting, to feel her so alive for just a few seconds. This is Inna, and I am doing right by her. If I can get better at saving her, with practice and hard work, she might one day have more time with me. I am not trying to save her life now. I know that she is beyond that. I would need to be a surgeon to attempt more than I currently do, and while I have contemplated it, a part of me is unwilling to punish her in her dying moments with experimentations and attempts. I have done it before, when she was outside, but there was a distance there. I think, now, about the direct pain she would feel; and how I would feel her dying breath on my face as I tried. It would hurt her. But to preserve her, to ease her suffering, that is something I can do. I am injecting her with the sedatives when she leans to me and speaks to me, the first time that she has done this in any of her cycles.

'Let me die,' she says. Her voice is barely a whisper. Barely human, really, from the sound. I stop what I am doing and drop the hypo, and I listen in case she says anything more. But she doesn't. That's it. Her eyes shut and her mouth stays open. Her words smell of her blood as it gargles it in her throat.

Let me die, she said.

'I have been,' I tell her body when she is gone, and I'm waiting for the next cycle to begin. 'Was that not enough?' In her next cycle, I just watch. As she dies, as they all die, as Cormac gasps at me, choking in his cell, I tell Inna that I am doing as she asked. 'This is what you wanted,' I say. She doesn't look at me. She floats on her back, with her head tilted back, and the blood floats like children's bubbles.

'I have to sleep,' I tell Inna as she dies another time, and I watch her. She chokes and coughs, lying there on the table. I say goodnight to her. She dies as I sleep. I talk to her as I shut my eyes, and tell her what I have done. Not that she will remember any of it. I sleep with the lid of the bed open, because I don't need the darkness, not really.

When I wake up it is to the alarm of Inna's screaming as she dies again. It will have happened all night: there must have come a point where my body was more susceptible to the noise. I drag myself from my bed and to their room, and I look at them. She always ends up the same way: face down, near the ceiling, a red balloon floated off and trapped in the branches of a tree. They have reached the end of a cycle as I enter the room, and I know I need to wash. I take a shower, watching their bodies the whole time. I am unwilling to close my eyes in case the cycle starts again. It's never happened with me in the room before, but there's always a first time. So I wash with my eyes open, the shampoo swirling around me in the shower-pod and stinging my eyes, but still. I dry myself and then shit, not taking my eyes off them the entire time. When I am done I stay watching them, naked in that room. They are all dead. Cormac stares at me, as if, as he died, he wondered how I could be so casual about the whole thing. As if I am the murderer here. I eat a bar, never taking my eyes off them. Even when I look at myself in the mirror – at my beard, so Robinson Crusoe am I – I am keeping an eye on them. I have to be prepared.

They start again as I reach the cockpit and examine where we are. No sign of it stopping, and no way to tell when it will.

I try to save Hikaru this time, but that's pointless, and he struggles so much, almost hitting me, that I think it is that he doesn't even want me to. That's how far gone he was. Maybe I should have realized the effect that this would have on us all.

I save Inna once more, and I carry her out of the room, to the table. This time I have decided to use the ship's supply of adrenalin to get more out of her. I plug her wound, and I stabilize her, and then, when she's on the table, strapped down, I take a hypo of adrenalin and have the intention to inject it into her heart. I want her awake, even if it shortens things. Even if the slightly fixed artery cannot take the increased blood-flow I will cause inside her.

I cut off her once-white vest, slicing it top to bottom with the thick-bladed scissors from the medical set, then discard the pieces. She is naked. There is the bird; and here, in the harsh brightness of the room, I can see every scar clearly now. Maybe I am less enthralled by the work done,

241

because over time I have come to see the flaws. How they reflect the light, almost, and how the blue that she's attempted to cover them with hasn't quite set. The synthetic flesh isn't blended properly; it's a different shade of skin tone. She could have had it dyed, had the scars hidden and smoothed over. I wonder why she didn't: how fresh this all was. Or maybe it was a choice, like Tomas' birthmark. She decided that it made sense to keep it, as a reminder.

The tip of the beak, her breast and her heart. I press the hypo to her breastplate, waiting until I hear it click, and then it does the work for me: like a nail gun, shooting into her. She inhales and jolts upwards. The blood starts pumping faster, and my gauzed patch-job is insufficient. It ebbs over and through, and starts running all over her.

'Mira,' she says.

'I'm here,' I tell her. I hold her. I keep my back arched, my chest away from her and the hypo that juts from her front, but I wrap my arms around her.

'What's happening?' she asks.

'You're dying,' I say. She panics and tries to struggle away from me, which only makes the blood flow faster. 'But I can make it stop,' I say. 'I can make it okay. Do you want me to help you?' I ask, and she nods. She dies in my arms. I don't know if this was the best way for her to go: how much pain she was in, whether she would rather have had something else. But it is what we have.

When she is dead, I take a scalpel from the kit, because I need to know. I slice along the line of the synthetic flesh, cutting it out as if it was a window, so that I might see inside her. At first, through the blood, it looks normal: pink and red and brown organs. But then the blood clears, and I see that they are synthetic: all transparent plastics, bags and pipes and

242

batteries. I want to know what nearly killed her; how much of herself she lost. I cut her more, and I look inside as much as I can. This is not her, I tell myself: it's a model. I pull aside the organs to see them all, and she is barely herself. Her insides are swapped and false. Underneath them all, her real organs. What is left of a stomach; a liver; a partial bowel. Joined and clamped together by technology, they all look normal, and then I see the part that is not: the cancer, rotting away at the stomach, the intestine. It is brown mould, brown and black, and maybe she knew about it, maybe she didn't, but it is pervasive and deep-rooted, and it would have killed her. Through all of her attempts to save herself, it would have been an end. I think about this ship, and how I keep trying to save her, but in the end, she will die anyway. We will all die anyway. For her, maybe this is better: the shock of Easton's blade; the blood; the table; me doing my best, or trying to.

I tell myself that I am a good man. That I have tried to be, because this seems a noble goal. I treat the bodies of those who remain in their beds as therapists, and I talk to them. I tell them that I would do anything to redeem what has happened. I cannot get them home, and so they die. But I would give anything to stop it. As long as I am in here, I know, they will do this, over and over.

I think about interjecting myself into the play: dying first, to stop them. But would that help? Could I? Can I? I think about going outside, and dying there, and maybe if I am not here the cycle changes, and everything alters, and they could live. Maybe, if I am outside, Hikaru never tries to cycle the airlock; and then I am the one in the loop, out there forever. They might find a way to save me, of course. They might work out how to give me an ending.

And then I realize it, and it's so apparent to me; and I am an idiot, because I did not see it sooner. I can give that ending to them. I always bring Inna back into the main body of the ship, and I try to save her. But what if I push her the other way, and I let her die? What then?

It isn't easy, that much is apparent, because there is nothing to gauge it against. When driving a car, there is the road; when flying an airplane, I would imagine, you have wind and drag and pull and an atmosphere to work against. Here, out here (or inside this thing, depending on how you want to think of the anomaly) there is nothing, so it feels like nothing. You push forward on the joystick and there is a rumble of the engines, but that doesn't carry into the stick itself. We should have taken another tip from our days of playing video games and built force feedback into it: a rumble through the stick that worsened the more pressure you applied. Instead, the rumble comes around us in the ship itself. But it feels like sliding on ice, I suppose. There's nothing to stop us: no brakes, not in the conventional sense. I worry about where the anomaly is, because of what we saw the *Ishiguro* do at its end. And I know that we cannot pass back through. I don't want to collide with it; I don't want to relive this without hindsight. That such a death, such a ruination, could be my end over and over? It's unthinkable.

So I have read about how this works, and in the cockpit I have plotted a course based on the maps that we kept before. I do not know how far we have drifted: inside the anomaly there is no sense of place. The pings reach nothing, rebound from nothing, so I am in a void. I travel as slowly as it's possible for us to go using the fuel, and I watch as the battery recharges ever so slightly, heading up towards the halfway mark, moving back towards something resembling safety.

I can hear the play in the other room, rehearsals for what I will make the final performance. I can hear their screams, but I try to concentrate on flying. In this blackness I cannot even tell if we are actually moving or not; if we are stuck in it, thick black tar tugging at our wheels. I bring up the old map, with the pin where the *Ishiguro* was – because that was the wall, or near as damn it – and I plot us as we head towards that, the computers doing the work for me, the distance and the speed, and telling me that we are moving. Reassuring me, even.

It isn't long until we pass the point where we were static before: I watch it on the map, move to boosters rather than engines. This allows us to crawl forward. I am assuming that the wall will have moved, but I have no idea how much by. We inch – really, moving in tens of metres – and we're soon past where we sat and waited the first time. I zoom the map out, and there, in the distance, is the moon, and Earth, where all this started. We keep moving.

I don't know how I am going to do this when we get there. I have a window of opportunity, I know that, though I can try multiple times. I will send Inna through the wall, a corpse and destined to stay that way; and Hikaru with her. I am not sure how I feel about Easton yet. How feral he is. He probably didn't even think about what he was doing. He was trying to save himself. You can't stay alive for as long as he has, in his physical condition, without developing an innate self-preservation instinct. I wonder if that carries through cycles like an injury? Changes to your psyche, to the way that you think? Brutal, base natures? I wonder if Easton's journey made him what he is now, in that room, stabbing Hikaru. It's constant, every cycle. Never a flicker of doubt about what he should do or how he should react. I wonder if being as alone as he must have been made him desperate to survive.

And then I wake up when I feel the anomaly wall pressing against me, inside the ship, and I know that I have crossed the boundary, and I am scared. In that second I slam the booster into reverse, pushing us back, and I sit and shake, because that could have been worse; and because, when I look at the map, at the computer's calculations, we are so far past it. We have moved on so very far; but that cannot be my problem now.

I lock the ship into place as I hear her scream and cry, stabilizing and anchoring it with the boosters, and then I pull my helmet on. I check the seals this time, actually bothering to take the time to ensure my own safety: I have no desire to die out there an infinite amount of times for the rest of my life.

I wait for Easton to die. I watch it happen, to make sure, and as he does I take one of the final few stims: for the clarity, to drag my eyes open, to keep my here and now. Easton dies. There are no tricks: it's the same as every other time. His body floats, loose and yet stiff at the same time, and I open the interior airlock door and I drag it out. I tie it down to the rail at the far end, still unsure as to what I should do. He deserves peace, I tell myself. And what happens to his cycle if I remove the other players from the equation? Does he go insane and hunt me down? Is that how this ends? Either way, he is tied, and then I take Hikaru's body and Inna's, and I put them into the airlock space. I change my mind about Easton. I unclip him. I am not sure exactly what it is that he deserves, but this is what he's getting. I can offer some sort of peace, and I should. I clip them all to the tether rope, and me at the end, in case I need to pull myself back to the ship, and then I seal the internal door to block off the rest of the ship. I open the external airlock door, and we're outside. Or we are in this. We are not on the *Lära* any more.

I push them in front of me, all three of them, and they feel like nothing. We move through space, a train, and I talk to them as I go. I tell them that it will be all right; that I am doing this because it is all that I can do. It is my fault that they are out here, and that they have died, and that their families, their loved ones, will maybe never know. Or, I pray, maybe they will. Maybe they will be picked up, seen by something. Maybe there will be closure. Isn't that all any of us seek? An ending?

Because I don't want to give this a chance to reset itself, I watch them constantly, never taking my eyes off them, forcing myself to not blink, to keep focused. We move forward and forward, and nothing changes. In the distance, I know what these things are: Earth, waiting for us. I push the bodies, a pile-up, and Inna is facing me. I look at her as we go, and she is right there, held in my arms. I tell her things: that I will miss her, and that I am sorry, and then I feel it against me, and she is suddenly gone through. I did not see it coming. I had hoped, I think, that I would follow. The rules would change and I would be free, but I do not. Instead I feel it here, in front of me. They go, momentum carrying them. I wonder how far it will take them. I wonder if they will follow it on the path I have set, and, somehow, they might travel back to Earth; and then they might burn up in its atmosphere, as they head home.

I press myself to the anomaly, and I decide that the others deserve this as well. I go back to the ship, and I pull myself back to the living area and their beds. The beds are sealed, so I undo them. I try not to look as I pull their bodies out: I hold them by their sleeves. They look the same, because there's no bacteria in their beds, no air, nothing to let the rot set in. I pull them through, one by one. Lennox, Tobi, Wallace. I think about my mother as I pull their bodies to the airlock. I think about what she looked like after she was gone, and they called us, and said, Do you want to see her? Spend some time with her? Say some words? We told them that we had already said all that we had to say; and that her body would know nothing of what we would want to say to it.

I set the cycle and open the doors, and we are outside. I repeat myself, pushing them through. There is no ceremony, and they are gone. As I am floating, I think that I could pull my helmet off: that I could choke here, and maybe I would die and drift across; and maybe I would be on the other side, and I would stay dead. I think this but there's no way, I know, that I could ever do it. I am too afraid of death. I am too scared of that infinite nothingness.

And to think that people used to dream of an afterlife. That, for them, paradise was what happened when this was over. Somewhere that was worth dreaming of, that was worth thinking about instead of life. Instead there is nothing. I would bet my own life that there is nothing, and it is a bet that I would win; and the only reason that I would make that bet is because I am so sure that I would live after it.

I push the anomaly wall with my hands, and I set my

boosters going, one more attempt, and I struggle against it. When it doesn't move, when it doesn't change, I turn back to the ship, and I see the stretch of the expanse around me. I am so alone here, and I have never seen anything worse than this, and how incredible and mystifying and wonderful it is, and how deep; how black; how terrible.

14

The *Lära* is quiet without them here. They have left their blood from their final cycle: staining the walls in seemingly improbable places. There has been no reset of that: it is indelible. I tell myself that I really should clean it off, but that it will be a task. I am better at the floating, the swimming around. Not good enough yet, maybe. (Then a voice inside me asks what I am doing it for: whom I am cleaning the ship for. It is a voice I have to ignore.) But it's so quiet. I wasn't really aware. It feels like a lie, that it's more silent, and maybe I'm just noticing it more. They say that, that empty houses creak more than full ones, somehow. This house is the emptiest of all.

I sleep. I don't dream, or if I do it's unmemorable, and when I wake up I am still strapped to my bed, and the lights are still as they were, and the cycle hasn't restarted or anything. I am alone, still. I sit in the lab and look at the maps, of where I am now. I think about running calculations about how far the anomaly has moved – or grown – and where it could end up. I wonder if Tomas knows what I do about it. If he's got enough information to do research. I wonder if he changed his mind and launched our backup. They could be heading towards us, roaring through space, maybe even captained by Tomas. He could be explaining that they cannot go through the anomaly, because they won't come back. They will be careful. They won't dare take the risks that we did. (And even then, as I look on it, did we even take risks? Or did we just live this out as it made sense to do?)

I try and talk to him. 'Brother?' I say, into the ether. I hope that he's listening, but there's nothing. It makes sense for me to wait here, I tell myself, but of course I am wrong. Even as I think it I know that it is madness. Still: another day here, another night. However long they are.

I think that I might go back to using clocks.

I ask myself why I got into this. Why Tomas and I decided that it was something we should do. What on earth I wanted from it when I was a child, what I thought that it would be like to be a scientist. As we grew up and it became a realistic possibility, why did we not see it? That it was not about the questions or the answers, not really. It was about investors and results and returns. But what is the point of this if not to gather answers? About who we are, about our place in the universe? This is our eternal question, Tomas would say to me: man's eternal struggle. Why us? Why did we grow out of the ooze, why did we develop hands and eyes and consciousness? Is there really a chance that it was an accident?

Don't you want to know more? he would ask me, and I would say, Yes, of course. But he was more desperate than I. He was more inquisitive, more willing to do what we needed to do. He said, This cannot be all, and the anomaly might be part of something. It's a discovery, Mira, and we cannot throw away a discovery without knowing everything possible about it.

I lie in bed and think about Tomas, and what he would do. He is probably at home. Maybe they have had a funeral for me, because he knows what he condemned me to. Maybe he was there, with his baker, in another of his dark suits and thin ties with his glasses on, and maybe there he was smoking one of his cigarettes, and he said something, read a passage maybe, about me. Something poignant, from literature, about space and the stars and the notions of loss and loneliness; something that would speak to me now, and mean something, and ruin me were I to hear it. He wouldn't have cried, but his baker would have. She would have put on a show enough for both of them. And who would have been there for me? Maybe some of the researchers, or the attendants from the NISS. Maybe some of my old classmates, if they even remember me. Maybe one or more of our stepfathers might have put in an appearance, out of duty. I wonder if Tomas would stay for the wake.

At my lowest, I wonder about Easton, the journalist. What he must have seen. I wonder how he was old, and how the other version of him, the one that was jettisoned, was so young. I wonder what it means for the logic that I had assumed about the anomaly, and the effect that it has upon us. Where I had assumed that we were all in a loop, always dying, always living again, I wonder what he has been through: that the events of his life show on his body, not resetting as with Inna and Hikaru, but still there. I wonder if, in those final few days, as he died on my ship, if he felt his choking, his suffocation every time he awoke and had to play it again; if the only thing he could do was to take part in the deaths the way that they were happening, and if he knew that he was no longer alone, and now he was part of our loop, our cycle, our new way of him dying.

I am at my lowest when I think of this because it is another question that I will never have an answer to; another way in which I am just a failure, desperate and clawing for a truth.

I am wary to not stray too far from the screens, and the cockpit. We hadn't expected that the wall would be solid. Maybe we would have compensated, built some anti-collision technology into the ship if we had known. We met with manufacturers of every type of addition we could have stuck into this thing, all the little details that some might ignore but that engineers and money-men were trying to get us to shoe-horn in. Things that belonged on cars or airplanes. We ignored most of them. We said, The ship is going to be built for use, for practicalities and work. Anything else is a bonus, but we won't pay for those.

Sleep comes easily to me now, so I do it all the time. It lasts for hours and hours, and it is still and peaceful, and it rejuvenates. I wake up and feel rested for the first time in as long as I can remember. I don't know why I am not stressed; probably acceptance. My body has, however, begun to ache, so I exercise when I can. We have devices to do this, but very few, so I hold onto the table and force myself into squats, into working my arms and legs. I shower and I shave, finally. I look at my face and I think about how I am essentially becoming more human now, as it matters the least. How fastidious I am still, even though there is nobody here to judge me. Regardless, I judge myself.

Eventually I snap and I try to clean the ship as well. I

wash the blood off the walls in the room, where I can still almost see the ghosts of them going through their cycle. Going endlessly through their motions. I put gravity on – I can't see how to make a bucket of water and a sponge work any other way – and I stand on the benches and try to get it all. It runs when I wet it, making wide pink stains down the white walls, and I have to try and clean them up as well. Where it has stained and smeared the cold walls it has dried, like you find on the underside of paint-can lids, and that runs as soon as you wet it. My work multiplies, but it's the only way to get it done. I work corner to corner, hunting it out. I have no idea how Hikaru and Inna could make this much blood between them. I wonder, as I wet each individual part, if it's Hikaru or Inna's.

When the walls are pink and I can't get any more away I drag the hose from the shower cubicle in the changing area and put my thumb against the end, running the water and spraying it across the room to try to get the walls as wet as I can. It only works on the nearest, but the pink runs down and it seems like the stain isn't permanent. It gives me an idea: I wet all the other walls, soaking them, filling my bucket – actually a kidney bowl, the only thing I could find – and I throw water at them. When every wall is as wet as they can be, like the room has been hit by a localized storm, I put myself outside it in the corridor, seal the internal doors, and then set the airlock to open. Both doors, no safety measures. Suck all the liquid out of the room. I watch it on the video: it peels itself off the walls, almost. It's not perfect, but it's enough. When the room is nothing but space, I shut the doors and go back in. It's so white, and so bitterly cold.

I turn gravity off again, and I clean the whole ship, top

to bottom. I go through the drawers and see what we decided we would need, the stuff that we never touched. Cases of tools and replacement parts in the engine rooms; medical supplies, enough to run a full operating theatre; all this food, and so much of it Hikaru's bland, bleached awfulness; all the measuring tools in the lab, all the instruments and methods of data collection; games, in case we got bored. What chance to use any of those things? I rifle through the drawers, where everything is vacuum-packed and magnetically held down, and I laugh at this. Tomas and I had gone through so many different possibilities, different eventualities. We had decided that we needed to prepare for them all. We were idiots. This trip was a waste, I tell myself.

We have champagne in the cupboards, in these individual cartons. They were for when we discovered what the anomaly was. One of Tomas' suggestions, a way to celebrate our achievement. A last minute thought. I take one down and suck the sickly, fizzy liquid out of it in one go. And then another. And another. I tell myself that I'm a bad person for doing this. For even starting this trip, for initiating this stupid fucking concept in the first place. I have their blood on my hands. Five people's blood, and their families' hatred of me should and will be deserved. Tomas will bear the brunt of that, when we disappear. They will say that we should have prepared better. They won't care that we were abandoned, because they will never know. It will be buried, some secret that people will never realize. All they'll know is that the anomaly is something we didn't expect, that we can't account for. It can become a mystery. I drink another of the champagnes. Each is the equivalent of a glass. I can feel my head swimming more. I do not drink at home, usually. To celebrate something, birthdays or whatever, maybe a glass here and there. Drinking in space. Drinking in space! They'll ask why we didn't prepare for every eventuality, which is something that Tomas does not and will not have an answer to. He'll say that we prepared for what we could, but is that even true? The eyes of the world were on us, the great scientists, meant to explain what the unexplainable is, meant to reassure, and we couldn't even bring six people in a fucking capsule home. They've been doing that for years: since the middle of the last century. That's how long we've been sending people up here for, and it's something that we should have become good at. Instead we pushed ourselves and took leaps rather than working on perfecting what we knew, rather than removing risks. We took more. We said, Death found these people at this place. We should seek out death. We should try to stare it in the eyes.

I drink another of the flasks. I tell myself that I should save the rest. I should bide my time. I think about what happened, and I replay it all in my mind. I think about my last time with Inna. I think about her body, and peeling her apart, and seeing inside her. I wanted to know how bad it had been, and if I could have helped. My final stepfather once said, Put your skills to good use. Don't fritter it away, how intelligent you boys are. How good you are when you work on something together. Fix cancer, he said, rather than fucking around in the stars and with ships and with things that will never do anybody any good. And when our mother died, he came to the funeral even though they were not together, had not been together for many years, and he said, I told you so. He stood at the funeral and he said, You stupid assholes. You stupid fucking children. See what you could have done. Tomas and I knew how irrational it was: his suggestion. It would not have helped anything. We knew that he was being insane, because it was likely that we wouldn't have found a definitive cure.

There is nothing for me here. No way out. I look at the readings, of how long I have left, and I know that I cannot just sit here and wait for death to come to me. I can discover something myself: I can do what I came here for. I unclip myself and pull myself to the cockpit, and I turn on the engines and point the ship away from the wall of the anomaly. I plot a straight path, a straight line, deeper into the anomaly, into where – if my calculations are correct – I might find a centre, eventually. We will accelerate and then coast, and then I will see how far I can go in here. If this thing has an answer, I am going to head towards it.

The ship shakes, and so do my hands, and then I settle into the seat, and I have gravity back, and I feel, for the briefest of seconds, normal: moving forward, sitting, human.

There's nothing in here, the deeper you go. After a day of travelling I can see nothing. It's quite incredible, to look at it. I surround myself with screens in the lab and take the best 360-degree view that I can, and all I can see is blackness. If I turn the lights out and rely on the light from the screens, even though I know that they're broadcasting and connected, the only light comes from our ship and engines, burning at the bottoms of the screens. In the distance, as far as I can see, there is absolutely nothing.

And I think, How can I be so alone? How can I be this absolutely alone?

I think that I should sleep again. I am not tired, but this is what I have now. The ship is still accelerating, still slowly

gaining speed, and there is still weight in here. I walk to my
bed and I lie down and I shut the door and I talk to myself,
just to hear my voice; and in here, closed in, it reverberates.
In here, it's trapped. I think that I am talking to myself, and
also that I am talking to Tomas. This is for him as much as
it is for me: if he accidentally hears me, through the crackle
of static inside the anomaly.

'I am so useless,' I say. 'I have squandered it all. I have done
what I should not, and it's a waste. If you could see me now
you would say that I am broken, a foolish man who rode some
foolish dreams. And you're just as bad as I am,' I say, 'because
those dreams were ours. We allowed them to be here. We
allowed them to be all that we were. We were distracted, and
we failed.' I need a drink, water. I am too lazy to get up, even
though I am not tired, and in my throat I can feel the sick
rising from the champagne. Here, it's worse. Here, everything
is worse. 'I would tell you how my day was, but it was tanta-
mount to nothing.' I feel the vomit in my mouth, so I open
the door of the bed and cough it out. It floats; another thing
that I will have to clean up. I shut the door. 'I am ruined,' I
say. 'I wish that I would die, because then this would be over.
It couldn't be my choice, because I am so weak that I will
always choose life: even here, where death means nothing, and
life means nothing, and when I go, there will be nothing.' I am
picturing myself as an old man: dying of some horrific disease,
and then waking up and dying again. Perhaps my heart gives
up, or perhaps a cancer of my own. Or maybe in my sleep,
just that I stop working, and then I start again, a new cycle,
and I stop and start and stop. Perhaps that is already happening;
because how would I know? 'This is no way to live,' I say. I
am sobbing, and then I hear it: a voice, talking to me.

'Brother?' it asks, over and over. It's Tomas' voice, slinking through the nothing. I hear it as an echo, crackle-filled and pale from the speakers. Barely there at all, and if I wasn't listening, maybe I would have missed it. It is as an echo, almost nonexistent. 'Can you hear me?'

'Yes,' I say, but I'm not sure that it isn't a lie. I call to him, but there's no answer. In the darkness, with the bed shut, I say his name over and over. 'Where are you?' I ask.

There is no answer, and I wonder if it was just a ghost. If I was never meant to hear it in the first place.

I wake up and I say his name, first thing, in case. But there is no answer, not even the hiss of a connection. I wonder if I imagined it, last night. If I dreamed what it was that I wanted to happen. It is possible. I have never had an imagination, not really, but maybe this time. Maybe now is when I develop one. I get out of bed and discover that I am weightless again, so we must be going as fast as we can, now coasting; and I move to the cockpit and bring up the map, because I want to see where the computer thinks that we are. We have no way of knowing the centre of this thing, but if it is close to a sphere in shape, maybe we can guess. I start the program doing its work, and I lean back and shut my eyes, and then there comes a crackle from the speakers.

'Brother?'

'Yes!' I say. 'You're there!'

'I can't hear you,' he says. 'I can only hear static.' His voice fades in and out of the nothingness. I try and talk with him more, but there's nothing coming back to me. It's quiet again. It was definitely clearer than the night before, which makes me wonder if the anomaly is thinner than we thought. Maybe I'll be reaching the far side of it soon enough? Maybe that's where the signal is coming from. There's no anomaly wall, nothing to stop me leaving it. The other side of the membrane, an easy slip-through for me, and back to the real world. This is the first time that I have felt hope in a while, I think. 'Hello?' I ask.

'I'm here,' his voice says, and then it's gone again, fading into the crackle. I don't stop the ship, or turn around: I know that I have to keep going forward. Maybe I am heading towards an exit; maybe that is how I can hear him.

There is nothing left for it now.

I talk to him, to fill the silence. I think that I could go insane here alone if I was given half a chance, so I keep talking to him. His voice flits in and out of the conversation; occasional bursts of dialogue with me that amount to answers, monosyllabic or thereabouts, but still: this is a conversation. The relief I feel at that. I am just so glad that I am not alone any more.

In the morning, the first thing I do is to look at the computer's calculations. It has finished extrapolating where the middle of this could be, and it is so far away still. Past that, the other end of the anomaly. What might be an exit. There is no concept of being able to tell what is around me, and no way to tell if the ship's instruments are correct. No points of reference for anything. In the olden days, a ship could plot a course by the stars, because they were unchangeable, the constancy. I am here with nothing around me, nothing at all. The distance looks as if it could be feet away, maybe, or thousands of miles. There's no horizon. The map could be so wrong and I would never even know it.

I want to say, I am coming back to you. I want to say, I knew that you would not abandon me.

*   *   *

The ship is slowing down. I find it hard to tell, but it is slowing. I set the computer to track it and it does, and I do the math myself, seeing the numbers as they should be and then as they actually are. We are – I am – slowing inside here. There is drag inside the anomaly.

This should be a breakthrough. It should be a wonder: that this thing that doesn't exist in any real way that we can tell, this anomaly in the truest sense of the word, it has a form of some kind. It is real, and must be tangible. I celebrate, by myself, that there is evidence. There must be something I can collect to prove this; maybe I just don't have the tools yet. But still, there is work to be done.

Then I am alone, just me and my discovery. I try to tell Tomas but the line is dead, and I think about what it means as the ship slows and slows, and I realize that I will have to switch on the engines constantly, to keep us moving forward. That I will be burning fuel all the way to the edge of the anomaly. I have no choice: eventually I will run out, and the batteries will discharge over time, and then I will die.

Where will I begin from? Here? This moment of realization? I try to call Tomas again, over and over and over, and then I set the engines to burn to counteract the drag: only a small amount, to keep us coasting, top up the speed and make it seem like there's nothing slowing us down.

Me. Nothing slowing me down. That is the easiest thing to forget, through all of this.

We would always be in touch. From the tin-can telephones we made in the garden as children – running from his bedroom upstairs to the tree house, where I would sit and attempt to communicate with him – to the telephone call he made to me the night after he met his baker. She was asleep in the bedroom that they would eventually end up sharing, and he crept to the kitchen and opened the fridge, so as to have an excuse, and he called me. He whispered.

'She's nice,' he said.

'Good,' I told him. I was alone in my room, and I had been asleep. Or I told him that I had, I cannot remember which, accurately. 'You can tell me about her tomorrow.'

'I want you to meet her tomorrow,' he said. 'You can come with me, and we'll have lunch.'

'It seems very early,' I said. 'How do you know you won't have forgotten about her in a week?'

'And it would matter if I had?' He sounded affronted. 'I like her. You could make the effort.' This was so soon after our mother died, and he was over-compensating. He had found a woman who made the kitchen smell like a stereotype should, and who wanted to take care of him. Who appreciated how hard he worked. 'She wants to meet you.'

'I'm surprised you even mentioned me.'

'Of course I did. I told her all about what we're working on, and how important you are.'

'You broke the NDAs?'

'Don't be ridiculous, they don't count with her. She's a baker, Mira, not a spy. She doesn't care. She thinks it's amazing, you know, what we're working on.'

'You've jeopardized everything,' I said, 'for this woman you barely know?'

'Oh, goodnight, Brother,' he said. He hung up the phone and ended the conversation, a conversation that was mine to end. I think that's when it fell apart for us, because that's when we stopped talking, apart from when we were at work. He said to me once, a few months after that, that my jealousy was ruining our relationship. That we were brothers and surely that was more important than whatever animosity I felt towards the woman that he loved.

I tell him what has happened anyway, and I tell it to him every few hours in case he hears me. I send it out there to let him know what to expect, and how to prepare. When I finally get something back from him he sounds so exhausted and resigned. I say, 'I'm so pleased to hear from you.'

'I know,' he replies, but he sounds as if he doesn't feel the same. He is tired and sad, I think, as if he knows something that I do not. It's the static, I tell myself: it warps everything. To him, I wonder how I sound. If I sound as eager as I fear, as happy to speak to him as I expect I do.

'Are you far away?' I ask when I get the chance.

'Not far,' he says.

'You're here for me?'

'Yes,' he says, and then his voice is swallowed again. I spend the night surrounded by the screens as large as I can make them, in that blackness, and when it doesn't feel real enough I go to the airlock and open the external door. I press my face to the plastic window of the internal one and I watch through, no sign that we're even moving at all. I stay there for I don't know how long, but it's not out of pity: more a feeling that, despite how terrible it is out there, how I cannot understand what it is, we – that is, Tomas and I, working together as we should be – have beaten it.

I don't hear from him the next day. He is silent, even though I get static, and I wonder why. It makes me worry that whatever plan he had has fallen through, and that I'm now alone again.

It doesn't change how I spend my day. I spend it worrying:

about fuel, air, Tomas. I can barely eat for the worry, so I try one of Hikaru's white bars, one of the noodle bars. It's so bland that I keep it down easily, and then I feel guilty. I think that this cycle is better than the one he died doing.

Tomas speaks to me the next morning, and there's a clarity to his voice, to the transmission. He says, 'This will all work out, you know.' He is trying to make me feel better, and to bolster my spirits. He is my brother.

'I know,' I say. 'You sound closer.'

'I am.'

'And I am,' I say. It's nice. I smile, and I'm sure that he will be doing the same. It's something synchronous; we always liked it when that happened. People would ask us if it didn't annoy us, as twins, that we were lumped together. We would say that it made us feel better: that there were always the two of us in a situation, and we were so close that we knew we would never feel alone in our reactions. We always thought the same, until Mother died, until the baker, until this project pushed us apart. I say, 'I'm glad that you didn't forget about me.'

'How could I?' he says.

'I thought that you were abandoning me before.'

'No,' he says. 'I couldn't do that.' He still sounds so sad. I wonder if he has had just as much trouble getting to me as we had getting here in the first place.

'Do you swear? That you won't abandon me in here?'

'I swear,' he says.

'How long until I see you?' I ask.

'Another twelve days, by my calculations,' he says.

'Twelve days? That's all the fuel I have!'

'It's going to be close,' he says. 'Very close.'

'And you're heading towards me as well?'

'No,' he says. 'I can't. It's just you, Mira. It's all on you.' And then he's gone, and I am alone again. Twelve days. I can do this. I have gone longer, I tell myself, when it was self-imposed.

'Do you ever think back to when we were children?' I ask him. I have always assumed that he never did: that he was too preoccupied with moving forward. Constantly moving forward, never dwelling on what happened before. 'I think about it,' I say, 'because I wonder what made us who we were. What made us different.'

'I think about it,' he says. There's such a fuzz on his voice, but so unmistakably him. 'I think about it all the time.'

'Because it mattered to you? I thought that we had a good childhood.'

'We did.'

'So what happened?' I ask. The static is too strong, I think, because he doesn't answer. So I lie there and try to sleep, and to forget about the gnawing inside me. Suddenly I find it difficult again. There is pressure on me now; and maybe I will miss something, something important. Maybe he will tell me something, and I will not hear it.

15

I don't know if Tomas' plan to rescue me involves me alone, or me and the ship. I tell myself that it would be nice to take this all back, considering who it is named after. It's fine to have a backup, but it will have a different name. He will have named it something pompous and inglorious, I should imagine. A seemingly well-chosen word like *Bravery* or *Temerity*. Something that sounds like a ship's name but that he feels represents a facet of himself and the trip we have made. Or that he will have made. *Discovery*, maybe. Maybe that's too impressive. He'll want some level of boastful subtlety. There is a part of me that wonders if the rescue he is conducting was part of this: that it's a glory he will attain for himself, that I will have no part of. I wonder if he knew what would happen with the anomaly, and didn't tell me. I suppose that it's something I will always have to wonder.

I clean everything top to bottom again. I want the ship to be in pristine condition when he sees it: to show that, while I could not save the crew, I have saved this. The investment;

our creation. I clean out the beds that my crewmates' bodies were put into. I change into one of the spacesuits, because then I can shut myself in their beds and breathe through the oxygen tanks, and I don't need to worry about taking in their death. Besides which, the suits are comfortable. I can wear this through, and when he sees me, I will look as though I belong out here. I am a professional.

I eat when I like. I try and talk to Tomas: this is a constant process, where I call for him and try to get him to answer. He crackles in, and he makes excuses, which is typical.

'It's hard to get a connection,' he says.

'Did you have to adapt the radios to the anomaly?'

'Yes,' he says.

'How did you do it?' I ask. I feel like I'm constantly suspicious.

'I don't know,' he says. 'They just told me that they got it working.' He's lying. There's nothing that he won't understand when his staff explain it to him. And, for that matter, that he won't have asked about. They will have said it was working; he will have wanted to know how. He's an inquisitive mind.

'What's keeping you so busy?' I ask.

'Research,' he says. He sounds exhausted, as if he's not sleeping. If he's anything like me, he isn't, not at this stage of his trip. And he is exactly like me.

Eleven days. He is more talkative today, and I ask him how he is. He says, 'I'm fine. I'm tired.' He doesn't ask how I am, but I tell him.

'You don't know what it's been like,' I say. 'Out here, all alone. And how they all died.'

'I know,' he says.

267

'No you don't. You haven't even asked about Inna and Hikaru. You haven't asked me anything about what happened.'

'Oh,' he says.

'Don't you want to talk about it? Don't you think we should?'

'No,' he says, then, 'I've seen some parts, from the camera footage. I assumed you wouldn't want to go into it.'

'I have had nobody to talk to.' I think about how weak this connection between us is: how much data could they have really streamed? 'Where are you?'

'The far side of the anomaly,' he says.

'Why is the connection so bad?'

'You can't expect it to be perfect,' he tells me. 'Not where we are, in this situation.' He crackles. I feel like I am in some ancient comedy movie, and the man on the phone is faking driving into a tunnel. I don't trust Tomas. I say it aloud – 'I don't trust you,' I say – but I don't know if he's listening, because all I get from his end is the static.

Ten days and the darkness is getting to be too much. The lights from the ship feel too artificial, and all I want from the minute that I wake up is to see something else real. I try to call Tomas but there's no reply, so I think about what we have. I stare at the engines. I surround myself with screens of the outside, but it makes no difference. It reminds me of car drives when I was a kid, in storms. Parts of Europe where they didn't have road-lights, and my stepfather would some-times switch the lights off on the car to scare us. He would make a noise, and wobble the car, knowing the road so well that he knew how safe we were. Tomas and I would howl in that laughing-scared way. Fuck.

I push myself to facing the floor. I am finally becoming

adept at this, mastering how my body works here. I can see how it's an art. I ache all over, but that's probably an effect of how little I've been resting. And this puts such a stress on your bones. The bone loss is minute, but it's there. Atrophy of muscles, loss of bone, wearing down of tissue. A slackening of what holds you together. I think about Easton, and what a zombie he was: barely even human. There is so much that I wish I could have asked him about his trip. That mystery, only partly solved. I wonder how this will play out from here on. I tell myself that I have no interest in ending my life like him, stuck in some loop I cannot escape from. Instead I will escape altogether.

I can see nothing, though. There is something, I think, and then I realize it's a reflection, the light from above making the floor shine through the projection of the screen. That makes me laugh: what here isn't just reflection? The cycles; the darkness; so even.

It's been such a short amount of time without company, and yet I already understand how Cormac could go insane.

Tomas will be waiting in the ship for me. It will not be the perfect trip that he envisioned, and I will be blameless in losing the crew of my trip, because the anomaly is so far beyond comprehension that it renders all blame ineffective, all concepts of understanding new. He will say, I've missed you. We'll embrace. Do you know that we haven't had an embrace since Mother's funeral? He apologizes for what happened, for abandoning me. He explains: that it was never meant to be permanent, but that it was necessary. It was our goal, he said. (Even in my fantasies he is selfish.) He says, As soon as it happened I rerouted everything to save you, Brother. All of our resources, every single man and woman we have here working on the goal of saving you. You've been on the front page of every news-site, he tells me. He shows me them, the stories floating in the air on the screens. They proclaim me a Hero. I will ask about my crew, and if I am a pariah now. He says that the families understand. They gave their lives for the greater good, he says, ever the utilitarian.

On the ship I will recover. We're going home, Tomas will tell me. We'll sleep that part of the journey: travelling faster. I'll have a bed, and we will climb into ours, next to each other, and he will tell me what's been happening as we go to sleep. He'll tell me about the rescue effort, and how he decided to personally man the ship, and how the research part of our career – of our lives, when we get down to it – is complete. We have discovered the anomaly, he tells me, and that's enough. We know what it is.

What is it? I will ask him, and he'll tell me. He'll have it all worked out. All the work we did, the research. The thousands of hours. I'll tell him that I have never felt like much of a scientist, and he'll say, Don't be ridiculous. You're as much of one as I am. Look at what we have discovered, he'll tell me. All you are now is a name in history, and whatever else you are from this point, that doesn't matter. You can go and be quiet, if you like. You can take a life away from this. I'll ask him what we will do, and he'll say, Whatever you like. We're brothers, and we're meant to do this together.

And I will tell him about what happened to me after he left me in the anomaly. I'll tell him about Inna and Hikaru and their cycle, and Easton, how we found him. He will tell me that it's okay that I don't feel guilt. That I don't really feel anything at all. I'll tell him about Inna's tattoo, and that she was ill. I won't tell him about the scar that made the bird what it was, because that's mine. Mine and hers.

He'll tell me to sleep then. There is something so comforting about that, being given that permission, so I will. I take his advice. He is older than I am, but not by much. And when we wake up, I can look out at the Earth coming towards us. It'll be a marble first, and then bigger, and then we will be descending. We will come in like a plane, doing everything we can to slow our descent. This is the part I haven't been looking forward to, I'll tell him, and he'll say, After what you've been through, this should be a breeze. I will notice that his birthmark is gone: dug out and rebuilt or recoloured or something, and that he looks exactly like I do. I'll ask about it, and he'll say, There was no point in either of us being more special than the other. I wanted parity. That will bring us closer together, and everything else the past however-many years will cease to matter.

When we land there will be a press conference. They will ask me how hard it has been, the trip and the deaths and being alone. I'll say, You don't know how hard. The hardest thing. But then they'll celebrate, and they will stop asking about Inna, and they'll laud us for what we've done. A podium finish, like racing drivers, with champagne, myself and Tomas. Applause.

At home, the baker will be there, and she will have made a cake. I can forgive her, I think. (I question my own fantasy, that she is still here. Maybe I don't hate her as I thought.) The cake has my name on it: Mira, in stars. The next day Tomas and I go to our mother's grave and we stand over it, and he says that he forgives me for how her life ended. He says, I am proud of you, Mira. Her grave says, Beloved Mother To Sons, and nothing else. Not our names, our full names, as he inscribed them. He's changed it.

We work with the agencies to help them look at the anomaly. They want to know if it's still coming towards

Earth, and what it will do when it arrives. They sit me down and ask me to describe what we'll face. I say, I cannot. I leave. I go to the wilds, and we never speak of it, because we'll be dead before it arrives. Because we have to be. I don't know how that will happen, or where or when. But it will be coming.

The fantasy ends quickly. I am alone and alive and in the ship, and I can see the nothingness.

'Tomas?' I ask.

'I can't talk,' he says. 'I'm sorry.' There's not even the pretence of static, or the realness of static, whichever. He just cuts the call. He sounds devastated. Like this is all coming to an end, or that he knows that it is somehow actually not at all real.

Nine days.

I am lost and lonely, and I am a man who needs to be the opposite of these things. I am a man who needs people, I have discovered; or a specific person. Tomas' presence has lightened my mood, and my feelings. It has made me feel less as though this is inevitable. As if maybe I will get out of this alive.

I clean more, as if that is all I have to do. There is a part of the ship where the blood has crusted a seal, and I can see the line where it is. It has snuck inside the bowels of the ship herself, and I decide that I want to clean this. I cannot get the cleaning instruments into the gap enough, where the wall and the floor meet, which means I have to go inside the wall to reach it. In the engine rooms there is panel to allow the engineering team to reach the insides of the ship. All around the thing, around every room, there is at least a foot of space between the interior and the start of the hull. They could get into it, to fit everything, to make sure that the turbine – which circles every part of the ship – works properly. The panel is easily removed, and then I can see into the ship itself. It's like a secret: seeing how something works. I think of Inna, and I climb in. A tight fit, for a few feet, and then I'm behind the wall. It's warm and dark. The turbine is off, so I can be in here. Otherwise the ring inside the hull would rotate, like the drum of a washing machine, and I would be killed. I creep forward, knowing where to go. It's close. They press against me, the walls, and I edge into where it is even darker. There's no light bleed until you reach the edge of a room, and then I am tracking along the corridor. A dip as I reach the changing rooms, the airlock, and I have to enter a smaller passage, a crawl-space. It runs underneath the airlock itself, and it's hard: hauling myself down, trying to stay under there. Pressed up against it, on my back, pulling myself along. Under here, it smells of something stale and metallic, which means I am at the right place. I feel it with my fingers: the blood. I don't know whose it is, but I clean it as best I can. In here, it's so dark: I only make it lighter when I get the blood out of the crack and the light from the room can poke through.

Getting the blood all gone from the ship is good. It's better. It feels cathartic, as if maybe, for a second, I can pretend that this never happened. I go from room to room and check everything, and I finally cannot see any anywhere. The ship is clean, almost back to where it started. I am the only evidence that we have ever been anywhere. Me, and the empty drawers.

Tomas messages me as I am trying to sleep.

'I wanted to see if you are still there,' he says.

'Why wouldn't I be?'

'I don't know. Sometimes I think that you are less than real. I can't believe this.'

'You left me for dead,' I say. He is silent. 'Don't you have anything to say?' I ask him.

'I don't know,' he says.

'You could apologize,' I tell him.

'No I couldn't,' he says. The connection severs.

I try and work out where Tomas could be. This seems like a sensible way to spend my time: exercising my brain. Putting anything I have up here to good use. This was always my flaw, I think. I could never just stop and be. Tomas was able to do everything, to multitask, to do his dating and his fucking and his work and somehow get it all right. He was hampered: he was the imperfect one, the one who was neglected when I was a miracle. He had the birthmark: I was physically perfect. But then, he excelled and I did not. I was the one whom they did tests on when we were children, who had the extra time to do his exams. He is no less intelligent, they said. He just needs more care. I was the one whom Tomas had to look after. Everything about us leads to this: him as my salvation, and still I know he is lying to me. He has always lied, because it's easier for him. And why should I trust him, I want to know. I want to ask him, but the connection is dead, so I plot his route instead. I try to see where he could have left from and where he could be now, if I make educated assumptions concerning my own trajectory. Assuming he can see me, and it's just me that cannot see him. Assuming that he is here to rescue me, and not luring me deeper into this thing for his precious fucking research. Nothing but assumptions. He had a thing he used to say about that, a pithy little joke that he threw out to embarrass me when I used the word. When we were researching, I used it a lot. So much of science is based on assumptions. We assumed that the anomaly would be something we could just read from, something benign and yet explainable. I can hear his pith in my mind, rolling around.

He would say, We should have researched more.

After a day of working on it, I cannot fathom where he can be. The estimations of the anomaly are huge and all-encompassing, and I put a pin into the map to represent where we could end up, based on trajectory and speed and assuming that I travel at normal parameters inside this thing. Assuming I burn fuel normally and that the drag – and therefore my speed – is constant. He can't be there, because I can't work out how he would reach that point. I can't see how, from earth, in the time that he had; flying around it, riding its curvature, coming in from the rear. I imagine it as many ways as I am capable of doing and I simply cannot see it. There is something about this that all feels too inevitable.

So I try options: that maybe he left before he said, that we were talking from somewhere closer, and he was lying to me; that he is lying now, but somehow has managed to find a way to communicate with me from Earth, even though the lag is less; that I have been here for longer than I thought. The last one burns. It would mean that I have died somehow, and am part of a cycle. I wouldn't even realize, would I? I would be stuck here, somehow in this loop, and he might have been out here for months looking for me. Maybe years. I have thought about how they work: some consideration about what makes them begin, what defines them. I touch myself, feel my body, as if that might give me a sign. Maybe I have been here for more time than I realize, and he has found a way out. Maybe we are different ages; brothers now,

275

no longer twins. No longer even close to identical. We wear different skins entirely.

It nags at me. I cannot fathom him lying to me, not like this; though it explains so much. It explains the hesitation in his voice, the trepidation, the fear. What if I was in a loop and he has found a way to break it? What if they are trying to talk me out of the anomaly without me dying, undoing all their good work? I try to work out the fastest Tomas could get to the point he claims, if he slept the whole way, if they had somehow added fuel tanks, replaced life-support systems with backup fuel, made the ship more cramped. Maybe only brought a crew of three, say, to run it. A skeleton staff. It's still days and days out. Maybe he's telling me his projected time? Maybe the point at which we will coalesce?

I message him. I am determined to ask him. I message over and over, nagging him, not even saying anything but his name, calling into the darkness. Eventually he answers, after I don't even know how long.

'What do you want?' he asks.

'Where are you?'

'I don't know,' he says. He barely sounds like the same man. He sounds broken, more broken than I am, even. Not like a man who is on a rescue.

'You said that I was twelve days away from seeing you. Now it's only seven.'

'Yes,' he says.

'So how are you that far into space so quickly? How did you find the other edge of the anomaly?'

'I didn't,' he says.

'So where am I to meet you?' I ask.

'At the centre of this thing,' he tells me. 'I'm right in the middle, I think.'

276

James Smythe

'What's in the middle?' I ask him, but he doesn't answer. I think he has gone, because it's silent apart from a hiss, but maybe that's him sobbing in the fug, or maybe it's laughter. I don't know. I can't tell.

It preoccupies me throughout the entirety of the sixth day before I will see him: whether this means I am not to be rescued after all. What it means to me to be pushing through this darkness. And it has a centre, and it's six days away. In the lab I estimate the size of it. I draw it as a black circle, and it engulfs so much of space. It's gargantuan. It fills the space between where I am now and the far beyond. I wonder if it's moving or growing. I wonder if that's making a difference. I draw the circle darker on the map, not translucent, blotting out the stars. I leave the *Lära* there as a pin, but it will make no difference to anything.

I wonder how he ended up in here. If he came in after me, or if it was an accident. If, somehow, his journey mirrored my own. We have that a lot, where we find that we say we would have done things differently only to discover that in reality we would do them in exactly the same way. It's very easy to think that you're distinct and individual when you are a twin, but actually you are nothing of the sort. It's an accident to think the same way as another. I try and talk to him but he doesn't answer.

I wonder if he is as trapped as I am. If he has called this a rescue, sold it to me, but really he is alone out here. I wonder if he's adrift; if he has asked me to come to him to rescue *him*. The tables turned. He'd never admit that, not outright. He would thank me later. My fantasy of this is of me getting home, but maybe that's impossible. Maybe what's possible is getting him back. It is not getting home, but the two of us,

277

we could work out how to free ourselves. Between us we could muster the fuel needed, the ideas. How to extricate ourselves. He has a connection that works, the ability to message me. Maybe he's still in contact with home. We could send our data home, keep them informed, answer the question of the anomaly. Isn't that what this has all been about, really?

I tell myself that I should make peace with it. There are five days until I see him, and he seems to be holding up worse than I am. He makes contact today, and asks me over and over where I am. I say, 'I don't have any reference points.'

'Find some,' he tells me. So I sit and I stare, and I try to see anything out of any of the screens. I drag them to their maximum possible resolution, their highest zoom, and I try to find even a speck in the darkness that I can latch onto. I tell him where I am on the map, on my old star charts. Where I should be, if the anomaly is true: the distance from home, the distance to our closest planets. I give him coordinates, but he laughs them off.

'You think those are right?' he asks. 'You think that they mean anything?'

'How can they not?' I ask him. 'You said I'm now five days from you. There must be constancy,' I say, 'or you would not have been able to predict that so ably, would you?'

'You're so fucking naïve,' he says. 'That's your problem, it's always been your problem. You're too naïve, and you're a coward, and you refuse to see this for what it is.'

'So tell me what it is!' I say.

'I can't,' he says. 'Not yet.'

'Why not? Won't it help me? Help us?'

'You'll see,' he tells me. 'You'll see.'

* * *

On the fourth-last day, I see something on the screens. I don't know what it is: a dot, even at the largest zoom. I strain myself getting close to it. It's barely even a pixel, barely anything at all. It's something in the distance, and I am headed for it. I wonder if it's Tomas. I message him, and I talk to myself, to the quiet on the other end, that it must be.

'I can see you, I think,' I say. 'Can you see me? You should be able to, as a speck.' I give him my coordinates again, but he doesn't answer. I spend the day attached to a bench and watching the speck grow. It's barely visible. It grows as flecks of dust grow: it amasses until there is just even more of that very same dust.

Three days to go, and he wakes me. 'Did you ever think that this would happen?' he asks. He sounds ill. He sounds like there's something terribly wrong. I can tell, because his voice is not what it should be.

'No,' I say. 'We didn't prepare for this, did we?' I lie in my bed, strapped down. 'We didn't have a plan for this. No contingency.'

'No, we didn't.' He is gulping a lot.

'Are you lying down?' I ask.

'Yes,' he says. 'As are you.'

'I am.' He coughs. 'What's wrong?' I ask him, but he coughs more, and then there's a retch. Vomit. I can hear him spitting it up on the other end of the connection. I try and talk to him, to get him to listen to me, but he doesn't reply, and the silence floods in. It's another five minutes before he says anything.

'Are you scared?' he asks.

'Of what?'

'Of what happens now. What's going to happen.'

'No,' I say. That's a lie. I am waiting for his reveal: as he shows me that he is as duplicitous as I fear. That he'll stab me again, and this will be a test, and I will be his lab rat.

'Okay,' he says. He's warning me. He goes then, and I can't get him back.

The dust speck is now something else. A larger speck. A ship, I know. I can see it, in the same way as I once saw the *Ishiguro*. I can't even think how long ago that was. I still worry that it was longer than it seems, that I am playing tricks on myself. But this in the distance is a ship, definitely. I can tell from the shape, the rough shape of it. It looks like the ship that I'm on: meaning that it's the backup. I still haven't asked Tomas about how he got out here, and why he's here. Why he didn't just leave me to die. I watch the ship-speck get closer and closer. Forty-eight hours and I will be next to it, and I'll climb aboard. And whatever happens, I will be with Tomas, which is better than being in this alone.

I have another fantasy. Perhaps I shouldn't call it that, as that suggests a desire for it to become true. But:

He and I are on our ship. We are together and we are growing older. He is dying, of something or other. Hunger. Thirst. Everything is recycled, and there is only so much of this. We are stuck inside this thing, this anomaly, and we cannot escape. He sacrificed himself for me – maybe that's the part of this that I like? that I am attached to? – and that's that. I watch him die, and then, as he dies, he chokes himself awake. He fits and sputters and chokes and then wakes again, and then he dies and then he wakes. I have seen the cycles when this is unnatural, when it's forced onto people, but not when they just stop. When their bodies are done.

Will the anomaly force them back into life? Is that something that it can even do? Will they live forever?

I watch the ship get bigger and bigger. People throw déjà vu around, as something that occurs when they do something that reminds them of another time. That isn't it. Déjà vu, real déjà vu, it's a chemical imbalance. It's a reaction where your brain can't parse what's happening and it turns it around. It ruins a moment of peaceful memory for you by adding dizziness, nausea into the mix. Watching this now all I have is a sense that I have been this impatient before. The ship starts as something small and generic, and then I see it exactly as it is. It's this ship, exactly this ship. Even down to the lettering on the side. *Lära*, it says. My mother's name; and also the name of Tomas' baker. I said to him, Can't you see what she is to you? What you're doing with her? And he said, She has the same name. It's a common name, and what is it to you? So when I suggested we name the ship after Mother, he wasn't happy. I said, I don't care. I look for a suffix, for a Two or a B or something else, something distinct, to see what he has done to differentiate us. I want to see if this twin has its own birthmark.

Then it is the size of the desk, on full zoom. I can see it sitting still and immovable. The boosters are not on; they're not holding it in place, which means it's drifting. The lights are on, though. It's not a power loss.

'You're looking at me, aren't you?' Tomas asks, over the speakers.

'How did you know?' He snorts at my question. He's silent, then, despite my prodding. I say, 'If you won't talk to me, listen to me. I am only a while away. Are you in trouble?'

I don't get an answer for hours, and then he says, 'Yes.' But even when I ask what he means, he doesn't say.

* * *

I can count how long it will be until we are together in hours now instead of days. I am lucky, I think, because one way or another I will be out of here, and I will no longer be alone. I could have lost all sense of who I am in this, after the crew died. And to say it, I still feel no guilt. I wonder if that's my problem. That I should have felt more. I wonder if that makes me a bad person. Seems to me that if I had focused on it, I would have lost myself.

I look at the blackness. It's my hope that Tomas and I can put our heads together and save ourselves from this. But if we don't – if he's lying to me, if he's as stuck here as I am – then I am still okay. It's better to not be alone as you die, I think. That's what our mother said to me as I sat with her. She said, This tells me so much about your love for me, and I said, It should never have been in question.

I message Tomas. He is barely there: a shell of a voice, a fragment, broken and devoid. He says, 'You're nearly here.'

'I am,' I say. I try to sound excited: to lift the tone. 'I am only hours away.'

'You're anticipating reconciliation.'

'Aren't you?' He snorts. 'Listen,' I say, 'I want to know if you knew that this would happen. All along, when you abandoned me. I need to know, Tomas. You understand that?'

'I understand so much more than you,' he says. He sounds like he's a ruined man. I wonder what he had to sacrifice to come out here to me.

'You don't sound happy to be seeing me,' I say.

'How could I be?' he asks. 'Knowing what I know now?' Then he severs the connection, and he's gone. But his ship is there, right in front of me. There are so many things I want to ask him. I strap myself into the cockpit seat and watch on the screens in real-time as it gets bigger and bigger, and I get closer and closer to him.

His ship looks tired from this angle. I wonder what it's been through to get here. I want to hear all of his stories, every single one. How he got here so quickly; how he came to be inside the anomaly; and he hasn't mentioned a crew, so I want to know what happened to them; and why is he here? Is it for me? I hail him as I get closer, but there's no reply. I say, 'I need to come aboard,' but there's nothing.

As we get closer still, I ponder his suggestion that we are near the centre of the anomaly. How did he know that? How could he? There's nothing here to tell me that, and nothing to allay my thought that we shall never escape it. I wonder what state I will find him in. If he'll be as broken as his conversations with me would suggest.

I'm scared of damaging the ship – either ship – so I stop far before I reach it. Hikaru would have been able to do something better with this. Maybe drive us alongside it, allow us to almost connect the doors together. That's why he was a pilot and I am not. I stop the ship with the boosters, and it's harsh and hard, gravity back, thrown into the chairs, but they work. They do what we wanted them to do.

'Where are you?' I ask. 'Why aren't you answering?' It's so quiet on the other end of the line. 'Tomas?' I say, but he doesn't answer. I check my suit, take a helmet, attach it. I have a fully replenished tank of oxygen, and I seal the airlock from the rest of the ship, leaving the door open for me. And then I'm in space, or the anomaly. The darkness. It's so cloying out here. A foot in front of you looks like the far-off distance, looks exactly the same. There is no light in here – nothing from the sun coming through, and you cannot even see out, from in here: the darkness is too much. It's like fog, only there's nothing tangible here. Just nothingness, all around.

I move through it, though, towards the other *Lära*, and I circle her. I will miss this, just as I get better at it. I can really feel myself growing in these circumstances. Perhaps I was always destined to be out here and alone. I feel like I am beginning to discover exactly who it is that I am.

The airlock of this other *Lära* is open. Tomas is waiting for me, as he said he would be. I get to it and pull myself inside, and I seal the door, start the decompression. It only takes seconds, but it's still enough to make me anxious. I look for Tomas here, waiting for me, but he's not. He's nowhere to be seen, not in this room. It looks exactly the same as ours, which makes sense, because we built them to be the same. Hewn from exactly the same plastics and metals and moulds.

'Hello?' I call as I step out. I check the changing area, the corridor, the engine rooms, the lab, the lounge, the cockpit, but he isn't here. It is pristine, as if it has never been used. I spend time pulling myself around every room, ending in the lab. The only sign of life: my notes, my handwriting. The orange map that I made, with the anomaly on it and a pin in it showing where the ship is. 'Hello?' I shout, but the ship is, apart from me, empty. He's not here, and, as I look at this exact duplicate of the ship I have just left, I realize that he has never been; or he has always been; or he will be, now.

It was as I thought: inevitable.

Somehow, now, I am more alone than I have ever been before.

16

I panic, and am terrified. I leave this ship, because it is wrong, and it has no place here. It is a lie, as all of this is a lie, and I swim through the anomaly to my *Lära*, my original version, untainted, truthful and honest, and I cling to the rail when I am safe inside the airlock. I start the engines, the boosters, turning the ship in the nothing. We rotate, and I look for the other *Lära*, the facsimile, but it is gone, and I am in its place; the same position, facing the same way, drifting and fitting into the lie in its entirety. I stop the engines and I weep, because I have no other choice. I feel sorry for myself; I feel as though I am responsible for this. From day one, I have been leading towards this.

I have made my own bed, and it is the same as it has always been, ever since we came out here. Now, I must lie in it.

I have to test this. I have to see if this is true, so I sit at the console and I open the radio and it is at the right frequency, of course it is, because it is the same frequency; and I say his name – my name – into the darkness, to see if I will answer.

'Brother?' There is static and nothingness. A gap, a pause, a wait in the air. 'Can you hear me?' I ask, knowing that he can. He replies. I can only hear myself in his voice, now. Nothing of Tomas in it at all. People always used to say that we sounded the same but I could never hear it. I can hear him asking more questions, but I don't have answers. I don't want to ruin him; I'm not even sure that I can if I want to. He still has hope, or he does now. I remember that feeling. I had it once, but now it is gone; or replaced, by whatever I will leave this ship for in fourteen days, and not come back to.

He is so happy to hear from me. I say his name and he bursts with joy. I don't remember sounding like this, but then, that's not surprising. Back then I was preoccupied with getting somewhere. Now I am stuck. I have to wait. I have to meet him before I see whatever it is that I am going to see. The connection isn't good, so I tell him about the static. It fades out and in, and I think that I should stop talking to him. It's easier. I can barely bear to hear his voice, because it does remind me so much of Tomas.

I wonder what Tomas is doing now. Fuck him, fuck him, fuck him.

He asks me about when we were kids. Our childhood. He doesn't know that it was the same. He asks if I ever think about it, and I say that I do. I cannot lie to him; not any more.

'All the time,' I say. He's so desperate. He thinks that it means something, that we are close. Tomas thinks about our

286

best times. He is so pathetic, I think. I am just like this, fawning at the altar of the one who would have surrendered me to this abyss, this maw. He wants to think that Tomas thought well of him, when in fact it was nothing but abandonment. I was a sacrifice to science. I wonder if he still thinks of me. If he wishes he could do it again.

The slow-fade of my mood as I try to forgive him. I reach out to my memories of how Tomas and I were and I try to think of a reason that I shouldn't harbour the grudge that I do, that I will, until the day that I die. Who am I kidding, I think; I am already dead. I don't say a word to the other Mira, because I am so angry. I want to tell him not to trust Tomas – not to trust me – but I can't. Because there's something else. There was a version of me here, and then it was gone. When I found the new version of the ship, or the old version, or the copy, I was not here. I must have gone out there into the darkness. It's a lure in the purest sense: the fish approaches the line with no idea what it's getting into.

I want to placate him. I can't remember our exact conversations, so I rely on my gut. That seems to make the most sense.

'This will all work out, you know.' I hope that I sound convincing. I am talking to myself as much as I am talking to him. I decide that I have a part to play: that of my brother. He wants to know that this is all right. I remember enough: that he was suffering. So I put the mask on, and I channel Tomas Hyvönen, master of all he surveyed; the brother who had something to prove, and proved it over and over, at the sacrifice of all others. Mira, the Mira coming through space with eagerness and hope, says that he thought he was abandoned, and I, a false Tomas, give him peace, for a moment at least. I tell him that I could never do that. I swear it to him. He asks how far away he is from me, and I tell him. I know exactly how far.

I don't sleep. I can't. I am worried about getting this right. About what it means, whether I'm in a cycle or not. I mean, I am. But at what stage, and whether I can break it. And if, therefore, I'm going to die. I'm going to die and somehow see myself.

Where do I go when I leave this ship? What happens to me? The other version of me wants to talk about Hikaru and Inna, and I cannot bear it. I don't want to think about them. I just want to move on. I want to tell him that he gave them an ending, that he finished their journey for them. That that should have been enough. Maybe I don't know him as well as I thought I did?

That thought alone makes me laugh. I remember that I wondered if there was something wrong, as the person I thought was Tomas signed off unnaturally. Now, I stifle my laughter as I do it. I think about how confused I am leaving myself. When he is gone I stare at the anomaly. That's all there is to do when you are perfectly still: stare at it.

What's left? After this, what is left?

I feel sick. I drank too much. I have finished the champagne. I have not eaten in two days, and I don't know why. I shout at Tomas, as pointless as it is. I scream his name into the ship, and I tell him what I think of him. I call him so many words. He has put me here. He is responsible for their deaths.

288

He is the one who should feel guilty, not me. Not for any of this.

'Tomas?'

'I can't talk,' I say. And then, 'I'm sorry.' Because I am apologizing to him, not Tomas. I am not the sort of man to abandon you. I will try to help you: that's who I am, now.

I still haven't slept. My body won't let me. I haven't shaved, haven't washed. I am becoming who I will become, and it is not who I was. I cared, before. Do you remember that? Once, I gave a shit.

I question this: that maybe I am imagining it all. That I am still alone. This is me and my psyche, and we're battling. This is a struggle, a tug of war that I am having, and losing. Winning would mean sanity. Winning might mean no longer being alone, because being alone means that there is nothing. Nothing left at all. It would make sense that I would imagine myself as Tomas, maybe. Maybe I should paint my face: the birthmark, blood-stained, covering my head.

'I wanted to see if you are still there,' I say to the other Mira. I want to know that he is real. He asks me why I – Tomas – left him to die. I cannot give him a satisfying answer. I can only let it hang there, and wish that I could tell him. I wish that I could tell him why our brother decided that we were not worth saving.

Still no sleep. I see things, out there, in the anomaly. I put screens everywhere I can around the ship showing the camera views of the outside. I don't know which direction is which, other than this. And there, in the darkness, I see something. A glimmer. It's there and then it's gone. I pull the screens up, look at them. Try to find it. There's nothing. I am seeing things, I tell myself. All that's there is the black that's always there. Why would there be anything else? How could there be anything else?

He talks to me and I reply, but I am barely present. Barely functioning. I want him here so that I can go out and see what it is.

Maybe that's why I left? Because there's something else out here with us?

I can't see it. He messages me, but I ignore him. If I miss it for even a fraction of a second, I am worried that I will not know what it is.

He asks for my help, and I want to tell him that I cannot offer him anything. He pesters me, an irritant suddenly. Is this how Tomas felt about me? Am I channelling him entirely, his feelings, his moods? The other version of me is still days away, and he sounds nothing like the man that I am now. I have slept, finally, but it doesn't feel like it. It feels like I'm past something, like I'm not even meant to be here. I can't explain it better than that.

Maybe I can. Like I've cheated death, maybe. I am on borrowed time, and yet time doesn't seem to be linear, not here. Time is like anything else: language, or air, or me. Perfectly malleable.

I see it again. I don't know if it's real, but it pulses with colour. It is so bright against the black. It gives this all a sense of being real: that the anomaly isn't just nothingness.

Then it's gone, and I am alone again.

* * *

This, whatever it is, is mine. It's mine and mine alone, and Tomas has nothing to do with it. And he will never know. He said, We are going to discover something for humanity! and I will do it. It was me who discovered how the anomaly works! I can answer that fucking question: it is a fucking demon, playing with time. It is all we do not understand, and we never can. And this thing, this light, this glimmer, I will explain that as well. Here is the question: What is it? I do not know, but I will discover the answer. Everything must have an answer.

I feel sick, and I try to eat, but I can't keep it down. My body is rejecting everything. It feels like I am not meant to be here. I feel like my mother did. She said, once, that the cancer felt like it was eating her. I watch myself on the screens as I vomit, as I lie on the ground and it passes through me, and I think, I am meant to die.

He speaks to me, but I placate him. I am sick. I don't want to tell him that I am sick. I have so little time to wait, now.

I tell him that I know what he's doing. I almost tell him to turn around. But that thing, whatever's out there: I need to know why I stepped out then. I must see it, and I think that he will have to reach me for this to complete. A loop is nothing if you cut the string.

And everything becomes obvious to me, and laid out in front of me. I can see it all: I can see how I move on from here. As I see the *Lära*, the other one, the original one, this one, I also see the glimmer, in the distance. It's not too far, I don't think. I can probably reach it.

I have two options. I stay here and I see. I break this. Or

I step out and I look for what it is, for that glimmer, tempting me, a penny in a stream. He speaks to me. I am sick of him as he is. Can't he see it himself? I ache. My chest hurts, and my head. It's eating inside of me. I wonder, if I cut myself open, would I see the blackness that took my mother, and that threatened to take Inna once in her life? I would be too gone to be replaced; all around me would be black and rot, and I would die.

I am not meant to live past this. I am not meant to be here. He says, 'I need to come aboard,' so I tell him that it's okay, and I put my helmet on and check that the oxygen is charged, step into the airlock and open the door.

I am gone.

17

Two hours is a long time. It's time enough to get away from the *Lära*, and from the me that's discovering exactly how useless he is. And from here, I am uncontrolled. I am free, perhaps for the first time. All that I know is that I was here, and I made my way out into this. I feel almost delirious with the freedom: that I can go anywhere. I have hours left, and the world – this void of a world, this space inside an anomaly that has ruined, stolen, changed my life – is my oyster.

So I move in the direction of the glimmer that I saw, because there is nothing else. I am alone, and I have always been essentially alone, and I will die utterly alone. This is not an exit or Tomas finally come to rescue me. No, he is at home, with his baker, and I hope that he is not sleeping. I hope that there is a connection between us deeper than science, and that he is seeing somehow through my eyes for my final waking minutes; that as he sleeps he will dream this dream. He will be here with me as I sleep for the last time. He'll wake up screaming, and she will comfort him, his Lära, but he'll know. He'll lie to her about what he saw, because he will know what it was and what it means. I will haunt him as he presents his findings to the world. I won't let him rest.

In the distance, the ship is nothing much any more. Like a car from an airplane. The newer version of me won't have checked the scanners, because I did not, so he won't know that I'm here. He'll be getting to grips with what he must do now. He will be panicking, back on his own version of the ship, readying to leave, watching himself fall into place. I cannot remember how long that process took. Will take.

In the distance, I can't see the glimmer, but that's all right, because I have seen it enough to know that it's there. A replicatable accident. If something, a situation or reaction can be replicated, that's enough primary evidence for its existence.

It reminds me of something: when this all started, and I didn't sleep in the bed as we launched, and I blinded myself with the light, that white glow. Sunspots. It's almost exactly the same as that, but this time I cannot explain it. I wonder if I am being played with, some tricks and games that I barely understand. Does it matter? Does any of this?

The suit is astonishing. It's perfect for what we needed. I can barely feel the heat of the boosters on the back of my legs, even after this long using them. They weren't meant to be used constantly, because the battery packs in the suits were single use. They were meant to last us the whole trip. Not that that matters now.

I can't see it, still. I shout out to it, inside my helmet. A voice inside my helmet tells me to take it off, and shout that way. Challenge the anomaly. A voice says, It's alive, Mira. It's playing games just as Tomas was, and I laugh that off. It's so easy to dismiss idiocy. I know that I'm dying. I know that I'm not what I was. I think, in fact, that I have never been what I was, or what I thought I was. I have been coat-tails and clinging on, and this whole time I have been a pawn. Tomas had never really lost one of our games before this one, you know. Before it was decided that I would be coming up here. Not once. Bunk beds, Spider-Man or Batman, which side of Mother we would sit, who did the pitch, who signed the cheque. If we decided it by game, he never lost, but I kept going back because I was sure that I could outsmart him. Our mother once said, You're the same. You look the same, you have the same interests, you think the same way about things. You're the same, you two. Or maybe she meant it as, You too. Telling me that I am just as skilled as he is. And I wanted this. I wanted the dress up, playing at being an astronaut, the thing in space. The thing that was dispos-able. He wanted the control, and the power, so he gave me the win. It was easier to lose a game and let me think that I was the winner. He wanted his suit and his horn-rimmed glasses and his whisky and cigars. But more than that: I was a test. I was a sacrifice. I was part of this, and he needed to be at home to realize everything. He says goodbye. The brutal final words of a scientist to his brother; not a scientist, but a lab rat.

I shout, 'I wish that you were here, Tomas!' and I mean it as instead of me, but perhaps alongside me would be equally fine. I could tell him to his face. I could beg that he repented and that I forgive him. He would not, though. He would see this as what it was: his choice.

My eyes wet, I think that I see the glimmer again, so I push forward. My stomach hurts. I haven't eaten in a while. Or had anything to drink; that was probably an oversight. I have no idea what I'm going to find here. It could be anything. I wonder if, back on Earth, they know that this is growing, or moving, or whatever. That it's coming towards them. I wonder if Tomas knows how to deal with it. Maybe I have been useful. Maybe I will be a hero, because my being here will give them an answer. He will be the one to tell them, of course, and he'll tell them about my sacrifice. There's no way he'll let my name die out. He'll think of something appropriate, I'm sure, because he will want it to reflect well on him. He will say that I was a scientist.

How deep is this? I keep going. When you have no point of reference it feels like you are staying still, so I keep looking at the *Lära*. I am going further and further. Before, when I spoke to myself, I said that we were meeting in the middle. I suppose that was true. I wonder why I said it.

I have hidden the numbers of how much air I have left from the inside of the helmet, because I don't want it to be a count-down. I only want a rough idea of how long I have before I cannot find the glimmer any more, before that hope is gone, and that will be enough. Because I know that, at that point, there will be nothing to be done about it.

When Tomas and I stopped talking for a while after our mother's death, he said to me, You think you know best, don't you? And I had to tell him that I didn't. That such thoughts weren't even close to me, nowhere near me. I said to him, She knew what she wanted, and I am only her son. I wanted what was best for my mother. I have always wanted to help those in pain. He said, There were other medicines, and I told him that he was mad. That she was suffering. Now, I wonder if this is my penance. If he thought that I was suffering, somehow. This is him making my pain cease. Does that make it better, if I think of him as that? As somehow rendering my name endless, timeless, part of history? Knowing

I could never achieve as he does, and will in the future? He has given me something else. I wonder if that's how he sleeps, after he sees the dreams of me dying. He tells himself that he did this for my benefit. He is benevolent.

I have to make my peace with him, somehow. I do not know how.

So I move on, and concentrate on other things. Inna. Hikaru. I am so glad that I was able to do right by them, and Wallace. His poor children. At least they might have a chance of knowing his absolute fate now, burying him. That matters. I wonder what he would have made of this, had he seen it. He was so much weaker than I thought, so desperately afraid of what we had found. We should have picked up on it. We should have known that he was a powder keg; and Hikaru, that he was liable to break down. That Inna was dying, or had come so close before.

But perhaps Tomas knew. Perhaps this was it: a crew of expendables, a crew that weren't meant to live past this? Capable – no, perfectly able, at the top of their game, even – of completing the mission, but with no mind as to whether they came back. Led by me, the weakling twin. The one who did not achieve without his brother's say. The one who stayed behind the curtain, but not because he was the one with all of the power; but because he was afraid.

I think about how they died. I watch it over and over, in my mind. Here in this darkness there is not much else to watch. I think about how much air I have left, and how it is going down whether I like it or not. I estimate an hour gone, even though I wasn't going to do this. I could check. Everything is a countdown, whether I like it or not. Here is a timer until we lift off. Here is how long it will take to reach the anomaly. Here is how long you have got left. Twelve days to see me. Now wait twelve days until you can leave. Two hours until you die. Time moves slower, it seems, the faster the countdown. As if you give yourself more time to think.

I wonder if they will try this again? To reach the anomaly and to see what they can see? Probably not, assuming that Tomas knows everything I know, that I have worked out. Instead, he will try to work out how to stop it. He will prepare the world with tales of atmospheric interference, or say that it will herald meteor showers. He is an expert, the only expert, now. They'll listen to him. They'll ask him how they can ready themselves for the oncoming anomaly, and he'll up his research budget. He will be able to write his own budget, in fact. He might sacrifice more of us, in the other ship. More expendables, thrown into the abyss to see what he can gain from it. He will claim, if anybody accuses him of anything, that it's utilitarian. For the good of the people of planet Earth, that's why he does it. He will tell them all that it's no less than we deserve: a man who is willing to get things done. And I suppose they'll thank him. They should, probably. I don't know, maybe he was right. Maybe he knew where it was heading all along, and this was his way of . . . I don't know. It doesn't matter. It doesn't matter any more.

What matters now is the people back there. If this reaches Earth, what happens? Does everybody cycle? Is that how this ends? In perpetual life? Do we ride it out until it passes? Will it ever pass?

How much bigger can this get?

Behind me, the *Lära* is tiny, now. He will be waiting, counting down the hours. Talking to himself. I am past the point where I can regret this and return. There is only forward. I am getting tired. I wonder if that's natural. This must burn energy. The suit is designed to only take so much, and I'm only human. I think about Inna again. I always return to her. I think about her on the table that time. I wish I could think about the good things more, that my mind wandered there. But I think of her, like my mother. I think of those plastic organs.

I haven't seen the glimmer again. I can't see anything, now, not really. My eyes aren't what they used to be. Now the *Lära* is out of sight. I think that maybe I can see the light from it, maybe, but it's probably me fooling myself. The blackness is so thick, so encompassing, I doubt I can see past it. I turn and then realize that I have lost my bearing. Have I turned back enough? I start to panic, because there is only one reason that I am here now, and it's that glimmer. I breathe too quickly and have to calm myself. Breathing fast makes my supply go down. It's not a set time. Everything seems a mistake.

I never wanted to die with regrets. I move forward, because I cannot die like this. Where will I start my cycle from, assuming I start one? Where will I begin again? It would be cruel to make me go through this all over again. I think, if ever you questioned the existence of a god, here is your proof. This is cruelty; this is nothingness.

I am sobbing in my suit, and the glass is misting. I try and hold myself back, because I know that my gasps are ruining me. The air is thinning. It is becoming nothing. It's not even time to make my peace.

I want to tell my mother that I love her. And Tomas, for all his sins. He would say that I have sinned worse than he ever could. That at least my death had purpose. He would say that I brought this on myself. So there is nothing here, and he would say that he knew that. I would tell him that I was so sure, and he would say, It was a trick of the light. It was seeing faces in clouds. You're good at that, Mira. It's how you've always been. I would argue, saying that there are no clouds here to see faces in. The glimmer must have come from somewhere. And he would stand back and look smug, because that would have been his point all along. I know so well how his mind works, exactly how he thinks.

The air is so thin, and I have to breathe twice where I previously needed one, huffing in the air that is left. I think of Inna, dying. I can still see her face. I cannot stand to think that I will die. I stop the boosters, because I would rather know where I am. I turn around. I try to find the glimmer. This cannot have been in vain. It cannot.

Nothing. Just the nothing.

My tears, and my pain. I wonder if this was destined. Pre-ordained, somehow. How I was always meant to go. I am going to choke. I am going to die. I want, more than anything, this to be an end. Only me: I am the only one who will feel this. I am singular, and distinct, but then I see him: another version of me. He is here, and he is dead; drifting. Realization. He is in the suit. I see him, and I turn around, and there is another, fighting against it, choking. He is me in a minute's time, from the future; and behind him, me coming forward, looking for this, from the past. One is a future that I will suffer through, one that I have already done. Around this, there are other versions of me: drifting off into the nothing. Some of them have been here a long time, I think. I know: I see their faces, and they are not me. As Cormac aged, so have they. Unexplainable, but this is where everything changes. I am in a sea of myself. I struggle to keep the tears in, to stop myself hyperventilating, and I manage it.

James Smythe

'You're stronger than this,' I say to myself, but then I try to breathe, and I cannot. That was my last. I hold it. My head aches, and my eyes feel dead inside my head. I look around, trying to count them all, and I lose track of where I am. I am not righted; I am not in any direction. I am everywhere, and everything. I think that I am dead, that I am gone.

Then: the glimmer. It has been here the whole time, above me, below me, all around me. It unfolds itself. My eyes are heavy, and I can barely keep them open, but I need to. Because here is what I was looking for this entire time. I was wrong, and Tomas was wrong, and none of us knew. We were unprepared, and we will always be unprepared.

It is a parcel, a rip, a hole and it unfolds itself into space and delicacy. Everything was so dark before. It peels backwards and inside it there is light: pure, absolute light; and I stare at it, up close, forcing myself to look. I tell myself that this isn't real, but I want to believe it; that inside this anomaly there is something so pure that it is made so that I do not understand, and have no need to understand. Outside, rushing away from it, I can see veins, thin red and white lines, spooling off as branches and rivers, splayed and rushing. Living things have veins, and blood, and life in them. It makes sense to me that there are things we cannot understand; that there is life that we cannot conceive. Maybe things that we should not, as well; that are not for us to know. I know that this is one. I have seen things that no other man has seen. I have my answer to the question: the question of what the anomaly is. It is final, and it is my answer alone, and I think that nobody else will ever know. Perhaps that it okay. Perhaps that I have an answer is enough.

*   *   *

301

The Echo

As I die, as I feel death coursing through my body, I look away from the heart of the anomaly, and down at the blackness below. It looks like I could fall: like there is nothing at all below me, and I am already falling, down and into forever.

Then it says, 'I am here for you.'

And I say, 'I know.'

I shut my eyes. It envelops me.

Acknowledgments

Thanks to my amazing editor Amy McCulloch and the team at Voyager UK; Diana Gill and Voyager US; Laura Deacon and Blue Door; and all the sales, marketing, publicity, design and everything else people that worked so hard on these books. Thanks also to Sam Copeland, my agent, and all at RCW.

Enormous thanks to Kim Curran, Will Hill, Tom Pollock, James Dawson and Nikesh Shukla, all of who made me want to be better at this.

Lastly, thanks to my family for the unending support.

Here's an exclusive extract from

THE MACHINE

by James Smythe

Available now

blue door

1

She opens the door to a deliveryman, and the Machine, which has come in three parts, all wrapped in thick paper. Each of the parts is too big to get through the door.

We'll have to try the window, the man says.

She shows him which one it is, along the communal balcony. It's already at its widest, to let some air into the flat, to try and counteract the invasive heat from outside. Still not wide enough, so the men – the first has been joined by another from the van, having just heaved another thick cream-paper-wrapped packet the size of a kitchen appliance from the van, and left it leaning against the bollards – tell her that they'll have to take the window out.

We've got the tools for it, this other man says.

Beth stands back and watches as they unscrew the bolts on the attaching arms, and then lift the whole sheet down. Others in the estate have stuck their heads out of their windows, or come out of their front doors to watch. Next door, the woman with all the daughters stands and watches, and her girls run around inside. The littlest one stands at the woman's legs, clutching onto her skirt.

Gawpers, the first man says. Always wanting to know what we're up to.

The deliverymen don't know what's inside the packages. They're just paid to deliver them. Beth wonders if she's going to be able to assemble it herself, or if she's better off asking them for help. Slip them a fifty, they'd probably stand around with her for an hour and figure it out. She doesn't know how easy it will actually be: if there will be wires, or if it's just a case of plugging the pieces together. The man she bought it from said it would be simple. They struggle up the stairwell with the first piece, stopping to mop their brows. They still wear dark-blue overalls, in this weather, and their now-sweaty palms leave dark-brown prints on the paper wrapped around the Machine's pieces. The first piece makes it through the window maw, twisted in the frame as if this is one of those logic games. Manipulate the pieces.

Right, the first man says. Where do you want them?

In the spare bedroom, Beth tells him. She indicates it through, pointing the way past the living room. The room is light and airy – or as airy as it can be nowadays – and decorated like it's a master, with an expensive-looking bed. Wallpaper not paint, with a different dado rail, a thick yellow colour contrasting with the impressed patterned cream of the walls. The room looks untouched, like nobody's ever lived in it. The bed is made, the sides of the duvet tucked in below the mattress. There's potpourri on the dresser in a simple golden metal dish, but not enough to stop the faint smell of dust. The sunlight, through the window, hits the dust, a cone of it floating in the air.

Anywhere?

By the back wall. I've cleared a space for it. She rushes past, ducking down in front of him, making sure that the space is still clear, then helps him lower the first package.

What the bloody hell is this thing? the man asks.

Exercise equipment, Beth tells him. That's an answer suggested by the man who sold the Machine to her. In his email, he told her that he would write that on the form for the collection, and on the customs form. He was French, and Beth had had to translate his email using the internet, only the occasional word making her stumble. Still, she got the gist.

Jesus, the deliveryman says as he puts it down – the French seller has marked the packages with arrows, showing which way up they're to be carried and stored – and stretches his back. He's wearing a thick black harness around his waist, which he pats. Lifesaver, he says. They make us wear them now, for the insurance. We take them off in the van, when we're done. Fucking hot though, wearing this along with the rest of the get-up. He stretches again, more exaggerated this time. His friend shouts from the window, where they see he's positioned the next piece – this one long and thin at one end, bulbous and clunky at the other, meant to stand tall, taller than any of the people in the flat – halfway through the window. He's straining to hold it up. Beth sees that the arrows (marked with thin, shaky writing that says THIS WAY UP) are horizontal. She wonders if that'll affect it in any way.

Come on, the man says, can't hold it. The other one takes the inside end and they work it through.

Same place? the first removal man asks. Beth nods, and then he asks for something cold to drink, which she prepares – iced tea, in the fridge – as they both struggle with it through

309

the tight doorways and narrow corner into the room. She's got two glasses on the side ready by the time that they're done with that piece, but the first man – clearly the superior of the two, older and wiser and with a company t-shirt on under his rote blue overalls – waves them aside. Last piece, then we'll have them, he says. Beth watches them both at the van, which they've parked at the bottom of the estate, by the bollards that prevent cars driving right up to the buildings themselves. They look at the last piece, which is nearly the same shape as the first, only somehow wider, more unwieldy, and they both laugh. She knows that they're talking about what it is. Speculating. They'll know it's not exercise equipment. They've handled exercise bikes before. They do this for a living, and the wool can't be pulled over the eyes of those who will know the weight and shape of an exercise bike or a rowing machine. She watches as they finally heave the last piece up between them, up the stairwell and into her flat through the window space. Their sweat drips from their heads and onto the concrete slabs, and the Machine.

It needs to be a certain way, she says. Would you mind? They shrug, and she tells them. The pieces have been labelled with numbers showing where they connect, drawn on the outside of the wrapping.

This is like Tetris, the first man says. The younger man laughs. They back up and look at it when they're done, and the wall is essentially filled by the wrapped packages. The light that came through the small window is totally blocked now, and the room is suddenly darker, thrown into the shade of the still-wrapped packages. You all right with this now? the older man asks. He hands Beth a sheet from his back pocket, and a pen. Sign this and we're all good. They gulp their drinks back as she signs her name three times, and then leave the glasses on the side. They replace the window back in minutes. These things are all designed to be taken apart and put back together so quickly now, the first man says. Everything's a bloody prefab, right? He smiles at Beth as if she doesn't live here, as if she'll be in on the slightly snobbish joke with him. To her surprise she laughs, to back him up.

I know, she says. Thanks for everything. I really mean that.

No problem. She waits until they're back in their van – they stand at the rear of it for a few minutes examining what they've got left on their sheet of deliveries, and where they're heading next, wiping their foreheads on their sleeves and on a towel, gasping for air – and then watches them drive away. Then it's just her and the flat and the Machine.

2

The paper pulls away from the Machine with relative ease. She's surprised that it didn't tear during the move. A few bits she has to attack with scissors but most of it rips away easily, and then she's left with the Machine itself. She stands back, on the other side of the bed, against the far wall. She sizes it up. This one is bigger than she remembers.

The pitch-black casing is grotesque, she thinks. It seems so vast. She hasn't joined it together yet, not where the clips and bolts require, but she can see it as if it was complete. On its side, a coiled power cable waits, like an umbilicus. The Crown has a dock above the screen, in the centre, and the whole thing seems unreal. She looks at it for too long, at how black it is. It almost fills the entire wall, and the shadow it casts is deep enough that she can't see the wallpaper past it. This was the only place it could go, because of the shape of the room. She tries to move as far back as possible and take it all in, but it isn't possible. It's like a cinema screen when you sit near the front: never entirely encompassed by your vision.

312

She knows, to the day, how long it's been since she last saw one of these. The last one was very different in some ways: it was smaller, she thinks, and the Crown wasn't docked as it is in this one. It was wireless, where here there's a thick cable that looks like it's got sand stuffed inside it to keep it taut, and other lumps and bumps along the length of the pale-coloured rubber. The Crown itself is less flashy as well. This is definitely an older model, but she wasn't looking for a new one. In the newer models, you couldn't change anything. Firmware updates were automatic. The guides on the internet told her that she needed one she could change, and this was all she could find. Even then it was hidden away amongst useless husks and books and videos. She had to email the man directly to ask if he had any working Machines, and it took four emails (making her jump through hoops) before he trusted her enough to tell her his prices. This one was the oldest of the old. She still paid through the nose for it. But it was the only one she had found in six months of searching, and she hadn't spent any money for the last few years beyond the essentials. This was a long-term plan, and she had saved accordingly. The email where he wrote the figure she would owe him made her cry: not from the immensity, but the relief.

She goes closer to the bulk of it. She remembers the one that Vic had during his treatments, and the way that it used to vibrate. They explained to her, once, about the power needed to run it. It's one of the most powerful computers in the country, they said to her. (She supposes that, were they to be invented now, they would be put into a smaller package: something the size of a briefcase, maybe even as small as a telephone.) It used to vibrate right through the floors, and Vic would sit in the chair next to it and his teeth would chatter as he clenched them together, because he was bracing himself. The early sessions were the hardest. This Machine here isn't even plugged in yet, and yet Beth puts her hand on it and would swear that she can feel the vibrations. The metal itself – that's what it's made of, some thick alloy that she couldn't even name, that isn't like anything she's got in the house, not aluminium cans or the wrought-iron picture frame or the steel of that lampshade, but something else, like the material that the thing is made from was this shade of black to begin with – is coarse and cold, and she would swear carries some sort of residual shudder. She takes the plug from the side and uncoils it, and runs it to the base of the bed, where the room's only sockets are. So much is wireless now and yet this needs hard-wiring. The ones that Vic used before were actually attached to the wall, part of the complex that they had to visit. They were monitored.

She goes to work on the bolts. They're all hand-driven, none requiring custom tools, which is good. Some of them have connectors that need to be touching, but the deliverymen got them mostly lined up for her. All the insides are driven by conductive metal rather than wires, which makes them easy to assemble. Foolproof, even. The pieces sit perfectly flush when they're connected and lined up, and it takes a bit of effort – heaving them a centimetre this way, a millimetre the other – but they satisfyingly click together. She can't even see the lines between pieces when it's done: it's like a solid lump of black metal from the front, no seams, like something carved from the world itself. It looks, she thinks, almost natural. Like rock.

She drags the plug from the side and plugs it into the wall, and then strokes the screen. Doing this is like instinct. The screen flickers to life. There's the familiar triple tone of the boot noise – ding-ding-ding, ascending and positive, full

of optimism – and then the screen is awash with light. Beth
hadn't realized how covered in dust it was. She doesn't know
when this thing was last turned on, but the clock has reset.
She pulls her sleeve down over her hand and wipes the screen
off. She'll do a better job later, but she wants to check that
this all works before she gets her hopes up. The interface is
exactly as she remembers, all big colourful buttons and words
driven by positivity. Nothing negative. Even in the act of
taking away they were reinforcing. PURGE, COMMIT,
REPLENISH. She presses a button, through to sub-menus.
There's a button that offers her the chance to explore the
hard drive, which she presses, but the drive is clear. That's
what she'd hoped for. She didn't want somebody else's memories lingering here. She heads out of the room and into the
other bedroom, her bedroom. Compared to the Machine's
room, it's chaos. Clothes everywhere, on the floor and bed,
– she sleeps around them, making nooks in them where her
body lies – and the walls stacked high with vacuum-packed
bags full of clothes that she hasn't worn in years, or that she
kept of Vic's. She keeps the hard drive under her bed, because
that seemed like the safest place. If she got burgled, she didn't
want them to take it thinking that it would be worth anything.
Pulling it out – it's been in a box with remnants of who she
was before, old library cards and birthday cards and
childhood photographs – she walks into the room and sees
the drive appear on the screen as she gets closer. It's a first-
generation capacitive wireless device, able to pick up on other
wireless items in the vicinity and read their drives. A new
option appears on the screen: a cartoonish image of a hard
drive. She presses the button – her hands are shaking, because
she's worried that the drive might have wiped itself or
corrupted over the past couple of years (ever since she backed

up the contents from an older drive one New Year's Day as she worried about it, worried about the life-span of these things) – and there it is: a folder named after her husband. She presses his name and waits as it loads.